Also by Jane Ashford

THE DUKE'S ESTATES
The Duke Who Loved Me
Earl on the Run
Blame It on the Earl
A Gentleman Ought to Know

THE DUKE'S SONS
Heir to the Duke
What the Duke Doesn't Know
Lord Sebastian's Secret
Nothing Like a Duke
The Duke Knows Best
A Favor for the Prince
(prequel)

THE WAY TO A
LORD'S HEART
Brave New Earl
A Lord Apart
How to Cross a Marquess

A Duke Too Far
Earl's Well That Ends Well
Once Again a Bride
Man of Honour
The Three Graces
The Marriage Wager
The Bride Insists
The Marchington Scandal
The Headstrong Ward
Married to a Perfect Stranger
Charmed and Dangerous
A Radical Arrangement
First Season/Bride to Be
*Rivals of Fortune/The
    Impetuous Heiress*
Last Gentleman Standing
Earl to the Rescue
The Reluctant Rake
*When You Give a Rogue a
    Rebel*

THE
DUKE'S
BEST FRIEND

JANE
ASHFORD

sourcebooks
casablanca

Published by Sourcebooks Casablanca, an imprint of Sourcebooks
P.O. Box 4410, Naperville, Illinois 60567–4410
(630) 961-3900
sourcebooks.com

Printed and bound in the United States of America.
OPM 10 9 8 7 6 5 4 3 2 1

One

KATE MEACHAM MOVED THROUGH THE ORNATE ROOMS
of the Austrian embassy like a tiger patrolling its territory,
she thought, or a fierce, sleek sea creature sliding unseen
through the depths. Her grandfather had introduced her to
gatherings like this glittering Saint Nicholas Day reception,
and she had learned to use them to soak up tidbits of useful
information for him. Grandfather, an illustrious diplomat
loaded with accolades and honors, had taught her that few
people in the realms of power took much notice of a young
woman, except perhaps to admire her face and form. They
gazed right past a youthful lady to discover someone of
actual significance. And sometimes they revealed secrets
that they thought she wouldn't understand.

A pang of grief shook her. Her grandfather had died
almost a year ago. She still missed him terribly.

Kate scanned the crowd for one particular tall handsome
figure. She'd been wanting to speak to Jerome Delaroche for
some time and was surprised he had not contacted her when
he returned to London.

At last, she found him, chatting with a circle of young
attachés in one of the back parlors. His dapper, square-jawed
figure stood out even in this impeccably turned-out group.

She joined them and gradually, subtly, separated him from them. When they were far enough away for private conversation, he said, "What are you doing here? I thought you'd been banned from diplomatic receptions."

"What? Nonsense. Who told you that?"

Jerome shrugged. "I heard it somewhere."

A way of saying he would not tell her. Her attendance had been discouraged since her grandfather's death, Kate admitted silently. But there had been no formal protest. Yet. "Of course I haven't been banned." She still had the support of some of her grandfather's friends. "I expected to see you as soon as you returned to London, Jerome."

"I've had a great deal to do."

"What sorts of things?"

"This and that."

Kate frowned. He must know she wanted all the details of his recent overseas journey. "I gave you the information that led you to Gibraltar. And won you a commendation, I expect. I should like to know how it went."

"I cannot tell you. It is a confidential Foreign Office matter."

"Which never would have come to light without me."

"How *did* you find out that fellow was spreading dangerous rumors?"

"I hear things."

"By venturing into places you should not go. And doing things you shouldn't."

"What are you suggesting?"

"Nothing."

"There's no need to hide your teeth. We've known each other since we were infants."

"I'm not certain infants can be said to be acquainted."

"Do you suppose I seduce my way to secrets?"

Jerome looked away. "Of course not."

"That's fortunate. Because I don't."

"I never thought so for a moment."

But she thought perhaps he had. Or had heard others speculate on the idea. Some people's minds went immediately in that direction. As if a woman had no other resources.

"Who is looking after you, Kate? Now that your grandfather is gone?"

This was chancy territory. She stifled her irritation at the idea she required looking after, like a child, at the age of twenty-four. "You needn't worry."

"As you said, we've been friends all our lives."

Kate nodded. As children, they had run wild during visits to the country. On school holidays, they had pored over globes and atlases and imagined being sent to the ends of the earth on adventures. They'd mourned together when all four of their parents had died in a shipwreck at the Cape of Good Hope. A location that had been grossly mislabeled, Kate thought.

"I shan't be able to help you," Jerome went on. "I shall be rather busier in future."

"Do you have a new position?" Her information, and his clever action on it admittedly, had probably brought him a promotion. Kate tried to be simply glad and not envious. A young lady—no matter how well born and educated and talented—could not go on diplomatic missions. As the world saw it, she was an ornament in embassies, companion to a man, her husband, and little else. "Happy to have helped," she said with only a brush of sarcasm.

Jerome moved from one foot to another in uncomfortable silence. Kate wondered what could be the matter with him. Jerome was the smoothest fellow she knew.

"The thing is, Kate, I've offered for Emma Lisle. We're to be married in March."

"Emma Lisle? That ninny?"

He looked pained and offended. "She's a gentle, sweet girl who cares about *me* rather than my missions."

"And will be no help on them."

"I don't require help! Nor do I wish to be a counter on the board of your ambitions." He frowned and lowered his voice. "We are not compatible, Kate."

Kate stood there, confused, until she realized that Jerome had assumed she'd been angling for a proposal. As if a woman could not associate with a man, offer him aid, for any other reason than the hope of marriage. "You can't think that I…"

"I'll work hard and devote myself to diplomatic work, argue the cases, hammer out the agreements, but when I finish and come home, I want a peaceful place. Emma will give me that."

"Peace is not brainless," Kate replied. At once she regretted it—the words and the acid tone.

Jerome's jaw tightened. "Unfair, Kate. Very nearly cruel."

She bowed her head. He was right. Emma Lisle was a kind, pleasant girl. She shouldn't have said that. "I know. I'm sorr…"

"You must admit that you are not at all suited for diplomacy."

"What?"

"Such work requires tact and patience and…a convivial nature. You possess none of those."

"How can you say that? I do."

He raised a skeptical eyebrow.

Patience was hard to master, Kate admitted silently. "Grandfather said I had a quick mind and plenty of courage."

Jerome nodded. "Indeed. But you are also abrasive and foolhardy. You don't think before you speak. And you… smolder."

"Smolder?"

"You're doing it now. You shouldn't look at a man that way. It makes people think you're no better than you should be."

Kate was stunned. She had thought that Jerome liked her.

"Coming here, pulling me away from everyone else." He looked around uneasily.

"I didn't pull you!"

"People will assume an intrigue. Especially now that you are…unsupervised." He shook his head. "You would be a disaster in an overseas embassy, rouse all the wrong sorts of attention. You must find something else to do with yourself. I'm sorry that I cannot help." Jerome turned and walked away. His departure seemed oddly final.

There had been quite a few such terminal moments in the last year, since her grandfather's demise.

Kate raised a hand to her forehead. The movement was echoed in a long mirror on the wall. Jerome had been standing in front of it. Now Kate faced her reflection, a tall, square-shouldered woman, with honey-colored hair and violet-blue eyes, a reasonably fashionable gown, judged quite pretty by those who were supposed to know. She looked angry, as well she might after that. Is that what Jerome had meant by *smolder*? She didn't think it was. Not at all. He'd practically called her a lightskirt. How dare he?

She gazed into her own burning eyes. *Had* she considered marrying Jerome? On some deep level where plans were hatched, ambitions weighed? Kate shook her head. She'd thought of him as a surrogate brother, sometimes annoying but loyal and reliable. Clearly she'd been mistaken.

Her reflection in the mirror wavered a little, shaken by her misjudgment and his accusations. While her grandfather lived, she'd had a place. His mere existence had opened gatherings like these to her, even though he rarely attended himself. She'd revered and loved him. She missed him acutely. But he was gone. And with him, seemingly, had gone her social standing. Over this last year, it had felt as if her life was melting away like snow in a lingering thaw.

Jerome's words echoed in her mind—find something else to do with herself. How was she to do that, exactly? Grandfather had given her a most unconventional upbringing. She had none of the accomplishments of young ladies of her background and class. Girls like Emma Lisle, for example.

The image in the mirror stared back at her. Kate straightened like a soldier coming to attention. She hadn't wanted those skills. She would not be judged by them. She would think of something. She always did.

An older couple appeared in the glass beside her. "Hello. Miss Meacham, isn't it? We met at the Castlereagh ball."

Where she had not been invited, Kate thought, any more than she had been tonight. Getting in there had been a bit of a coup. She groped for a name. These were the Grindells, she recalled. He was a minor functionary in the customs office.

"Are you here all alone?" asked Mrs. Grindell.

"Oh no." Technically, it wasn't a lie. There were people all around her.

"Very sorry to hear about your grandfather," said Mr. Grindell. "A marvelous man."

"Yes, he was."

"We didn't see you at Russian gala," he added.

"Of course it was full of foreigners," sniffed Mrs. Grindell.

Hardly a surprise at a foreign embassy, Kate wanted to say. But she did not. Despite Jerome's insulting opinion, she was capable of tact. "I was out of town for a while," she replied instead.

"Visiting friends?" asked Mrs. Grindell nosily.

She had been supporting a friend. An acquaintance. A newly met connection. They had helped foil a dastardly plot involving long-lost documents, a ruthless foreign agent, kidnapping, and a cunning trap in which she had played a crucial part. It had been extremely invigorating and would remain one of her most cherished memories. She longed to hear about the aftermath. If she hadn't given a false name in the matter, she could inquire. But if she had used her own name, she could not have joined in.

"Where are you living now that your grandfather is gone?" Mrs. Grindell had the look of an inveterate gossip.

Kate had no suitable answer to that question. It was time to slip away. She wouldn't accomplish much in her current mood. Kate looked around. "Oh, there is the Austrian ambassador."

The Grindells turned eagerly, as she'd known they would. She was unimportant in the scheme of things, a mere diversion until someone of significance came along. She used the distraction to slip behind a larger group of guests and then around them to the edge of the room. Casually she made her way down it, her gaze distant but purposeful, as if she was on her way to meet someone unexceptionable. Her chaperone, perhaps. The imaginary older female who made Kate's existence socially acceptable.

Hiding a sneer, she slipped into a hallway and through a door into the back premises. She knew the geography of all the major diplomatic residences—how to insert and extract herself without the bother of front entries and invitation cards. Lower servants didn't question a lady walking with assurance. As long as she kept moving. And majordomos could be evaded. Sneaking made things like cloaks and bonnets awkward, but she'd always found a place to leave hers until she returned for them.

What could Jerome have meant—that she'd been banned? How would they? They wouldn't dare. She would not be dropped into oblivion simply because she was an unattached female!

Henry Deeping looked over the selection of periodicals set out on a long table at his London club. He could not aspire to the heights of White's or Brooks, but this cozy room was a refuge on a chilly December evening. He chose a newspaper, requested a glass of wine, and sat down.

The place was nearly empty. Like most of the other members, Henry had planned to be with his family for Christmas, enjoying the festivities of the season, only returning to London in the new year to take up his first post in the Foreign Office. But the capture of a dangerous agent near his family home in Leicestershire, and the discovery of potentially explosive documents—incredible as that adventure now seemed—had brought him back to town early.

He had helped corner the agent, escorted the captive to town, and now he was kept kicking up his heels at others' convenience, occasionally summoned to answer questions about the sequence of events that had already been covered in written reports. On the one hand, he was pleased to have attracted the attention of his new Foreign Office superiors. He'd been commended for his deft handling of the situation. On the other, he was sorry to miss the family holiday. All of his friends and connections were far away.

Yet as soon as he thought this, he was proven wrong.

A tall, athletically built man strolled into the room, his pale pantaloons and exquisitely cut long-tailed blue coat proclaiming him a nonpareil. "There you are," said the Duke of Tereford. "I tried your rooms first."

Henry had known James since they were twelve-year-olds arriving at school, facing a new place with a mixture of bravado and trepidation. He'd sat with James in classrooms and run beside him on playing fields. They'd had adventures as young men on the strut in society and plunged into deeper waters on several memorable occasions. When James had come into his inheritance and assumed a dukedom, Henry had been glad for him and only a little envious. Well, perhaps more than a little. In one stroke James had acquired title, fortune, and a life work. Not that he had wanted the latter at the time.

He felt a familiar sense of eclipse as James sat down. The duke was known as the handsomest man in London. Henry was aware that his own tall thin figure, pale skin, and dark hair and eyes were not nearly so striking. He looked well enough, but he was no Adonis. "I'm surprised to see you back in town at this time of year," he said.

"The town house is cleared and repaired at last," Tereford replied. "It's ready to be furnished and made ready for next season and for Cecelia to spend a great deal of money."

"Are you actually posing as a put-upon husband whose wife overspends?" Henry asked.

Tereford smiled. "No. It's more likely to be me."

"As everyone knows." James's inheritance had come with a flood of responsibilities that had threatened to overwhelm his friend, but had instead been the making of him, Henry thought now. Through a very fortunate marriage.

"Not everyone surely?"

Henry gave him a satirical look and received a grimace in return. "Cecelia is certainly the more sensible one," Tereford said.

"You know, from what I have observed lately, I think you work together as a very efficient team."

A tremor of emotion showed on the duke's face, and as quickly disappeared. "Thank you."

Feeling that he should say more, Henry added, "I was wrong to doubt the wisdom of your marriage. I'm sorry for anything I might have said that…"

"I know, Henry."

The look they exchanged spoke volumes without the need for actual words. It encompassed years of friendship, good-natured teasing, and many occasions when they had stood up for each other. That history let Henry see that something was bothering the duke. He raised his eyebrows, indicating an openness to confidences.

"I am to be a father next year," Tereford said.

"Congratulations!"

The duke's answering smile was wry. "Thank you, but I'm terrified. What do I know about fatherhood? My own was not a good example."

"You aren't like him," Henry said. James's father had been a cold, sarcastic person, and his biting criticisms had been particularly hard on his heir. Henry had never observed the least sign of softness in the man, and he'd often pitied his friend when he endured one of his parent's thundering scolds.

"Not like him anymore?" the duke asked.

"You never were."

"Was I not?" Tereford looked concerned. "I've been called selfish and arrogant."

Henry couldn't deny it. James had shown leanings in that direction. He'd pointed them out a time or two. "Not since you married, I daresay."

Tereford's expression grew tender, then uneasy. "When I am presented with a child…"

"What's become of that family you had living in the town house while it was being repaired?" Henry interrupted.

"The Gardeners?" Tereford asked, surprised.

"Right." Henry had been astonished when he'd discovered that Tereford had taken in an indigent family to watch over his London town house.

"Mrs. Gardener is making ready to move to the country," the duke replied. "It is what she wished."

"There were several children."

"Ned and Jen and Effie. Ned is an apprentice tailor at Weston's now."

"You get along quite well with them."

"I do?"

Henry nodded. He had seen it, and been startled.

"Well…" The duke still looked uncertain.

"You'll do very well. Wait and see."

Tereford bowed his head, more abandoning the topic than agreeing. "Are you in town for Christmas?"

"Yes. It's taking a great deal of time to resolve the Leicestershire matter."

The duke nodded. He had been involved in that as well, an anomaly in a somewhat motley crew.

"I think the Foreign Office feels that my job has started," Henry added. "And my time is no longer my own."

"A memorable beginning."

Henry nodded. He should count himself fortunate. He needed to make his way in the world, and his uncle had very kindly volunteered to help him. It was true that Henry had expressed no desire to be a diplomat. Such things happened when one was quiet in a noisy family. Someone popped up to tell you what to do. And he hadn't refused. Diplomacy was a respected profession. It offered sensible, practical possibilities. Quite unlike his own grandiose dreams. He shoved that thought into the oblivion where all its fellows lay.

"We're here so that Cecelia can see the best doctors," said the duke. "You must spend Christmas with us."

"That would be pleasant." Henry felt his mood lift. The Terefords were very good company as well as friends. "Perhaps the duchess can advise me. My uncle says I need to find a proper wife if I wish to succeed in diplomatic circles."

"We've given up matchmaking," Tereford replied.

"We?" Henry smiled at the thought of him doing any such thing.

"I was…drawn into a few courtships. But no more. Cecelia agrees."

"Don't I deserve assistance?" In fact, Henry was not eager to marry for the sake of his career. That seemed a cold, sad endeavor. But he enjoyed teasing James.

"Do you really require it?"

"I was joking."

Tereford examined him with benign curiosity. "Have you heard anything from Miss Brown?" he asked.

"What? No." Henry had not been able to forget the acerbic

young lady who'd pushed her way into the Leicestershire affair while seeming to disdain them all. She'd had some undefined connection to the Foreign Office and almost certainly was not actually named Brown. But he didn't see why James would mention her now. "I wouldn't expect to do so."

"Ah, well, I suppose you could find her again."

"I don't want to find her. Why should I?"

The duke shrugged. "You didn't think her rather interesting?"

"Not in the least." She'd been irritating and insulting. As a pretty young lady, she'd taken advantage of the rules of chivalry to behave churlishly. And why was he thinking about her looks? Or anything about her? Naturally Henry did not wish to see her ever again.

Two

KATE MEACHAM SAT IN HER GRANDFATHER'S FORMER study and looked over the monthly bills. Grandfather had left her his small house, where she'd lived with him since her parents' death, situated in an unfashionable neighborhood near the British Museum. His income from investments had come to her as well, and they were enough to sustain a frugal young woman if she didn't wish to do anything ambitious for the rest of her natural life. If she was prepared to spend decades in small routine tasks.

Kate sighed. She did wish to do all sorts of expansive, adventurous, impossible things. Of course she was grateful for this refuge, slightly shabby and stuffed with books and bereft of its animating old owner as it was. She'd have been lost without it. She felt a bit lost anyway, she thought in her secret heart.

A brisk knock rattled the closed door. Mrs. Knox came in without waiting for permission and stood looking down at Kate, hands on her ample hips. Her round face, creases etched by frequent smiles, was solemn today. "I know you miss him dreadfully, Kate. We all do. But something must be done about your situation. People are beginning to talk."

"What people?" Kate asked.

"Neighbors. Mrs. Sanders."

"That tittle-tattler!"

"She doesn't matter too much, but if word spreads…" Jerome's insults came back to Kate as Mrs. Knox shook her head. "You can't live all alone."

"You are here."

"I'm a servant." The older woman said it calmly, without resentment.

She'd been as much second mother to Kate as housekeeper/cook, but her antecedents were low, as the world saw it. Mrs. Knox had taken pains to learn educated speech and manners, but society did not count her as a suitable chaperone. "Society is an idiot," said Kate aloud.

Mrs. Knox gave her a resigned look. She was accustomed to strong opinions in this household, along with discussions that ranged beyond the bounds of strict propriety.

"What is the terrible danger of a woman alone?" Kate asked. "I am the same person I've always been."

"You are indeed."

"Which is perfectly…" Her voice trailed off. She couldn't call herself perfectly respectable. Or perfectly anything, really. Except fed to the gills with limitations perhaps.

"I won't be brushed off, Kate. There is the matter of the breeches."

"Breeches?" Kate repeated, hoping this wasn't what it most likely *was*.

"Going out at night dressed as a young lad. The lord knows where. Until all hours. Yes, you thought I didn't know about that. But I do."

"I haven't done anything improper," Kate began.

This earned her a frown. "How can you say so? The mere fact of it is a scandal. As you know very well."

"I can't get useful information sitting in the parlor with the mending!"

"Useful to who?" Mrs. Knox asked.

This was a sore point. No one had asked her to go looking. No one wanted her to, even though Jerome had made good use of the rumors she'd uncovered. In fact, like Jerome, most everyone wished she *wouldn't* go looking. Or they would wish it, if they found out. What a furor that would rouse. She didn't want to think of it. "Grandfather's contacts will speak to his young assistant." His painstakingly assembled network shouldn't just go to waste. "And I know the signals."

Mrs. Knox sighed. "He did you no favors, teaching you such things. You ought to have been put in the way of meeting your own sort. You ought to have had a come-out."

Kate shuddered at the idea. "I don't think there *are* any of my sort. Can you imagine me simpering over teacups in a stuffy drawing room?"

"Only if you were seeing yourself as a spy gathering intelligence," replied Mrs. Knox with another sigh.

"Oh, then." Kate grinned at her.

"You won't jolly me out of this. Something must be done."

"Grandfather let me do as I pleased."

"That is not quite true."

Kate looked down, acknowledging the reprimand. He'd listened and advised and guided the course of her life. He'd been the wise balance to her rash impatience. She didn't know what she was going to do without him.

She pushed back the grief, and the anger, summoned resolve. She would find her way. What other choice did she have? "All right. I'll think of something."

"I know you will."

Kate appreciated the confidence in her tone and the smile as the older woman went out. She gazed at the door as it clicked shut. Mrs. Knox, Sally the maid of all work, and fourteen-year-old Johnny the errand boy/footman in training relied on her now. For their sake as well as her own, she needed to keep the household functioning. But surely life could offer her more than mere survival. She could not face an endless, trivial rut winding down through all the years ahead. The idea was insupportable.

But she did not actually wish to be excluded from polite society due to the irregularity of her living arrangements. Jerome's comments about a diplomatic ban came back to her, more threatening this time, and Kate felt the chilling touch of loneliness.

———

Standing near a wall at the Swedish reception for Saint Lucia's Day on December thirteenth, Henry Deeping looked for a single familiar face. He'd been ordered to come here. Apparently, it was part of his job at the Foreign Office to help fill out British numbers at gatherings like this. He hadn't expected any assignments until after the New Year, when his uncle would be back in London and would present Henry to his many allies in the diplomatic community. These receptions would grow easier then, with plenty of acquaintances to meet. Now, they presented a challenge. Did one push oneself forward, forcing introductions? Was that permissible in this situation, as it would not be among the *haut ton*? How was he to know?

He wondered if this might be the point. Were his new superiors testing him? Were they watching to see how he fit himself into a new circle? He hadn't spotted observers, but he supposed they might be here. Or perhaps he was being overly imaginative. Probably he was. It was a secret, besetting sin—the sagas that tried to unfold in his mind at the least provocation. He was not important enough to rate watchers.

He looked over the array of characters who filled the room. They came from all over the world, and many had unfamiliar mannerisms. He could enjoy watching them and gauging their personalities from the way they behaved. But could he charm them? Was that his task?

A footman carrying a tray of champagne glasses entered from an unobtrusive doorway a few yards down the room. A female figure slipped out in his wake, and Henry was startled to recognize her. It wasn't another servant. It was the young woman he'd recently been discussing with the duke. She'd called herself Kate Brown during that tussle with the covert agent in Leicestershire in November, though it had become clear in the end that name was false. And now, here she was again, more grandly dressed than she'd been in the country, but unmistakably the same young lady—tall, square-shouldered, with honey-colored hair. What was she doing here? Why had she entered in such an odd way? Henry couldn't help but stare.

She seemed to feel it. She turned and looked at him. Their eyes locked, hers a vivid violet blue. She didn't look pleased to see him. Well, he felt the same. He and Kate Whoever She Was had not hit it off. She'd seemed ready to give him a sharp setdown at the least excuse. No, Henry thought. Without any excuse at all. *He* hadn't given her any. He'd been polite and accommodating, even when she'd insisted on inserting herself into the Leicestershire matter, where she hadn't been wanted or really needed. He didn't mind sarcasm. His sister, Charlotte, excelled at it. But this young lady had gone beyond the line.

She looked as militant as ever as she moved off, cleaving the crowd. It seemed she intended to ignore him, which Henry heartily approved. Did people actually shy away from her? He watched the pattern of the crowd. He really thought that some of them did, as if a cat had entered a dovecote.

Suddenly she veered in his direction. A tall, fashionably dressed young man with a peevish expression angled in from the other side of the room, clearly bent on intercepting her. They eeled through the crowd, she evading, he pursuing, coming closer to Henry with each swerve.

They reached his vicinity at the same time. Kate Whatever abandoned her flight and turned to face the fellow. "Are you here alone again?" he asked her. "It's outrageous, Kate. You must stop this."

"I don't see that it's any of your affair, Jerome," she replied.

There was that imperious voice, Henry noted. And the flashing gaze. She had a certain annoying magnificence. Like an ill-tempered lioness snapping her fangs to warn everyone to steer clear.

"If you don't stop these…invasions, I will have to speak to someone," said Jerome Whoever.

"You wouldn't dare!"

"It is the responsible thing to do. How did you even get in…?"

"I'm not here alone." The young lady took a step sideways and grabbed Henry's arm as if it belonged to her. "Have you two met? Jerome Delaroche, this is Henry Deeping. And vice versa." She made a fluttering, dismissive gesture.

The man turned to Henry, looked him up and down. "Deeping of the Leicestershire matter?"

Henry nodded. She had his arm in a steely grip. He couldn't get loose without causing a scene.

"Gibraltar," Delaroche murmured, pointing at himself.

Henry had heard something about a recent action there. They'd been talking of it when he was called in to the Foreign Office. He'd been surprised to find that gossip appeared to be endemic inside its walls.

"How absolutely *splendid* that you've heard of each other's successes." The lady's tone was biting. Lioness indeed, Henry thought. She would have been glad to savage them. "*Do* congratulate each other on your commendations," she added.

Delaroche looked sour. "How do you know Mr. Deeping?" he asked her.

"If it is any of your business, which it certainly is *not*, I am a friend of his sister, Charlotte."

That wasn't precisely true, Henry noted. But it wasn't entirely a lie. She had become acquainted with Charlotte in Leicestershire, and they had seemed to get along. Hardly a friendship, but… He received a flash of warning from those violet eyes and decided to say nothing. He didn't want to become embroiled in the dispute brewing here. It had a long-established air.

"And so he brought you here?" Delaroche asked her.

She raised her chin and gazed at him. She hadn't uttered any outright falsehoods, Henry thought. But she'd made space for them and allowed them to take root. "Shouldn't you get back to Miss Lisle?" she asked.

Henry recognized the tone. It implied that the person in question could go to hell instead. When she turned her gaze on him, its fire confirmed his interpretation. "Jerome is recently engaged to Miss Emma Lisle," she said.

"Ah. Congratulations." It came out like a question, though he hadn't meant it to.

Delaroche scowled at her. He seemed about to say more, but then he turned and walked away, joining a pretty girl in a pink gown, who smiled up at him adoringly.

"*Pfft*," said Henry's companion.

She was still holding his arm. She didn't seem inclined to let go. A diplomat would not shake her off and flee the reception, Henry supposed. He would be more dexterous. "If I am your escort, I imagine I should know your real name," he observed with what he felt was commendable restraint.

She turned that smoking gaze on him again. "It's Meacham. Katherine Eloise Meacham."

"Meacham?"

"As in Sir Michael Meacham, yes." She was still obviously irritated. "He was my grandfather."

Henry blinked. Sir Michael Meacham was a legend in the Foreign Office. His uncle had mentioned him. Sir Michael had been an expert on British foreign policy, consulted by political leaders of all stripes. The exploits of the man's youth, in Africa and Asia, were almost mythical. Henry wondered what it could have been like to be his granddaughter. "Why did you use a different name in Leicestershire?" he asked her.

"Once people hear Meacham, they think of nothing but him. It would have roused too much attention."

"Because you weren't supposed to come to Leicester-shire?"

"There was no permission involved."

Henry paused briefly over this interesting sentence. She might wish to suggest that permission was not required in her case. But he suspected it meant she hadn't asked any-body. In fact, he was certain of it. He wondered what excuse she'd given her guardians for the journey.

"I went to support Miss Palliser," she added.

"The scholarly lady translator whom you hadn't even met until you heard I was looking for such an expert," Henry said. "Heard from where you were lurking behind a potted palm."

"I wasn't *behind* it. It merely happened to be between us."

"And you happened to be eavesdropping."

"It was an accident." She glared at him. "I *happened* to know of her skills too, because of her father's friendship with my grandfather. You wouldn't have found her without me."

"I would have found some…"

"And she turned out to be perfect for the purpose. Of course I went along to lend her support."

"Miss Palliser didn't seem to require support. She appeared entirely competent and self-possessed."

"You wouldn't have captured that agent without me," said Miss Meacham, shifting her argumentative ground.

"And Miss Palliser and my sister. Actually it was chiefly them, if I remember the sequence of events correctly." Which he did.

Miss Meacham dropped his arm. At last. She started to speak, then stopped. Henry watched her swallow an impulse to annihilate him. It was obviously a struggle. He wondered why she hesitated until she said, "How is the investigation going?"

She wanted information as a starving man wants food, Henry realized. She would squash her temper to get it. "I can't say a great deal," he began.

"Don't you dare give yourself airs after mere days in the job," she snapped. Interrupting was just one of her annoying habits. She had others.

"Because I don't know a great deal," he continued as if she hadn't spoken. "I show up when I'm called for and answer questions. I receive portentous hems and haws in response and watch people exchange smug looks. I haven't seen the agent since we brought him to London. I still don't know his name."

Miss Meacham grimaced. "They love their secrets." She looked out over the crowd. "They hug them to their breasts and gloat over them."

"I suppose there are concerns for national security."

"Are you a spy?" she demanded. "Am I?"

"No. At least, *I* am not." When she glared again, he said, "A joke, Miss Meacham. Humor does exist."

She wrinkled her nose. "Indeed. But that wasn't it."

Henry's patience was exhausted. "What are you doing here?"

She looked away.

"You *are* here alone. I saw you come in." He nodded at the unobtrusive door. "Mr. Delaroche suggested that you aren't welcome. People stand back when you pass them."

"They do not!"

"Some of them do, Miss Meacham. I observed it."

The look she turned on him this time was uneasy. "When Grandfather was alive, I was welcome. Now that he is gone, I am…nobody."

Henry examined her expression. She seemed both mournful and irate, which couldn't be a comfortable combination. He felt a twinge of sympathy. He had been feeling rather like a nobody himself in this crowd of strangers.

"Which is simply despicable," she added with her old asperity. She gazed out at the chattering people, seemed to think of something, and turned slowly back. "You are here to mingle and show the flag," she said to Henry. "Offer up congenial conversation."

He acknowledged it with a shrug.

"But you have only begun at the Foreign Office. You don't know many people here."

He nodded.

"I do. I could present you."

"Ah…" Henry wasn't certain her sponsorship would be an advantage. In fact, he suspected it wouldn't be. But really, the granddaughter of Sir Michael Meacham must be respected, after all the man had done for his country.

"We could tell everyone that you were a friend of my grandfather. And he consigned me to your... No. He told me I could depend... No. He asked you to bear me company in my grief." For a moment, she looked genuinely stricken. Then she tossed her head like a thoroughbred pestered by a fly.

With a growing fascination over the workings of her mind, Henry said, "I don't think..."

"A connection to Sir Michael Meacham would add to your consequence among the diplomats," she added.

"It is a lie."

"I'm sure Grandfather *would* have liked you had you met."

Henry was almost diverted by this beguiling idea. But not quite. "Why would you do that?"

"Well, I would want something in return."

There it was. "What?"

"To go along with you to any other gatherings like this," she replied. "Officially *invited*."

"But you wouldn't be."

"*You* are. And you are welcome to bring a companion. Look at Jerome and his fiancée." Miss Meacham threw the pair a piercing glance. "She has no official position. And no one cares for that."

"But they are... We scarcely know each other. No. We don't know each other at all." A short stay in the country while everyone was fully occupied with chasing a kidnapper hadn't allowed time for cozy chats. Even if he had wanted them, or she had encouraged it.

"Well, that is easily remedied." She smiled up at him.

The effect was nearly blinding. She seemed a different person suddenly—even prettier, softer, beguiling. Had she ever smiled at him before? Henry didn't think so. He would remember. "I don't know if I could sustain the deception," he said. He felt that matters were sliding a bit out of his control.

"I will help you, of course," she said.

"You don't mind lying?"

Miss Meacham gazed up at him impatiently. "However will you manage to be a diplomat?"

"What?"

"They don't go about blurting out the truth, you know."

"Discretion is…"

"The better part of valor," she interrupted. "That was Falstaff playing dead, you know. Hardly a sterling model."

"I wasn't going to say that." Smiles aside, she really was a maddening young lady, Henry thought. "Wouldn't it cause talk? If we are continually arriving together?"

"Talk." She brushed this aside with a gesture. "There is always talk. It will pass. I could teach you things I learned from Grandfather," she added.

This was a temptation. "Like what?"

"How to make the best use of this sort of event. How to listen with your back."

"With my…"

"Look at them all nattering away," she went on, gesturing at the crowd. "And swilling champagne. Their tongues are loosening, but not stupidly so."

"All right," Henry said.

"They will begin to be a little too free with their close

colleagues. Just a little. But if you or I went to join in, the talk would die."

He nodded to show he understood.

"But if we stand nearby, talking with another group entirely, that's a different thing. They will go on twittering amongst themselves. One need only listen to those behind one's back."

"Isn't that noticed?" Henry asked.

"The trick is to make a remark now and then to keep up the appearance of conversation. But really to concentrate on those behind you. I've picked up quite a few interesting tidbits that way."

"So you don't have to stand behind a potted palm."

"I was not *behind*..."

"That seems a bit underhanded," Henry interrupted. There was a certain pleasure in goading her, he realized.

"Well, a diplomat is a professional sneak, Mr. Deeping."

"Very amusing."

"Did you think that was a joke?"

"I think it is incorrect. A diplomat is a bridge between nations."

"Is that what you think you were doing in Leicestershire?"

Henry hesitated. "That was an unusual circumstance."

"Perhaps not so unusual." Another smile and her glowing eyes silenced him. Henry felt a strong tug of attraction. Miss Meacham was outrageous. And...riveting. There was an acute brain behind that lovely face. And a wealth of daring. He didn't really like her, of course. That is, he hadn't. Before. She was not quite what he'd thought.

He discovered he was wondering what she would do next. He might not like it. But it was likely to be interesting. Different from the commonplace daily round. Did she too have a rogue imagination? He'd found them rare. And precious.

"So, shall I make some introductions?" she asked.

Henry let himself be led away.

Three

WALKING INTO TEREFORD HOUSE A FEW DAYS LATER, Henry Deeping marveled at the newly decorated rooms. The building was in the most fashionable part of London, just off Berkeley Square.

Henry entered a serenely lovely drawing room decorated in blue and gold. The paneled walls were freshly painted. The furnishings were elegant. The figured carpet was pristine, and the air smelled of potpourri. James leaned on the mantel where a fire crackled. Henry recognized elements from James's old rooms augmented by his duchess's exquisite taste.

"What do you call a group of geese?" the duke asked him as he came in. "We cannot remember."

"A gaggle," Henry replied.

Tereford nodded. "You always know the right word."

"I've heard it is an imitation of the sounds geese make," Henry said. Though didn't geese honk? That noise wasn't much like gaggle.

"Where?" asked the duke.

"What?"

"Where did you hear such a thing? I cannot quite imagine it as a topic of conversation."

"Perhaps I read it. Or one of Charlotte's friends told me. Probably Sarah Moran. She's always full of odd facts." Blaming the hint of an eccentricity on absent friends, Henry sat on a brocade sofa next to the duchess. "You've achieved an amazing transformation," he said to her.

"We have, rather." She smiled as she looked around the room.

One could not have constructed a handsomer couple, Henry thought. Dark-haired James and his golden wife. Both dressed in the first style of elegance, as always. The Terefords might have served as an illustration of what was meant by *haut ton*.

"James has invited you for Christmas dinner, has he not?" asked the duchess.

"He did. Thank you."

"I want to ask any friends who are in town. Many people are in the country, of course. But I've started a list. It's time we began to establish traditions for our family." Her hand rested briefly on her midsection.

"Are you sure you feel up to entertaining?" asked the duke.

"I've been a little ill in the mornings," his wife told Henry. "But I am better and better as time goes by."

"So much so that you will swallow roast goose?" James asked. "Though not a whole gaggle, of course."

It might have been one of his old sardonic taunts, but Henry saw deep concern in his friend's blue eyes.

The duchess looked uneasy for a moment, putting fingertips to her lips. "If I cannot, I will enjoy seeing others feast." She picked up a sheet of paper from a small table at her elbow. "My father and Aunt Valeria will be coming. I'll be sure to seat you beside her, Mr. Deeping."

"Oh. Ah." The duchess's aunt despised society so thoroughly that she occasionally pretended to be deaf to avoid making conversation. She kept it up even though her deception was now well known.

The duchess laughed. "I was joking. We must find some livelier company for you. Have you suggestions? I'm happy to invite any friends of yours who are in town."

For some reason Henry said, "I saw Miss Brown at a reception recently." Both Terefords looked interested, and Henry wondered why his first thought had been to mention that complicated young lady to them. But there was no taking back the words. "Only she is not Miss Brown," he added. "That was in fact a false name, as we suspected. She is Miss Meacham."

"Meacham," the duke echoed.

"Her grandfather was Sir Michael Meacham," Henry added.

"Good lord."

"Who is that?" asked the duchess. "The name seems a little familiar."

"He was an éminence grise of the Foreign Office," said James.

"A fount of wisdom and rather a legend in policy circles," Henry added. "My uncle admired him."

"How interesting. I thought there was something unusual about her."

Henry didn't know why the duchess gazed at him as she said this.

"I will certainly invite her," she added.

"Invite?"

"To Christmas dinner. Isn't that why you mentioned her?"

"No, I…" Why had he? It was true their encounter lingered in his mind. It was true that he often found himself wondering what she was up to this very minute.

"No?"

The idea of seeing her was…alluring. It wasn't as if he was extending the invitation. The Terefords had made her acquaintance in Leicestershire. They might have thought of it themselves. He shrugged.

"Do you have her address?" the duchess asked.

Henry shook his head. He knew so little about her. He did wish to learn more. But in the face of the duchess's bright curiosity, he said, "Why would I?"

"I expect I can find it," said James.

His wife nodded. "There is Miss Palliser as well. You must know how to reach her, since you found her to make those translations."

This time Henry nodded.

The duchess made notes on her page. She tapped it with her pencil. "Who else, I wonder?"

"I am imagining Miss Palliser conversing with your aunt Valeria," James said to his wife. "Somehow, I think they would get on."

"If they find a common subject…" The duchess looked doubtful.

"In your invitation to Miss Palliser, suggest she bone up on beekeeping."

"Very amusing, James," said his wife.

"Perhaps I can't come after all," Henry teased. "I have just remembered…"

"You have already accepted," James interrupted. "You can't disappoint Cecelia now." He smiled mockingly at Henry.

"Merlin," murmured the duchess.

"Cecelia! You wouldn't."

"We need more gentlemen," said the duchess with a lovely smile. "Oh!"

"What? Who?"

"Someone amusing."

Tereford looked resigned. Very fondly so, Henry noticed. His old friend had changed quite astonishingly in the last year.

Not far away in miles, but a world apart in the eyes of the fashionable world, Kate Meacham again sat in her grandfather's study. She looked over a list of people he had gone to for information. Surely someone among them would have heard whispers about the agent she'd helped capture in Leicestershire. It was wildly frustrating to know nothing about what was happening with the fellow. But most of these sources could not be approached in her own person. It would have to be the breeches again, if Mrs. Knox could be got around. Kate wasn't certain that she could.

There was a tap on the door, and Sally looked in. "A caller, miss," the maid said.

Kate blinked. They never got morning callers, here in the social hinterlands. "Who is it?"

"A lady. Palace-er she said her name was. She didn't have a card."

Kate rose and went down to her small tidy front parlor. There she found Miss Daphne Palliser, looking just as she had in Leicestershire in November when she was translating important documents. In her thirties, stocky and brown-haired, Miss Palliser wore one of her plain sensible gowns and the spectacles that magnified her gray eyes, giving her an owlish air. She was a formidable scholar, impatient with polite conversation, and certainly not someone who paid morning calls.

"Good day, Miss Meacham," she said. "Or am I supposed to say Miss Brown still?"

"That ruse is over," replied Kate.

Miss Palliser nodded. "No doubt you are surprised to see me."

"Oh. Well, I…" They had worked closely together through a dramatic period, but they were not really friends. There had been no leisure to learn much about each other. Kate adopted her guest's direct manner. "I am rather. Do sit down. Would you care for something? Coffee? Wine?" As a political statement, in opposition to British policies, Miss Palliser did not drink tea.

"No, thank you." She sat. And then looked uncertain, which was not like her at all.

"Is there news in the investigation of the Leicestershire matter?" Kate asked her. Miss Palliser's scholarly abilities had been instrumental in solving the case.

"I wouldn't know," the older woman responded dryly. "The Foreign Office regards me purely as a tool. If there is some question about a passage, they call me in for a consultation. Or they did at first. They have found scholars of their own to interpret the documents. *Gentlemen* scholars. And they certainly don't tell me anything."

"It's maddening. They wouldn't have anyone to question if it weren't for us."

"They prefer to forget that ladies are capable of decisive action." Miss Palliser nodded. "Mr. Deeping might know more."

Kate shook her head. "I asked. He is not being told either."

"Has he been placed with us among the people of no importance?" Miss Palliser's tone was bitter.

"So it seems."

The older woman brooded for a moment, then made a dismissive gesture. "Pay no attention to me. I am not in the best of moods. I have had a disagreement with my father. He has been ordered abroad to oversee some treaty negotiations. He is the Foreign Office's expert at minute detail and subtle nuance, you know. Which has always struck me as ridiculous, because when it comes to his own family, he hasn't the least sense of either. I doubt he could tell you my middle name."

She had mentioned something like this before. Kate made a sympathetic sound, mystified as to why she had called here to repeat it.

"Most of the time he appears to forget my existence," Miss Palliser continued. "Or perhaps he only wishes that I didn't exist. It's difficult to tell the difference. But now suddenly he is fussing. He cannot take me with him. There is no place for me on the expedition. The Foreign Office wouldn't approve." She threw up her hands. "I don't wish to go! I never have. We would not get on at all. But suddenly he feels he cannot leave his inconvenient daughter in London alone. I am thirty-four years old! Hardly in need of oversight. There are the servants. I have my work."

"Ah," said Kate, still bewildered. She had found Miss Palliser an interesting companion in Leicestershire, and she realized their unconventional positions in the diplomatic world were somewhat alike. But they had separated without planning to meet again.

"And now you are wondering why I am pouring out my grievances on your unsuspecting head," her guest said, as if reading this thought in her expression. "Well, it is why I have come, though now that I am here, I don't know…" Miss Palliser frowned at the floor. "It seems to me that we have certain things in common. Impatience with niggling social conventions, for example. And intellectual curiosity, though in different areas."

Kate nodded. That was certainly true.

Miss Palliser examined her. Kate reciprocated. "Ah well," said her visitor then, with an air of throwing caution to the winds. "I shall just say it. I wondered if you might invite me to come and stay with you?"

Kate's mouth dropped a little open.

"Quite temporarily," said Miss Palliser quickly. "I am looking for a way to satisfy my father, and I believe this might do." She began ticking off points on her fingers. "He is a baronet. Your grandfather was knighted for his service to England, and my father admired Sir Michael very much."

As had nearly everyone, Kate thought with a pang.

"So we are of similar rank and background. It would satisfy society's idea of propriety, and my father's, if we were chaperoning each other." Miss Palliser scoffed. "Though neither of us actually requires such a thing, we are thought to. Naturally each of us would continue to do as she pleased."

"Chaperoning," Kate repeated.

"I am speaking of something quite brief," the older woman added. "Until my father departs and is well away. He will forget all about me then, and I can return home."

As the request sank in, Kate wondered if this was a solution to the problem Mrs. Knox had posed. One she could bear. Not hiring some stranger to descend upon her settled household and preach proprieties. That would be horrid. She would not be lectured or controlled. And she had no funds to tempt such a person in any case. But Miss Palliser wasn't anything like that.

Kate had faced the fact that word of her situation would inevitably spread. Some friend of her grandfather's would realize that she was living alone. If Jerome learned of it, he would put his oar in, using the excuse of old friendship to cause trouble. Kate suppressed a spark of temper. For some reason, Jerome seemed to wish her ill. If he didn't want to work with her, then so be it. But then—*particularly* then—he had no right to interfere. Not that this would stop him. He had always had a pompous streak, she realized.

Miss Palliser was looking as if she regretted her words. She started to rise. "I beg your pardon…"

"Actually I have a problem very similar to yours," Kate said. "My grandfather left me this house and a small income, but my living here alone is causing gossip."

The older woman's frown eased, and she sank back into her chair.

"Perhaps a visit would be pleasant for us both." It wasn't good that this sounded like a question. "You once said I made rational conversation." Kate wasn't certain who she was trying to convince.

"So you do." Miss Palliser looked equally ambivalent.

They gazed at each other warily, and then, slowly, they both began to smile.

"There is a certain element of the ridiculous to this situation," said Miss Palliser.

"Two intelligent, capable persons who are treated like children," Kate replied.

"Or unstable chemical compounds that are likely to explode if left to themselves."

Kate laughed. "Well, why not? Let us try it out and see how it goes."

"As a trial to be terminated if either party wishes it."

"Yes."

"I have a modest income left to me by my mother," Miss Palliser added. "I can pay for my keep."

Kate's first impulse was to demur, but she couldn't afford

to do that. The household expenses were very carefully calibrated.

"I do require a good many books," said Miss Palliser almost defiantly. "More than any reasonable person should, according to my father."

"I have not formed a favorable idea of his opinions," replied Kate.

Miss Palliser smiled. "But to be clear, I shall be bringing several cartons with my clothes and such." She dismissed the latter with a wave of her hand.

Kate rose. "Come. Let me show you something." She led her visitor upstairs to her grandfather's old study.

"Oh," said Miss Palliser when she entered. "What a splendid room! It is just the sort of working place I have always dreamed of."

"You are welcome to work here," Kate replied.

Her visitor turned in surprise. "But don't you wish to?"

"I've found that I'm not comfortable here for long, with Grandfather gone." Kate had been noticing this more and more. "This was so much his spot."

"Ah." Miss Palliser nodded in understanding.

"I am happier at the desk in my bedchamber. And you may add as many books as you like," Kate added.

"Fill it right to the ceiling?" asked Miss Palliser with some amusement.

"Indeed. My grandfather has…had the finest sources on history and diplomacy in the country," Kate replied.

A gleam of greed showed in Miss Palliser's owlish gaze. "Annotated?"

Kate wasn't certain she would share her grandfather's private notes. But his marginal comments were fascinating in themselves. "Many volumes, yes."

Miss Palliser rubbed her hands together in anticipation.

"Will you teach me to throw knives?" Kate asked. Miss Palliser had demonstrated an uncanny skill with small blades during their recent adventure.

This drew a laugh from the older woman. "I don't mind trying."

Thinking such lessons might be worth having a near stranger in her house, Kate offered her hand on the bargain. Miss Palliser shook it. She departed soon after, and Kate went to give Mrs. Knox the news that she had secured a respectable chaperone.

Daphne Palliser lost no time in sealing the agreement. She and her belongings arrived the following day. Mrs. Knox directed the carter carrying in boxes and bundles while Kate took their guest to her new bedchamber.

"When it came down to it, I found that most of what I care about is books," Miss Palliser commented.

"My grandfather was the same."

"Not completely." She gestured at the building around them.

"He inherited this place from an aunt. I don't think he added a stick of furniture." Kate opened a door on the third floor. "Here is your room." The house was tall and narrow. A half basement held the kitchen, pantry, and rooms for Mrs. Knox, opening on a small garden at the back with a privy at the end. The ground floor held the parlor and dining room.

The next level was taken up by her grandfather's study with books overflowing into a library in the other chamber on that level. Four small bedchambers occupied the third floor, with servants' rooms on the top level above. A stair wound up the middle of the house.

The chamber was at least neat and clean, Kate thought, though probably not as spacious as the one Miss Palliser had at her father's home. The bed and wardrobe and small armchair were relics of a previous century. The flowered draperies and bedcovering were worn, though not actually ragged. Preparing quarters for Miss Palliser had made Kate look at her dwelling with new eyes. It was so clearly the home of a man who cared more for ideas than appearances. Cluttered and a little shabby. "I haven't really changed anything since Grandfather died," she said.

Miss Palliser nodded.

"I hope you will be comfortable. I don't know…" Kate's voice trailed off. Now that the die was cast, she didn't know whether this had been a wise choice. Though it had been the only one offered, she noted.

Miss Palliser looked as if she understood. Or was feeling just the same. "If we do not suit, I will move out at once." She smiled. "When my father is gone, he won't think about what I'm doing. Or know."

And if word had spread by then that Kate had a proper companion, she need not contradict it, she thought. Even if Miss Palliser returned home. She would have the illusion of a chaperone without the irritating reality. This benefited them both. And they did have many things in common.

They looked at each other—still wary.

"I've been lonely," said Kate, astonishing herself.

There was a short silence.

"I too."

Similar discomfort showed in both their faces. "Shall we set out the daily routine?" Kate asked. "Settle things as we both prefer?"

"A splendid idea," replied Miss Palliser. "A list?"

"A list," Kate agreed. "Let us go to the study."

Four

"I HOPE WE DON'T FIND WE'RE SORRY TO HAVE ACCEPTED this invitation," said Kate as she and Miss Palliser stepped out of a hansom cab onto the damp cobbles in front of Tereford House.

"Christmas dinner with a duke and duchess? How could we not come?" the older woman responded. "And they were quite cordial in Leicestershire."

This was true. But that had been in the country in unusual circumstances. This was London, and the Terefords were leading lights of the *haut ton*. Kate didn't have a high opinion of the fashionable set. Her grandfather had called them the froth on society's surface, ornamental but not solid or generally dependable.

"They would not invite us and then be rude," said Miss Palliser. "Who would do such an irrational thing?"

Kate couldn't say, but she still was far from easy about how this event would go.

A polished footman answered their knock and ushered them in. They stepped from a cold, wet December day into a grand entry swathed with holly and evergreens. Warmth enfolded them. Kate breathed in the scents of pine and oranges and the mouthwatering aromas of the coming feast.

Open doorways on either side revealed rich furnishings and draperies.

Relieved of their wraps and bonnets, they were escorted to a beautiful blue and gold drawing room hung with more evergreens and warmed by a crackling fire. They were greeted at the door by the Duchess of Tereford, whose sapphire gown and golden hair matched the chamber. "Welcome Miss Palliser. And Miss Meacham, I understand?"

Kate resisted apologizing. Yes, she had used a false name when they met. She'd had good reasons. She doubted this flawless woman could understand them.

"You are most welcome," their hostess continued. "I should like to be better acquainted with you both."

Her smile was lovely, and she seemed sincere. Kate saw kindness in her eyes. Miss Palliser shot Kate a sidelong look as if to say, "You see?"

"Come and let me introduce you."

As she drew them in, Kate examined the guests gathered in the room. Only the Terefords looked like members of high society. The rest were…oddly assorted.

They stopped first beside two older people near the fireplace. Both were plump and blond and dressed rather plainly. The duchess presented Kate and Miss Palliser and said, "This is my father, Mr. Nigel Vainsmede, and my aunt, Miss Valeria Vainsmede."

"I understand you are something of a scholar," Mr. Vainsmede said to Miss Palliser.

"I am," she replied with a confidence Kate envied.

"You must tell me about your work."

"I should be happy to."

Valeria Vainsmede sighed audibly. She did not look pleased to be here, Kate thought. Sharp intelligence glinted in the older woman's pale blue eyes but very little patience. "I don't suppose you know anything about bees," she said.

"Nothing of particular significance," Kate replied. "I was stung by one when I was small."

"I expect you were interfering with the acquisition of nectar," was the unsympathetic reply. "Or you stepped where you shouldn't have."

"Perhaps the bee was out of place."

"Extremely unlikely," Miss Vainsmede replied. "And scarcely worthy of death in any case."

"Death?"

"They die when they sting you," said the other with a glare that implied she should have known this.

Kate was sorry to hear it. She felt unaccountably guilty and was glad when Henry Deeping came to join them. It was only relief that made her heart beat a bit faster, she told herself.

He brought along another slender dark-haired man with a craggy face and a furtive air. The fellow limped and leaned on a cane. It took Kate a moment to recognize him. He called himself Merlin, she remembered, and had an eccentric history. He'd been part of their efforts in Leicestershire, in a somewhat peripheral and plaintive way because of a broken leg. She'd never seen him on his feet. "Hello, Merlin," she said.

"Oliver Welden," the man retorted. "I've left all that behind me."

"All what?" Kate wondered.

He waved this aside with a familiar crusty impatience. This had seemed to be his constant state in the country, and he didn't appear to have changed.

"Your leg is better," said Miss Palliser.

"It mends far too slowly," he complained. "I cannot begin my work as a Bow Street Runner until it is fully healed."

"They took you on then?" Kate asked. Merlin had been determined to join these famed investigators after learning of their existence.

"With Tereford's recommendation," said Henry Deeping. Oliver Welden gave a grudging nod.

"That should prove interesting," said Miss Palliser.

The man merely grunted.

"Come and meet the others," said the duchess.

She led them over to a young man and a boy who gazed around the room with open curiosity. The elder had a round face, friendly blue eyes, and somewhat prominent front teeth. Large bones in his hands and wrists suggested he hadn't attained his full growth. He looked to be in his late teens and wore his long-tailed coat with considerable panache.

"This is Tom Jesperson," said the duchess when they reached this pair. "He is an actor at the Drury Lane Theater."

The young man grinned and bowed elegantly. "Pleased to meet you," he said in an accent that copied the duchess's.

"Tom has been attracting favorable notice on the stage," their hostess added. "He is an old acquaintance of Charlotte Deeping and her school friends."

Kate wondered how Mr. Deeping's sister had come to

know a London actor. But the connection wasn't explained further.

"And this is Ned Gardener."

The younger boy looked nervous and a bit out of place in this group. He was perhaps no more than thirteen, Kate thought. He was slender, brown-haired, and would have been nondescript had it not been for his clothing. This was immaculate, the equal of any in the room, including the duke's, and clearly the work of a first-rate tailor.

"He is newly apprenticed at Weston's premises."

Pride shone from Ned Gardener's face, and he fingered the lapel of his coat with unconscious reverence. He bowed with less ease than his companion. His greeting was nearly inaudible. Kate's puzzlement grew.

They moved on to where the duke was charming two older ladies whose dress was rich but of a plainness that rejected the very concept of fashion. Kate was not surprised to discover that Miss Brill was head of a school for deserving girls and Mrs. Rice oversaw a refuge for families in distress. Others in the room included scholar friends of the duchess's father and their wives. Kate lost track of the names at some point, but Miss Palliser was clearly at home with this cohort.

They were called in to dinner soon after the introductions were complete. Kate found herself placed between Henry Deeping and one of the older scholars. The latter had already picked up his knife and fork in anticipation of the meal. His eyes were on the doorway where the feast would emerge.

The duke stood at the head of the glittering table and smiled down it to his wife at the foot. "We are pleased you could all join us on this festive day," he said. "Welcome to our home and happy Christmas." He sat, and servants began to bring in dishes and place them down the center of the long board.

The dinner was of course sumptuous. There was roast beef and venison, a crisply glistening goose and a fat capon. Potatoes, squash, brussels sprouts, and carrots supplemented the meat, along with ewers of gravy and baskets of bread rolls. The wine was plentiful and very fine.

Henry Deeping appreciated the bounty and the cheer. But he found his enjoyment was elevated by the presence of Miss Meacham beside him. He'd felt an unexpected leap of interest when she arrived. The sight of her lovely figure and a flashing glance from her violet eyes enhanced the occasion. "May I give you a slice of goose?" he asked her, carving knife poised over the platter.

"All right," she replied absently. She was looking around the table with a frown.

Henry put a serving before her. The bearded older man on her other side held out his plate with some urgency, and Henry cut him a larger portion. He accepted it with a pleased nod and began heaping mounds of every dish within reach around it. "Miss Brill?" Henry asked the lady on his left, indicating the goose.

"I do not consume the flesh of animals," she answered.

"I beg your pardon."

"It is not necessary for you to do so, though you might wish to consider your own choices." Miss Brill helped herself to a selection of vegetables.

Henry hesitated briefly, then took some goose for himself and reached for the gravy. When he offered the ewer to Kate Meacham, she fixed him with a steady gaze. He found he really couldn't look away. "Are we the scaff and raff of the ducal acquaintances?" she asked. "Is this some sort of charitable noblesse oblige?"

"I don't think…"

"Oh, not you. You are the duke's friend." She raised her eyebrows. "Though perhaps not his wealthiest or highest-ranked friend, eh?"

Henry stiffened. "The Vainsmedes…"

"The duchess's family, all right. But what about that boy?"

Henry followed her gaze. Ned Gardener sat beside Mrs. Rice, with Tom on her other side. She looked amused by their conversation.

"Tereford pulled Ned's family out of poverty," Henry acknowledged. "He gave Ned an opportunity he never expected. Ned is determined to make good."

"As a tailor."

"He wanted that above all things."

Miss Meacham made a skeptical sound. "All things. All the things Ned had the chance to observe in his limited circumstances. Which can't have been very many."

Henry could not dispute this. He sampled the goose instead. It was, of course, delicious. "Ned does love the work," he said then. "With the proper encouragement, he will talk about the 'hand' of various fabrics and the proper drape of a coattail for half an hour."

"While the Terefords float above us all without a care in the world."

"That is unfair," Henry replied, though he was uneasily aware that he'd had a similar thought when James had inherited a vast fortune. "Everyone has cares." A burst of laughter down the table made him add, "Except Tom, perhaps. He always seems remarkably carefree."

"An actor," Miss Meacham replied caustically. "He would be skilled in making you think so."

Henry gazed at the young man. Was his good humor false? It didn't feel that way.

"The duchess said he is an acquaintance of your sister."

"Yes. Tom…assisted Charlotte and her school friends in several adventures. You should hear Charlotte recount the tales. They found a hidden treasure and set fire to a, er, den of iniquity."

Miss Meacham blinked. "Did you actually say 'den of iniquity'?"

"Charlotte says her sarcasm comes from growing up plagued by four brothers," he replied. "What's your excuse?"

She blinked at him.

"Have I rendered you speechless?" Henry smiled. "That has been an ambition of mine for some time."

"To reduce me to silence?"

"Briefly. So that you think a moment before you bite my head off."

"I don't do that."

"Yes, you do. Ever since I met you. And I don't know why." He'd thought she despised him. He wasn't quite sure of that now. It seemed less likely. He realized that he would very much like to know her true opinion.

Miss Meacham concentrated on her dinner for a bit. Henry did the same, savoring the flavors while waiting for her reply.

"You are…"

"Yes?"

Their eyes locked. Hers were riveting violet pools. The babble of table conversation seemed to dim around him. Henry was aware only of her at his side. Her shoulder inches from his, her hand resting on the tablecloth, the angle of her cheek and curve of her lips. Then she blinked and looked down, and the spell was broken.

"You take things for granted," she said. "As a man you can do as you like."

"That is not really true. As I think you know."

"More so than I can," she muttered.

He wasn't going to argue that.

When he was silent, she glanced up. "Aren't you going to tell me that I am strident and ungrateful? That I should accept my allotted place with good grace and be a proper submissive lady?"

"No, I wouldn't do that. But I don't see much point in brooding on injustices." That could take one to dark places indeed.

"I do not brood."

"That's good then." He smiled.

She frowned at him.

A cloud of footmen entered to take away the ravaged

platters and bring in the second course. There were plates of small mince pies, Chantilly crème, syllabub, shortbread, and slabs of gingerbread. The finale was the Christmas pudding. Garnished with holly and flaming blue from brandy, it was greeted with acclaim and a round of toasts to the future and warm sentiments of the season.

"My grandfather loved Christmas," said Miss Meacham as she tasted a bite of the pudding. "He always made sure we had an invitation to a feast like this." She made a gesture. "Not as grand as a duke's table, but plentiful and jolly. And he took great pains over his gifts. He made a game of it with me. I wasn't to tell him what I wanted. Instead, we played twenty questions. I gave hints, he drew conclusions, and then bought my present. He went all over London to find books his friends had been searching for to give them."

Her mournful expression touched Henry. "I wish I had met him."

She nodded sadly.

"Did he always get it right?"

"What?"

"Your gift."

Her glorious smile lit her face. "Not once."

"But you pretended that he had."

Miss Meacham blinked in surprise. "How did you know that?"

Henry wasn't sure. The words had just popped out. "One does," he said.

"Does?" She was watching him as if he had said something odd.

He groped for an explanation. "Much of the pleasure comes from the delight of the gift giver. Don't you think?"

Miss Meacham gazed at him. The rest of the world remained background noise. If he wasn't careful, he was going to lose himself entirely, Henry thought. "I suppose you weren't very good at hinting," he found himself remarking. "Forthright statements are more like you."

"And you, apparently," she answered.

It was time to turn the conversation. They were surrounded by near strangers. They couldn't lean so close—when had that happened?—and devote themselves exclusively to each other. Henry could feel the Terefords' interested eyes on him. He straightened, took up his spoon for the pudding. "My family greatly enjoys the Christmas season," he said. As if they had been exchanging commonplaces.

"They would," replied the always unexpected Miss Meacham.

"I beg your pardon?" Her tone had sounded critical.

"You have an exceedingly pleasant family."

"You met them very briefly. And yet you seem to be blaming them for something."

"Don't be ridiculous."

"I don't believe I am. You sounded quite accusing."

Miss Meacham glanced at him, then looked down at the sweets on her plate. "I didn't mean to," she said finally. "Perhaps it's that…my parents died before I really knew them. They were often away even before they were killed in a shipwreck."

"Were they diplomats also?" Henry asked. That would explain some things about her.

"Yes." As if reminded, she added, "There is a Twelfth Night celebration hosted by the American ambassador next week. Have you received an invitation?"

Henry nodded.

"Good." Her gaze grew sharp. "You promised to include me. If you are going to argue that…"

"I am not going to argue."

"You aren't?"

"No. I will escort you. Though I am still concerned that our outings may cause some talk."

"Talk, talk. How I tire of that word! You are the responsible oldest brother, aren't you? Always taking the conventional route, obeying the rules. Never daring."

The phrases struck like slaps. Henry felt a flash of anger. "I dare."

"Really? How?"

"On the hunting field…" But he bit off that painful association.

"Jumping hedges? That is mostly the horse."

Henry gritted his teeth. She knew nothing about…anything. "I dare," he repeated, mostly to himself.

"Show me."

"I shall." He wanted to do it then and there. But how? Shaking a young lady at the holiday table—or anywhere at all, ever—was not daring. It was outrageous, insane. And he had not lost his mind. Not just yet.

"You may give me another spoonful of the Chantilly crème," said Miss Brill on his left side.

"Eh? Oh, certainly." Brought abruptly back to earth, and his automatic good manners, Henry served her.

"I do not think it necessary to eschew all the *products* of animals," she said. As if he had asked. "So long as they are well treated."

"How are you to know that?" asked the elderly gentleman on her other side. Henry had forgotten his name.

"I trust the duchess to take care," Miss Brill replied.

"She might be deceived."

They descended into argument, leaving Henry to brood on the fact that he was intensely, blazingly, conscious of Miss Kate Meacham on his right.

———

"You see your fears were groundless," said Miss Palliser to Kate in the cab as they rode home. "The evening seemed quite pleasant to me."

"Yes." Kate was conscious that her tone lacked enthusiasm.

"Did you not enjoy yourself? I found the company surprisingly congenial. Not what one expects from the fashionable set. Young Tom Jesperson was full of marvelous tales, and wonderful at recounting them."

"He is an actor."

"Yes." Her tone implied, And so?

"The guests weren't fashionable."

"Exactly. The Terefords matched the company's interests and degrees. Thoughtful of them."

She couldn't fault their noble hosts. Even though she

wanted to, for some reason. Pure orneriness, Kate decided. The occasion had left her fuming with…fuming.

"You appeared to enjoy talking with Mr. Deeping."

"He was sitting beside me. It was necessary to talk to him."

"Are you saying you did *not* enjoy it?"

Was Miss Palliser teasing her? Kate had not expected that from her owlish companion.

"You appeared thoroughly…absorbed."

"He is…." Not what she had thought him. Not easily categorized. Or dismissed. Definitely not dismissed. Why this should annoy her, Kate did not know. She had no excuse for wanting to hit something.

"He is rather interesting, I think," said Miss Palliser.

Kate turned, but she couldn't see her companion's face in the dimness of the cab. "What do you mean?"

"He has a polished surface. Which a diplomat requires, of course. But unlike many I have met, I believe his hides interesting complexities."

"Why do you say so?" asked Kate.

Miss Palliser's cloak rustled as she settled back on the hackney's seat. "When he first came to ask me to work on the translations in Leicestershire, he suggested it was a way to use my capabilities to the fullest. That was…unusually insightful in itself. But something about his tone made me ask if the investigation was doing the same for him. He replied that such a thing wasn't possible. And then he was very sorry to have spoken so freely. It was plain to see. I believe he was fatigued from his journey and let the words slip. Something in his tone made me think that he…seethed with hidden ambitions."

Kate was transfixed by the word—*seethed*. It suggested bubbling cauldrons or volcanoes on the verge of explosion. Suppressed passions? Had she felt these simmering depths in him herself? Was that why he irritated her so? Why she constantly goaded him?

Perhaps it was. Perhaps she wanted to see them loosed. The idea, the challenge, excited her. Not just the seething, but that he hid it so insistently.

If there was fire hidden in him, she wanted to find it, Kate thought. She needed to. But what would cause Mr. Henry Deeping to erupt?

"Rather the opposite of Mr. Welden," said her companion.

For a moment, Kate had no idea what she was talking about. Then she recalled that there were other people in the world. "Merlin?" What had he to do with anything?

"He seems to hide nothing with his grumbling opinions. And yet underneath…"

"More acid?"

"I wonder."

"You do?"

"I was wholly occupied with the translation work in Leicestershire. I don't remember anything about his history. Do you?"

"Not really." Kate had thought of little but tracking down the foreign agent. Merlin's eccentricities had not interested her. "I think someone mentioned that he had been a kind of hermit for a while," she said. Could that be right? It seemed unlikely.

Miss Palliser made a dissatisfied sound.

Kate was about to ask her why when the cab pulled up before her house. The conversation was dropped as they got down, paid the fare, and went inside.

———————

Two days later, Henry was surprised to receive an early evening visit from Jerome Delaroche. "I asked at the office for your address," the taller man said when he arrived at Henry's rooms. "I thought I might just drop a word in your ear."

"A word?" Henry asked. Was this a subtle way to hear about a diplomatic matter? He and Delaroche were not employed by the same department. And though they had been introduced, they were not at all acquainted.

"Might I come in?"

Henry stood back, ushered him into his parlor, and offered a glass of wine. Delaroche accepted and then sipped it as he examined Henry's quarters from one of the armchairs before the fireplace. "Pleasant digs," he said. "Been here long?"

"A year," Henry answered. He remembered something his uncle had told him—informal connections were as important as official channels in diplomatic work. Perhaps even more important. Much might depend on the contacts one established. Was this how such a network began? Delaroche had been in the job longer than he. He would let him take the lead and see where the conversation went.

After a short silence, his visitor said, "I wanted to speak to you about Kate Meacham."

Henry blinked in surprise. "Miss Meacham?"

"We have known each other all our lives, you see."

Was he worried about her reputation? Henry wondered how to reassure him without saying something the lady would not appreciate.

"I would advise you not to become embroiled with her," Delaroche added before he could speak.

This was not what he'd expected. "Embroiled?"

"I don't know how she secured your escort to that reception."

Henry said nothing in the pause that followed. He didn't really care for Delaroche's tone, and he did not intend to expose Kate Meacham to any possibility of censure.

Delaroche waited longer than was normal for polite conversation. "But I doubt whatever she told you was the truth," he said finally. "She was not invited. Specifically. And she knew it."

"Why not?" Henry asked. "Her grandfather…"

"Sir Michael spoiled her," Delaroche interrupted. "But he also exerted some control over her actions. Since his death she's been behaving…recklessly."

She *had* gone to Leicestershire under a false name, though Henry didn't think Delaroche was aware of that. She had sneaked into the reception where they met again. And others, apparently. This was a bit reckless. But he would not acknowledge that. "In what way?"

Delaroche threw up a hand. "I hate to consider the full extent of it. She has no concept of restraint. I don't know what she might do."

"So you are accusing her of…?"

His visitor shifted in the chair. "Isn't it enough that she shows up at quite exclusive events where she has not been invited? It's being noticed."

"So Miss Meacham was welcome at diplomatic receptions while her grandfather was alive, and now she is not?" She had said as much. It seemed she hadn't been exaggerating.

"Sir Michael made his own rules."

This wasn't really an answer to his question. Henry was finding the conversation distasteful. "Why are you telling me this?"

"So that you will refuse to help her."

"This is an order from our superiors?" If that was the case, he had difficulties.

Delaroche almost said it was. Henry saw the temptation in his expression. But in the end, he replied, "It is a request. From me." He frowned. "She's known to be a friend of mine. And some people are aware that she was the source for the Gibraltar information."

"Which was very helpful, I understand?"

"She could not have learned of that by any means a young lady should employ," Delaroche burst out. "She has gone wild. I don't know *what* she does."

Clearly, he meant to suggest improprieties without actually naming them. So that accusations could not be brought back to him. Henry felt a flare of anger and sympathy for Miss Meacham.

"Kate is intractable." Delaroche grimaced. "I really could not marry her. Sir Michael…"

"He asked you to do so?" Henry found the idea exceedingly annoying.

His guest made a throwaway gesture. "Not quite. When he grew ill, I believe he hoped… But I could not live with Kate. What man could?"

A man who appreciated intelligence and initiative, Henry imagined. Men who did not imply improper behavior without presenting a shred of evidence.

"I shouldn't have mentioned that," his visitor said. "Please forget it."

He had to know that was impossible. Every word he'd said had been carefully calculated, Henry realized.

"You need to think of your own advancement," Delaroche went on. "She will drag you into trouble. And that will do you no favors in the Foreign Office."

"It's very kind of you to warn me."

Delaroche wasn't stupid. Clearly he heard the censure in Henry's voice. He set aside his wineglass and rose. "It would be a mistake to cross me," he said.

"How am I crossing you?" Henry asked.

"By parading Kate around town and letting her make a spectacle of herself."

Henry wondered if Miss Meacham knew some disreputable secret about Delaroche. Was that what he feared?

"You'll find yourself up to your ears in scandal."

"I believe I can avoid any such thing." He was not a fool or a dupe. Of anyone.

"I was trying to do you a good turn."

Perhaps there was a grain of truth in that. But Henry

thought the visit had been much more about protecting Delaroche's interests than his own. Delaroche was associated with Miss Meacham in people's minds. He wanted her removed from public view and forgotten so that no hint of doubt could touch him. It was contemptible.

Henry frowned after he ushered the man out. Kate Meacham was unconventional. Reckless, yes, perhaps she was. Daring, he thought, the word coming back to him from their conversation at Christmas. She dared.

And he did not?

He sat down and poured himself another glass of wine. She'd called him responsible, conventional. That was what she saw. And despised, Henry thought. But what did she know? Less than nothing.

Less than nothing.

He took a swallow of wine. As a boy he'd yearned to be a hero. He'd built a treetop redoubt and defended it from dragons, sailed it through tempests with Sir Francis Drake. He'd careened across the countryside with Arthur's knights—a brother or two—in tow. School had failed to dim his aspirations. He'd fed them with feats on the playing fields and tales of derring-do.

He had been set on joining Wellington's army and fighting for his country. His family had put together the price of a cavalry commission. And then, just before he was to join his regiment, he fell during a neck-or-nothing hunt and smashed his left leg to flinders. Henry shrugged away a wince as he remembered the sudden thunderous pain. Catastrophe. He'd been utterly flattened. With the complications of infection and fever, the injury had taken more than a year to heal.

And even then the knee had not been the same. Unthinking, he rubbed the joint. It still pained him in the cold and damp, though it no longer gave way under stress.

Henry drank Madeira. The army hadn't wanted him after that, and his spirits had been as crushed as his leg. It seemed as if his family's ancient calling—breeders of the finest horses in the land—had turned on him and ruined all his hopes. The call to heroism had been a silly illusion. Darkness had descended for a while then, a gloom so deep it had nearly destroyed him. He didn't speak of that. Ever. Many of his London friends didn't even know. Those who did, like James, followed his lead and were silent. One did not venture back into that place, he thought.

He tossed off the rest of the wine, shoved the glass away. That was the past. He had clawed his way back. He had regained his balance—gotten back on horseback both literally and metaphorically. His uncle had stepped forward and offered him a worthy profession. And if using words to fence rather than sabers seemed paltry, well, that was a limited view. He was…content.

He had been. Really. He never thought of that time. Until an opinionated young lady had burst into his life and dredged up these memories with her accusations.

Daring, Henry thought, as one might name an old friend who had passed out of one's life. His uncle would snort at the word. He was an intensely practical man, and he expected Henry to follow his lead. As he would, Henry noted. That was the plan. What did Miss Meacham expect? Piratical antics? He shook his head and turned away toward bed.

Five

At the Twelfth Night party to mark the end of the Christmas season, the American embassy rang with singing and the rhythm of dancing feet. The effects of plentiful hot spiced wine were obvious in the raucous games. Kate watched a bewildered young Polish attaché dragged into bobbing for apples amidst gales of laughter and noted there was nothing stuffy about this celebration. She felt more at ease among the diplomats than she had in months.

Only gradually did she realize that the steady presence of Henry Deeping at her side might have a good deal to do with this. In some ways he reminded her of her grandfather. He felt like a sheltering wall in a high wind.

As soon as this thought emerged, she turned on it with startled suspicion. She mustn't begin relying on anyone else. Certainly not on a young man who only stood beside her because they had made a bargain. Nothing more. She didn't know him at all.

And yet it seemed to Kate that she did, and that Henry Deeping could be trusted to stand against the social pressures that threatened to sweep her away.

"I had not expected to see sober diplomats snapping at

apples like oversized turtles," he said with the smile that transformed his thin face into something very special.

"I don't think many of them are sober," she replied.

His laugh was charming and more gratifying to Kate than it should be. Something in her yearned toward him. She reined it in. She was not being reasonable. She'd best stick to business. She'd promised introductions. "That is the ambassador from the United States," she told him, pointing out a gray-haired man with a high forehead and straight nose. "Richard Rush. He is quite popular here. They say he has a 'gentlemanly' attitude. So he is forgiven for being our staunch opponent in the recent North American war. And for the fact that both his father and grandfather signed our former colonies' Declaration of Independence."

"You are very well informed."

"So unusual for a female?" It popped out, a relic of many other conversations.

"I did not say that. You have an irritating habit of putting words in my mouth, Miss Meacham."

"I just prefer to have opinions out in the open. However negative they may be, it is better than hidden prejudice."

"But that is not my opinion. I never said anything of the kind. You construct sentences full of pitfalls."

Kate rather liked the idea. "Like traps dug for animals to fall into?"

Mr. Deeping stared. "And be killed? No, that was not my thought."

She was still taken with the concept. "I know people I would have loved to slay with a well-placed sentence."

"Enemies, Miss Meacham?"

Kate shook her head. "I can respect an honest enemy. It's false friends I can't bear."

An odd expression passed across his face, as if she'd made him think of someone in particular. He started to speak, then pressed his lips together as if uncertain.

She would have pursued it. She liked winnowing out secrets. But they were joined just then by an enthusiastic Austrian determined to add them to a singing group he was assembling. Thoroughly lubricated by the spiced wine, he would not be denied. They must all learn his Teutonic refrains. With extravagant gestures, he herded them across the room, pulling others into his orbit as they went. Richter was his name, Kate remembered. She'd met him somewhere, though they'd never spoken at length.

Mr. Richter added them to his choir like a sheepdog chivvying its charges, then stood before them and raised his arms. "After me," he said and belted out a stanza.

It sounded more like a drinking song than a holiday carol to Kate, but it was certainly jolly. At his signal, she did her best to reproduce it.

"*Lauter*," exclaimed their director. "Louder. With feeling!" He bellowed out the next lines.

Kate met Henry Deeping's laughing eyes, and warmth washed over her. The enjoyment in those dark depths stirred her heart. He gazed at her as if they were the only two people in the room, as if he wished to share all he knew and felt with her alone.

"*Erklingen*," called Richter. "Sing out stronger." He beat time on his thigh.

Kate made herself look away and took a firm grip on her imagination. The man had merely smiled at her. Mr. Deeping was relishing the song, feeling the effects of the wine, nothing more. She mustn't misinterpret. Look what had happened with Jerome, how she had misunderstood him. And she had never felt anything like this for her childhood friend.

This, Kate thought. What precisely was *this*? It was foolishness, replied a stern inner voice. It was the sort of silliness she'd avoided all her life. And yet silly was the last thing it felt.

"*Alle zusammen*," shouted Richter. "As one." He raised his arms like an orchestra conductor and brought them down.

She would stop *this* immediately, Kate thought as she sang. She would keep to their bargain and expect nothing else. Had he said one single thing to encourage *this*? No, he had not. Resolutely, she sang. Determinedly, she pulled her thoughts from Henry Deeping. And his smile pulled them right back again.

It was not terribly late when they left the reception. There were still holiday revelers streaming past outside, and Henry was glad to see that the streetlamps had been lit. They walked a while, enjoying the crisp air after stuffy crowded rooms. Henry savored the touch of Miss Meacham's hand on his arm and wondered if he'd ever had a better time at any party. Perhaps not? Miss Kate Meacham was a beguiling companion, he thought. She was quick and lively and at ease among the diplomats. Her acerbic asides were like a stimulating dash of spice in a complex dish. And she was quite lovely. He stole a glance at her profile, knowing that she did not care to be judged by her beauty. Yet a man couldn't help but notice.

She turned her head as if she felt his gaze. Henry smiled. She blinked as if caught in a bright light and looked away. Since the end of the singing, she'd seemed a bit distant. Tired perhaps. He should get her home.

They had turned up Brook Street, and Henry had raised his hand to summon a hack when Miss Meacham's fingers closed on his forearm in a painful pinch. Henry looked down in surprise. "What...?"

"Look," she hissed, signaling with a subtle movement of her head.

He followed the motion to the intersection with Bond Street up ahead. A man strode across it, his figure illuminated by a streetlamp. For an instant, Henry was perplexed. There was something familiar. Then he recognized the fellow. It was the foreign agent they had captured in Leicestershire, the man he had thought securely in the custody of the Foreign Office and being interrogated by senior officials. He turned to Miss Meacham as the man passed into a pool of shadow. "What is he doing loose?"

She did not look at him. She kept her eyes on the figure moving up into New Bond Street. Henry followed her gaze, watching him pass from light into shadow under the gas lamps. Miss Meacham tugged on Henry's arm. "We must follow him." She pulled him along.

"But..." Henry looked around for pursuit, found none. What the deuce was going on? He moved along at Miss Meacham's side.

Their quarry turned right at Oxford Street, walking faster now. "Don't get too close," Miss Meacham said. "He will recognize us."

"Shouldn't we apprehend him? Take him back into custody?"

"Do you think he escaped? He does not move like a man on the run."

Henry watched the man amble along. "No, but he wouldn't wish to attract attention."

"I think an escaped prisoner would duck into a cab or be met by a confederate rather than stroll along Bond Street."

It was a point. "It is night," Henry replied.

"There was enough light for us to recognize him. I think we should see where he's going before we do anything."

Henry allowed himself to be convinced.

Warily, they kept pace, well back. When the man continued past Oxford Circus, Miss Meacham said, "He is heading toward my neighborhood. You don't suppose he could be going to my house?"

"He would have no way of knowing where you live. You didn't even share your real name."

She nodded.

"You should go home," Henry added. The streets were not so well lit here, and the problem would grow worse depending on which way the fellow went. It was not wise to walk in some parts of London at night.

"So you wish to send me off alone?" she asked with an edge of mockery.

He couldn't do that. A solitary woman out at night was

assumed to be a lightskirt. She would be subject to insult at best and possibly much worse.

Their quarry's head turned as if he sensed followers. Miss Meacham ducked into a recessed doorway and pulled Henry in after her. She threw her arms around his neck and drew his head down.

Their lips met before he could think. There was a reeling, startled moment, and then Henry's body responded to the sudden embrace, pulling her closer. She melted against him, her fingers twined in his hair, her mouth softly urgent. He was seared by desire as their kiss lit the world. Henry felt as if the air had gone molten. The thrill that coursed through him drove everything else out of his head.

Then she pulled back.

"We were supposed to *pretend* to kiss," she gasped. A streetlight showed that her violet-blue eyes were wide, her lips parted, her cheeks flushed.

"I beg your pardon. You surprised me." In more ways than one. In nearly every way possible. He was dizzy with longing.

"It was obvious!" She sounded as breathless as he felt. And she hadn't let him go. In fact, her fingers had tightened in his hair.

"I've never done this before."

"Kissed?"

"Failed to pretend to do so."

"The agent!" She leaned to the side, pressing closer against him. Henry restrained his hands as she peered over his shoulder. "He's there, but nearly out of sight. We must go!" She pushed at him.

Henry stepped back, every inch of him still on fire, brain still fogged. She slipped out of the doorway. He followed. And they resumed their cautious progress along the pavement, even though Henry's universe had tilted sideways.

Their quarry turned left on Gower Street, and then made a series of turns into increasingly dark and empty thoroughfares. The emptiness was both fortunate and awkward. There was no one to accost them. But they had to drop farther back so as not to be noticeable.

"He's going toward the Foundling Hospital," murmured Miss Meacham.

"What would he want with orphans?"

"I can't imagine."

At the corner of Judd Street, they had to pause. Even in the poor illumination, their presence had become too obvious. When they dared advance, it was just in time to see the man enter a house a hundred yards away under a lantern hung over the doorway. Henry couldn't tell whether he was welcomed or had a key.

They waited. The street was dark and silent.

"Shall we walk by?" he wondered.

"We mustn't be spotted. He knows us."

"I am aware." Henry breathed the cold January air and searched for his equilibrium.

After a while, when nothing else happened, they moved, keeping to the deep shadows. There was a line of shrubbery across from the house the man had entered. They sheltered behind it and watched the place. One of the second-floor windows showed a dim light.

"I've never done that before either," Miss Meacham suddenly blurted, a bit too loud for comfort.

Henry put a finger to his lips to urge quiet and murmured, "Done what?"

"Failed to pretend to…" She lowered her voice even more, leaned closer. "I don't go about pulling gentlemen into doorways. Or anywhere else. I find things out *myself*. Alone."

Henry couldn't see her face in the shadows, but she sounded shaken. He found he was glad of it. Because he certainly was. By her shoulder pressed against his, her breath on his cheek, her heady scent, this talk of kisses. "I assumed that was the case," he managed.

"Good." She bit off the word.

A figure moved across the light in the window. Only one, so they couldn't tell if the agent had joined others in this nondescript dwelling.

"I don't understand why he was released," Henry murmured. "There was no mention of that when I was called in for more questions."

"It is a very curious occurrence," Miss Meacham whispered.

"You think the case against him was dropped? But how could it have been? He was caught red-handed."

"I think something extremely odd is going on," she answered.

"I must report this at once," Henry said. He wondered how to find his superiors at this time of night.

"To whom? The people in charge of questioning him?"

"Who else?"

"But one of them may have helped him get free." Miss Meacham was silent for a moment, then added, "Someone must have."

"Mightn't it have been his confederates?"

"Who are they? Has he named anyone?"

"I haven't been told."

"He could have been set loose so that he would expose them," she went on.

"Ah." That hadn't occurred to Henry.

"Or he had help from someone within British ranks."

"Surely not."

"Do you think we have no dissension?"

Henry didn't know what to say.

"We should gather more information before we tell anyone what we've seen," Miss Meacham whispered. "You can inquire about how the questioning is going. See if you are told about an escape."

Part of Henry would have preferred to hand this puzzle over to his superiors and let them unravel it. But she'd said he didn't dare. He would show her that was not true. "All right."

"Ask more than one person," she added. "See if you get different responses."

"You think someone might lie?"

"If they helped him get away? Of course they would spin some tale."

"But you are suggesting treason."

"Intrigue rather. He is not a big enough fish for treason." Miss Meacham's profile was just visible in the dim light. She was watching the house like a cat at a mousehole. "If the

Foreign Office is in a turmoil over his escape, that tells us one thing."

"And if it is not?" Henry asked.

Miss Meacham turned to look at him, though Henry couldn't see her expression. "That will be more difficult to interpret," she said.

The light in the house went off. They waited. The street remained dark and quiet. The two of them seemed the only creatures awake. It was strange to be lurking outside in the city at night, Henry thought. It felt unexpectedly exciting.

"I don't think he's coming out again tonight," murmured Miss Meacham.

"It doesn't appear so."

"Of course, he might have walked through the house and gone out the back, and we have been watching someone else entirely."

"Ah." He should have thought of that. "I am not accustomed to skulking," Henry muttered to himself.

A low laugh escaped Miss Meacham, but she didn't speak.

"I shall escort you home." Henry wouldn't hear any argument about that.

She made none. She simply took his arm, and they slipped silently back around the corner and moved cautiously through the night.

"I shall return to Judd Street early tomorrow morning, while you go and ask questions," she said after a while.

"I cannot allow you to do that."

"Allow?" Her tone was crisply amused. "How do you propose to stop me?"

Henry had no answer for that, since he clearly couldn't. Not without rousing a storm of scandal. "I could ask you to refrain," he ventured.

"You could."

And she would not pay him the least heed. "Will you at least be careful?"

"I will. I will wear a veil." Miss Meacham sighed. "If only I had dogs. Or children."

"What?"

"People walk dogs," she told him. "And take children out for exercise. That neighborhood was safe enough, but it was not a place for loiterers."

"You mean to lurk there?"

"Lurking is far too obvious," she replied dismissively. "I know. I shall station myself near the Foundling Hospital and watch the street from there. The hospital often has visitors, philanthropists and so on, some quite eminent. People go in and out. I will blend in. You can find me there when you have asked your questions and perhaps discovered what is going on."

"I don't think that is a good idea," Henry declared.

"I did not ask your opinion," she replied. She pulled on his arm. "My house is this way."

Henry tried to marshal telling arguments as they passed the silent bulk of the British Museum at Montagu House. "I don't suppose I could convince you…"

"Highly unlikely," she interrupted.

"You are an obdurate young lady."

"You are not the first to say so. And worse." She stopped

in front of a small redbrick house. "This is it. I will bid you good night."

"I will see you inside," Henry said.

"Not necessary. My housekeeper will be on the lookout for me."

"As will Miss Palliser," he said, glad to remember that she had people to watch over her.

"Of course," she replied in an odd tone.

"They will wonder why we did not arrive in a cab," Henry added.

"Which is why I wish to slip in quietly before they notice how I came."

"You sound as if you've done that before."

"Are you accusing me of something?" Her tone had gone cold.

Remembering Jerome Delaroche's insinuations, Henry said, "No, of course not."

"Good." She bit off the word as she slipped away from him, a dark figure in the starlight. He listened to her footsteps, the scrape of a key, and saw her outlined by dim light when the door opened. Then it closed and she was gone.

He lingered for a moment, feeling a variety of things, not all of which could be identified. Then he headed off down the street, walking fast. Gradually he realized that his strongest emotion was exhilaration. The night, the adventure, the lady—they made a heady combination. Most particularly the last. He'd never known anyone like her.

From behind her parlor curtains, in darkness, Kate watched Henry Deeping leave. Even when his tall figure had disappeared down the street, she stood there. Now that she was alone, in secret, she could acknowledge that his kiss had set her blood afire. She'd liked it. More than liked. When she thought of that kiss, her skin tingled, her heart pounded, and her breath caught. She wanted to kiss him again. At length. More thoroughly. The idea made her dizzily giddy.

She wouldn't, of course. Society didn't allow such pleasures for respectable young ladies. And though she despised narrow-minded propriety, Mr. Deeping might not understand that she meant... What did she mean? What did she think she was doing? They had a spy to chase. This was no time to be mooning about.

Gathering her cloak close about her, Kate moved silently up the stairs to her bedchamber. She didn't need a light in this familiar place, and she encountered no one. Even Miss Palliser, who often read late into the night in the study, was abed. Kate was glad to see it. The older woman would have been deeply interested in the news of the escaped agent, but Kate wanted some time to regain her balance before plunging into that discussion.

In her room, she lit a candle at the dying fire, undressed quickly, and prepared for bed. She expected to toss and turn over the events of the evening, but sleep overcame her only minutes after she had snuffed the candle and pulled up the covers.

The dream came to vivid life not long after that, seeming as real as any mundane experience. Kate wore a loose silken wrap patterned with swirls of spring-green leaves. She could feel it sliding over her bare skin. It scarcely covered her as she reclined on an ornate chaise. Henry Deeping sat at her feet, leaning against the chaise, wearing a similar sort of robe in dark blue. His hand cupped her bare calf, and Kate knew that in a moment it would move upward along her leg in a maddening, languorous tease that would go on almost past bearing. Her head dropped back in anticipatory ecstasy.

And even as Kate *was* the reclining lady, she was also observing the scene and thus could meet Henry Deeping's commanding stare. His dark eyes drilled into hers, promising unimaginable pleasure. His hand moved.

Kate came awake with a gasp.

She was in her bedchamber, in near darkness, panting with desire.

She sat up. Every inch of her skin tingled with longing.

Against that burning, the room was chilly, the air like a splash of cold water in her face. The fire had gone to dim coals behind its screen. It was deep night.

Kate got up and pulled on a warm dressing gown— nothing like the silken robe of her dream—and slippers. She lit candles and added a log to the fire, stirring it with the poker until the flames caught. Then she fetched a ring of keys, went to a chest in the corner, unlocked it, and took out a wooden box the length and breadth of her forearm and perhaps ten inches deep.

She had found this box after her grandfather's death, hidden under his shoes and boots in the bottom of his wardrobe. When she had seen her father's initials carved into the top, she'd been angry with him. Then she'd opened the box and discovered why her grandfather had never passed it along to her.

She did so again now.

Candlelight danced over a painting on the top of a stack of heavy paper. It showed a couple embracing. The image was tastefully suggestive, not blatant, and it was beautifully executed by an artist of talent.

Discovering that her father had collected fine erotic art had been shocking enough. But when Kate found comments on the backs of some images in her mother's handwriting and realized that it had been a joint…pastime, she'd been astounded. And rather fascinated, since her parents had been near strangers to her. If it had been her grandfather's collection… That would have been uncomfortable. But the box had been covered with a thick film of dust. He clearly didn't look at it, though he never destroyed it either.

She'd examined all the pieces after that first discovery. And once or twice since then, truthfully. But never until tonight had she dreamed of them or been roused as she was now. That was Henry Deeping's…fault.

She paged through the stack until she found the image that had featured in the dream tonight, delicately limned in pen and ink. The man and woman in the scene looked nothing like them. The man's stare was compelling but not like in her dream. The art was striking, but the effect was not at all the same.

It wasn't the picture. It was Henry Deeping. He'd ignited something in her that came to life in the dream. Something that used the drawing to express…longing.

A flush heated Kate's cheeks. She put her cold hands to them as the heat flowed down her neck and chest. What would he think if he knew? If he could see her now? What did *she* think?

She would have to decide that when her turmoil was less. For now, she stood gazing at the drawing, flickering candle-light making it seem about to come alive, and thought of the man who had kissed her in a shabby doorway.

When the fire started to die down again and the chill grew, Kate replaced the box and returned to bed, but the dream echoed in her sleep and waking intervals through the rest of the night.

Six

THE NEXT MORNING KATE ROSE AT FIRST LIGHT AS SHE
had set herself to do. She had *not* intended to be heavy-eyed
and fuzzy-headed, but the dream had stolen her sleep.

She dressed in dun colors unlikely to attract notice and
put on her plainest bonnet. All the while, a lure beckoned
from the back of her mind, urging her to grab hold with all
her might, in the shape of Henry Deeping.

Just for an instant, Kate gripped the bedpost, dizzy with
desire. The impulse had not gone away. It wasn't just a fig-
ment of the night. Indeed, it appeared to be settling in as a
permanent resident.

The world her grandfather had given her had not included
the management of such longing. He hadn't mentioned the
topic, one way or another. And in her limited encounters
with the male sex, she'd never been…tempted. Tempted.
That's what she was now.

Kate breathed deeply—once, twice—and summoned
years of discipline and training. There was work to be done.
And in order to do it, she must be on her way. There was no
time to waste. Fortunately, Miss Palliser was a night owl, not
an early riser. Kate was not likely to see her at this hour.

She gathered her heaviest cloak, a thick woolen scarf, and

warm gloves, and went quietly down to the kitchen to get a bit of bread and cheese. When she turned to slip out, she discovered Mrs. Knox in the doorway, hands on hips.

"Are you going somewhere?" asked the older woman.

"For a walk."

"At this hour? The birds are barely awake. And it's mortal cold. What are you up to?"

"A bit of exercise?"

"I've known you since you were eleven years old, Kate. I can see plainly when you're plotting mischief."

"It is not mischief." There was no deceiving Mrs. Knox. But she might be diverted. "It is part of an inquiry for the Foreign Office."

"Which they asked *you* to undertake?"

"Not exactly asked," Kate admitted.

"Indeed. We both know that they don't want much to do with you since your grandfather died."

"I shall show them how wrong they are!"

"They're not the sort to listen to a young woman," said Mrs. Knox. "Or an old one for that matter."

"They cannot disregard what we have discovered."

"We?"

"Mr. Deeping and I. He is making inquiries at the Foreign Office later this morning."

"That is the gentleman you met in Leicestershire? The one who's squiring you about now? Though we haven't seen hide nor hair of him here." Her expression was sour.

Kate nodded. Mrs. Knox never needed more than a hint to put things together. "Miss Palliser knows him."

"And what's *he* up to?"

"I told you, making inquiries."

"No. With you." The older woman's gaze was sharp.

It was as if the kiss burned on Kate's lips like a signal flare. And the dream! Her cheeks grew hot. She wouldn't mention either of those things. "We saw the agent we captured in Leicestershire, walking free on the street. Which did not seem right. We are trying to learn why. Simply that."

Mrs. Knox looked unconvinced. "Where are you going now?"

"To watch the house the man went into last night."

"I don't think…"

"From a good distance," Kate added. She held up the veil she would drape over her bonnet. "It is near the Foundling Hospital. I won't be noticed. There are always people about there."

"I don't suppose I can stop you," said Mrs. Knox.

They faced each other, control of the household hanging in the balance. Kate didn't know what she would do if Mrs. Knox forbade the outing. Oh, she would go. But where would that leave them? Open rebellion might spark an equal response. Would her longtime mentor leave? She couldn't imagine the house without her.

In the end, the older woman stood back from the doorway. She looked disapproving, and her expression showed that this issue was far from resolved. But she made no more arguments now.

Kate picked up her things and departed in haste, pulling on the warm cloak as she left the house.

She walked briskly north, eating her sparse breakfast before putting on the veil that would obscure her features. It took only a few minutes to reach the precincts of the Foundling Hospital. This had been a fashionable charity for almost a century, since it had received a royal charter to care for abandoned babies. Sadly the London slums provided a steady stream of these, and the buildings had been expanded several times since then.

The morning was cold and clear, the air sharp in her lungs. Kate moved about the hospital courtyard as if she awaited an important meeting, managing to keep the doorway their quarry had entered in sight through the open railings. She could do nothing about a back door and hoped Henry Deeping would hurry. The Foreign Office did not open at dawn, however. It would be hours before he could possibly appear.

It was nearly three, and Kate had concluded that she would have to go if she did not wish to be noticed—and freeze to death—when his cab pulled up and he jumped down to join her. She was glad to see him, and not just because she was cold and hungry and tired of lurking.

"There was no sign of any disturbance at the office," he told her as the cab drove away. "I spoke to three people." He held up a hand to forestall the comment she'd been about to make. "Very carefully. All of them talked as if the man was still in custody."

"Who did you ask?"

He named them.

"Spinks ought to be trustworthy," Kate said. "Grandfather thought Abernathy a fool. Did you suggest the idea of letting the agent go in order to find his confederates?"

"No. I didn't want that remembered later when the matter comes out."

Kate nodded. It was a good point. Cleverer than she had expected. "What is going on?" she wondered aloud.

"I have to report this," replied Mr. Deeping.

"To whom? Who do you trust?"

"My superior, I suppose." He looked uncertain. "I don't know him well."

"If you speak to the wrong person, there will be trouble. You will probably be maligned in some outrageous way. Even tossed out."

He was silent for a moment. "Lord Castlereagh?"

He sounded doubtful, as was Kate. Her grandfather had known the Foreign Secretary well, and she had met him. But they were not really acquainted. Castlereagh would have no reason to trust her. And he was currently enduring a storm of criticism that must be very difficult to bear. "We need solid evidence, and details, before we go to him." She shivered as a gust of wind pushed at her cloak.

"How long have you been out here?" Mr. Deeping asked.

"Since just after dawn."

"You must be freezing." He took her hand. "Like ice! I must get you home."

"I don't require an escort at this time of day. You should stay and watch that house."

He glanced at it and away.

"If we can find out where the man goes, who he sees, we will know better what is best to do."

"Assuming he did not walk through that house and out the back as you said," Deeping replied.

Kate shrugged. If he had, they'd wasted their time. There was nothing to be done about that.

"The two of us cannot watch alone. We haven't the time. And we will be noticed."

"Enlisting the wrong person from the Foreign Office will ruin all," Kate said. She took a breath, ready to argue.

But he nodded. "I have an idea."

"What?"

"What if I were to ask Merlin—Mr. Welden, that is—and Tom to take a turn? Welden was involved in the Leicestershire matter. He will recognize the fellow. And my sister says Tom is one of the most enterprising lads she's ever met and quite trustworthy."

"That is a good notion," Kate said.

"You sound surprised."

He smiled down at her, and Kate's pulse accelerated. She was momentarily transfixed by the shape of his lips. A flash of last night's dream tried to intrude. "No, I..." Actually she admired the scheme. And the man. She had to find something to say.

The door of the house down the street opened, and the agent emerged. "Turn around," Kate exclaimed.

Mr. Deeping did so without hesitation. "Has he come out?"

"Yes."

Mr. Deeping pulled down his hat brim, keeping his head bent. "Is he walking this way?"

"Yes," she repeated. "We must move away. He will surely know you."

He muttered a curse. "We have no arrangements in place."

Kate took his arm and urged him through a gate into the courtyard of the Foundling Hospital. Mr. Deeping kept his back to the street while Kate watched through the mesh of her veil.

The man passed the gate. They gave him a few moments, and then Kate peered out into the street. "He is turning at the corner, going toward Russell Square, I think."

They waited until he had moved out of sight, then cautiously went after him, staying well behind.

At Russell Square they watched him go into the garden in the center and sit down on a bench beside one of the paths. He stood out a bit. The place was empty on this cold winter morning, the branches bare. They drew back so that he would not notice them, just keeping the top of his head in sight. After a few minutes, another man approached from the opposite side of the garden and sat beside him. They were too far away to see more than a dark hat and bulky overcoat.

"I will walk around the garden and get a closer look," said Kate. When Mr. Deeping started to object, she added, "You cannot come. He might see your face."

"Your veil is an unfair advantage," he muttered.

"Fancy that." She strode away, making a circuit of the square at a pace that was neither strikingly fast nor suspiciously slow. Merely a lady taking a bit of exercise in the bracing air. She faced straight ahead, but behind her veil, she slanted her eyes toward the bench. They glanced at her when she first appeared, but then took no more notice as they leaned together, talking intently. She walked around, observing them from every angle.

She would have liked to make another circuit, but that would draw too much attention. She returned to Mr. Deeping, who had retreated down Guilford Street to a spot where they could just keep the two men in view.

"I've seen the other one before," Kate said then. She frowned as Mr. Deeping looked inquiring. "Somewhere."

"At a diplomatic event?"

"Perhaps. It must have been." She shook her head. No memory came back.

After a time, the conspirators stood up. They bowed and separated, leaving the garden in opposite directions.

"Our man is coming this way," said Mr. Deeping.

"Returning to his refuge, I suppose. I will go ahead, so that he can't think I am following him, and make certain."

"But if he turns off…"

"We are in danger of being noticed, Mr. Deeping. This has gone on a long time." Kate was cold and hungry and puzzled. It was an uncomfortable combination. "You follow the other man, see where he goes. He will not know you."

She walked off before he could argue, returning to the Foundling Hospital and lingering in the courtyard long enough to see the agent return to the house where he'd stayed the night. She would have to trust that he remained there. She couldn't linger anymore.

Reaching home, she first visited the privy behind the house and then went inside to take off her cloak and bonnet.

Mrs. Knox arrived at her bedchamber as Kate was tidying her hair. "You are back," she said.

"And desperately hungry," Kate replied.

Mrs. Knox didn't move. "Where have you been all this time?"

"As I told you, watching a house where a foreign agent has gone to ground." Kate decided not to mention Mr. Deeping's presence.

"So you've been standing about in the street all morning? Do you want to cause a scandal?"

"I was in the courtyard of the Foundling Hospital. There were other people about." Kate chafed her hands together. She was terribly cold. "Some tea would be very welcome."

The older woman gazed at her for another moment and then sighed. "I don't wish to be fratching with you, Kate. And I haven't the authority of your grandfather. You can dismiss me from the household anytime you like."

"I would never do that!"

"But I wish you would listen to me," Mrs. Knox went on without acknowledging her protest. "I fear you're heading into trouble. And I can't bear to see that."

"I will take care."

"That is just what you don't do." The housekeeper grimaced. "And Sir Michael not here to restrain you any longer. What's your future to be?"

It was a question Kate didn't wish to face, newly complicated by Henry Deeping's entry into her life. Profoundly grateful that Mrs. Knox knew nothing about that searing kiss, Kate turned from the mirror and summoned a smile. "I *will* be careful. I promise." She put a hand on Mrs. Knox's arm.

The older woman laid her fingers over it and exclaimed. "Great heavens, you're frozen!"

"Tea?" asked Kate in the voice that had coaxed treats out of her surrogate mother for years.

"I'll go and brew some." Mrs. Knox shook her head as she turned toward the stairs. "And don't think you've put me off my worries. Because you haven't." She paused. "Miss Palliser was asking where you'd gotten to," she added as a parting shot.

―――――――

Since he didn't have to worry about being recognized, Henry followed the second man more closely than they had dared before. The fellow seemed deep in thought and paid no attention to other pedestrians, so Henry was able to catch a good look at his face. It was not familiar.

Reaching a busier street, the fellow hailed a cab, and Henry had a moment's anxiety before he found another and told the driver to go after the vehicle. They threaded their way west through the raucous streets of Soho and into more fashionable precincts.

When the leading cab pulled up before a well-known address, Henry was astonished. He thought it must be a coincidence, but the passenger got down, paid the fare, and entered as if he was quite familiar with its precincts. No one made any move to stop him. Henry stood before the building and stared for a full minute before he recovered himself and moved off. This was more than mystifying. It was unnerving. He was glad now that he hadn't told anyone at the office. The complications had become worrisome, possibly even dangerous. He turned away and hurried off to make some arrangements.

That evening Henry brought Oliver Welden and Tom Jesperson to Kate Meacham's house in a hansom cab. They were admitted by a plump, round-faced woman dressed like an upper servant. Though the lines etched in her face suggested smiles, her eyes were sharp as she stood aside to let them enter. She examined them one by one, with special care for Henry, it seemed to him. The housekeeper, he concluded. She felt solid and responsible and was clearly watching out for her charge. Henry was glad of it, even as he tried to hide any vestige of that searing kiss from his expression. Of course that simply made it more vivid in his mind. He felt as if desire was branded on his being, blatant in his face.

She took them upstairs to a study crammed with books. Miss Palliser sat behind the cluttered desk. It looked as if she had appropriated it for her own, and Henry wondered if Miss Meacham resented this. She didn't appear to. She stood before it as if she was accustomed to having it occupied. As they all sat in chairs set out in a semicircle, Henry wondered what her renowned grandfather would have thought of this group, and then decided that he might well have held odd meetings of his own right here.

"Who is watching the agent's hiding place?" Miss Meacham asked.

"Some friends of Ned Gardener's," answered Tom. "He

knows a deal of lads without much to do and happy to earn a few coins. They're used to staying out of sight as well."

"What were they told?" she asked with a frown.

"Only that the fellow was suspicious and we wished to know where he went and who he saw," said Henry.

"Ned'll help too when he has a free day," Tom added.

As an apprentice, Ned had few of those. Henry doubted that he would find the time to join their efforts.

"The lads don't like going too near the Foundling Hospital," Tom went on. "Afraid they'll grab them up and shut them away."

"They mostly take in babies," replied Miss Meacham. "But tell them they can stay at the other end of the street."

Tom nodded.

"I have quite a bit of news," Henry said. "First, rumors have begun to circulate around the Foreign Office that our agent has been moved to a secret location out of town where he will continue to be questioned."

"But he hasn't been," said Welden and Miss Palliser at the same moment.

They exchanged an appraising glance.

"He's right here in London," Miss Palliser added.

Henry acknowledged this with a nod. "As we know. And I was discouraged from mentioning him again lest 'word get out.' I was told my part of the business was over with, and I should concentrate on my proper job now that it has started."

"Who said these things?" asked Miss Meacham.

"Abernathy. He came round especially to speak to me."

She made a face. "Grandfather thought he was a fool. He

would say whatever he was told to without thinking about it or, heaven forbid, objecting."

Tom frowned. "Sounds like somebody at your place is covering for this agent fellow."

Henry nodded. "I was told to turn my mind from my 'past glories' to my current tasks." The superior tone from a plodding fellow like Abernathy still rankled.

"What are your tasks?" asked Miss Palliser and Merlin, once again in chorus.

They looked at each other as the rest of the group gazed at them.

"I have wondered what such a post would be like," said Miss Palliser.

"As one does when one has no chance of attaining a position," Merlin said.

"Precisely."

A grin played about Tom's lips as he watched the pair. "Do you send men off on secret missions?" he asked Henry.

"I write letters, make appointments, log in reports, and copy them for distribution," Henry told them.

Tom looked disappointed by this mundane litany. Henry started to tell him that some of the reports were highly confidential, containing information that could have explosive consequences, then decided he should not. That was rather the point, wasn't it? "But that is not my biggest piece of news," he went on. Everyone turned to look at him, and Henry realized he'd been holding back to generate a bit of drama. "I followed the second man we saw this morning." He looked at Miss Palliser to confirm she'd heard the story. Receiving a nod of comprehension, he said, "The fellow took a cab to Carlton House."

Silence, stares, and dropped jaws greeted this revelation.

"The Prince Regent's place?" asked Tom.

Henry nodded.

"Do you mean that he left the cab in front of the building?" Miss Palliser asked.

"A cogent point," said Oliver Welden.

Henry shook his head. "No, he walked in as if he belonged there. I didn't see the least hesitation. Certainly no one moved to question him."

People exchanged glances, turned back to him.

"But what could the prince—" Miss Palliser and Welden began. Seeing that they were echoing each other again, both fell silent.

"Oh," said Miss Meacham. "Oh. I saw him at the Castlereaghs' ball."

"The prince?" Henry asked.

"No. Well, yes, the Regent was there. But I saw the man you followed. I remember his face now. He arrived at the ball with the prince. Quite late. I don't know his name. But he was clearly a royal crony."

Everyone took a moment to digest this information.

"I have a low opinion of Prince George," said Oliver Welden. "But I cannot see what he would have to do with a foreign agent."

"I wonder if we have been mistaken about that," replied Miss Meacham. They all turned to her. "Or not mistaken, but too limited in our ideas."

She looked earnest and intelligent and quite lovely, Henry thought.

"I have been thinking about this supposed agent," she went on. "Whose name we still do not know." She glanced at Henry.

It made his breath catch. He shook his head. If anyone at the Foreign Office had discovered the name, they had not passed it along to him.

"We came across him working for a family in China," Miss Meacham continued. "We then assumed an association with the emperor's government. But what if he is simply for hire?"

"A mercenary of espionage?" asked Henry. Miss Meacham smiled at the phrase, which pleased him inordinately.

"A man with skills and connections in that realm, which he puts at the disposal of the highest bidder."

"But who would trust such a man?" asked Miss Palliser.

Welden nodded in approval, which was rare for him. "If somebody came along with more money, he'd be likely to turn."

"He might have some...villain's code," Miss Meacham said. "But I agree it would not be wise to put much faith in his type."

More glances passed among the group. The Prince Regent was not stupid, but his judgment was notoriously erratic, particularly in the choice of companions.

"We know the man is prepared to use violence to further his schemes," Miss Palliser said slowly.

"We saw that in Leicestershire," said Welden.

"You think the prince is in danger?" asked Tom. "I wouldn't want to see that."

"I think if this was a plot against the Regent, the fellow I followed would have taken much more care to stay secret," Henry replied.

"He seemed quite friendly with the prince at the ball," said Miss Meacham. "They looked like kindred spirits, in fact. Very cordial."

"The command to release the agent must have come from quite high up," said Welden and Miss Palliser at once.

They stopped and stared at each other.

"The prince is about as high as they come," said Tom.

And not someone to oppose, Henry thought. His Highness had shown a vindictive side on many occasions.

Miss Meacham held up a hand and ticked off points on her fingers. "We know the man we observed in Leicestershire is capable of violent intrigue," she said. "We do not know why the two were meeting. But we must suspect any transaction that involves our agent." She turned down another finger. "It would be best if we were not noticed. We must remain secret."

"Very competently summarized," said Welden with his talent for making a compliment sound patronizing. Henry remembered that he had been a schoolmaster at one time.

"But what are we going to *do*?" Miss Palliser asked. "We do not know whom we can trust."

"No one but ourselves," replied Welden. "That is the only safe course of action."

"It usually is," she agreed.

"We will keep watch," Miss Meacham answered. "See where these men go, what they do."

"Eventually someone at the Foreign Office must know of it," Henry said.

"Lord Castlereagh?" asked Miss Palliser and Welden together.

This time, it appeared they were coming to enjoy the unison. Tom seemed to find it quite amusing.

"The Foreign Secretary is weighed down by criticism from all sides just now," replied Miss Meacham. "It is so virulent that my grandfather was worried about his state of mind. We must be very sure before we draw his attention to any problem." She looked at Henry. "You agree?"

She might as well have said, "Do you dare?" Her violet gaze was a challenge and a taunt. Henry felt his body and spirit respond. He wanted to impress her. Yet he had duties. She must understand that, having lived with her grandfather. "We will keep watch and make notes of any developments," he agreed. "For now. Until we can be certain who should have the news. And then we must pass it along."

Miss Meacham looked disappointed. She turned away.

Henry felt a flash of annoyance. It had been a measured response. What did she expect? Was he to leap about and spout rebellion?

"This will give you good practice for the Bow Street Runners," Miss Palliser said to Welden.

He seemed much struck by the idea.

"I've got no role in the latest play," Tom said. "I can teach you about disguise. I'm good with paint and false hair."

Welden looked even more intrigued. Miss Palliser did as well. Henry felt a twinge of envy. His schedule was not his own now that he had taken up an official post. He wouldn't be present for much of this.

"It'd be good practice for me too," Tom added. "Starting next month I play an 'ancient prophet.'" He hunched over and made a grizzled face.

They divided up the hours of the day for further surveillance. Tom and Ned Gardener's friends would cover the nights. Welden, Miss Palliser, and Miss Meacham would take turns patrolling during the day, while Henry was in his office.

These things decided, the meeting began to break up. Miss Meacham lingered at Henry's side as if to say something to him. But then she didn't speak. He looked for the perfect words and found only, "Charlotte and her friends will be quite jealous when they find out about this. They love solving mysteries."

"You cannot tell them."

"I know that." Did she think he was careless? Or foolish?

"Do you walk with us?" Welden asked Henry.

They were unlikely to find a cab in this neighborhood at this time. It would be best to go together. Henry gave a curt nod and joined him and Tom. Miss Meacham's farewell encompassed them all, giving no one any particular attention. Henry's mood grew more foul. He didn't join in the talk as Tom explained that the real key to a disguise was not false whiskers but changing one's way of moving and standing. "You got to *feel* like a different person," he said.

"Inside?" asked Welden.

"And to the ones you're trying to fool," said Tom.

For his part, Henry felt vastly frustrated.

When the gentlemen had departed, Kate left Miss Palliser to her studies, which always ran into the night. She wished to go to her room and brood on the injustices of the world and society, but she found Mrs. Knox waiting for her. Without preamble, the housekeeper said, "This Mr. Deeping then."

"Yes, what about him?" Kate hadn't meant to sound sharp and sour, but she did.

Her surrogate mother paid no attention. "His family lives in Leicestershire?"

"Yes, they are well-known breeders of racehorses."

"Horse breeders!" exclaimed Mrs. Knox, looking shocked.

"Highly respected. His ancestor was knighted by King Charles the Second for outstanding service." Kate had heard this from Charlotte Deeping.

Mrs. Knox looked somewhat mollified. "What is his fortune?"

"I have no idea." This was not quite true. Kate knew that Henry Deeping needed to make his own way in the world. Like her, he had no large income behind him.

"It can't be too large."

"It really is none of our affair." She could see where this was going, and she didn't want to follow.

"But he has a post at the Foreign Office. Your grandfather would like that. And you are carrying on your grandfather's work of gathering information together."

"Merely that and nothing more," said Kate.

"Nothing?" Mrs. Knox's gaze was searching.

Her tone seemed to point directly at the issue of kisses.

But she couldn't know about that. Or the dream. Unless Kate foolishly let something slip. "Nothing," said Kate. What more could it be?

"Indeed."

Not trusting her talent for subterfuge against this questioner, Kate turned away before she could say more.

Seven

HENRY BENT OVER HIS DESK IN A LARGE CHAMBER FILLED with other young men like himself, carefully copying a field officer's report on allegiances in a contested area of central Asia. The content was interesting, and he understood that by copying it, he would add to his store of information on the state of the world. Still he would have preferred simply reading the words. The physical task was tedious. And his mind sometimes strayed to wondering whether he was gathering equally useful information with Miss Meacham and the others. And then to what they might be discovering right now, without him. And then, inevitably, to the many attractions of Miss Meacham herself. Most of the paths in his brain seemed to lead there these days. So when a shadow fell across the page he was glad to look up.

"Henry," said the dapper midsized man who stood there.

"Uncle." Henry rose automatically, and then immediately wondered if he should have. He was nearly six inches taller than his mother's brother. He'd felt odd about that since he attained his adult height. It seemed somehow disrespectful, which was the last thing he'd ever felt about Brinsley Gerard.

His uncle showed no sign of minding. He looked up with a pleasant smile. Nine years older than Henry's mama, he didn't much resemble her. Muscular, a bit craggy, with a mane of hair gone gray, his dress was plain but correct in every particular. A childless widower, he had interested himself in those of his nephews who were not immersed in the Deeping breeding stables. Henry knew that their uncle had advised his younger brother Cecil, and he had helped Henry gain his post in the Foreign Office, where he was well established. When he'd offered his aid, he'd told Henry that success here was based on reasonable intelligence, an ability to obey orders while taking sensible action in the absence of same, cordiality, and no desire for personal power. "We are not great magnates or very wealthy," his uncle had said then. "But we are part of the backbone of this country, and we can try to see that it acts with justice and fairness." He'd served on delegations all over the globe. Though he'd never been a soldier, he stood like one.

"I didn't know you had arrived in town," Henry said.

"I heard some things that brought me down a few days early."

Henry immediately thought of Kate Meacham. His uncle had a wide acquaintance in these offices. He certainly knew Delaroche. Henry wondered if the fellow had written to him. That could complicate matters which were already... complicated.

"Come along," said his uncle. "We'll have dinner at my club and talk."

Henry gathered his hat and coat and followed him out. The looks they received at this early exit suggested that his uncle had been identified. Henry's absence would be excused if anyone inquired.

Half an hour later they were seated in comfortable arm-chairs in a large club room, well away from the other members present. His uncle ordered wine and, when the servant had left it, said, "You were missed in Leicestershire at Christmas."

His uncle had spent the holiday with Henry's family, as he always did. "I was sorry not to be there," Henry replied.

"Instead you had an unconventional introduction to your new work."

Henry acknowledged this with a wry nod.

"I've read a report about the matter, but tell me how it seemed to you."

He did so and answered a series of shrewd questions. He very nearly added a hint about recent events, but just then his uncle said, "So that is how you became acquainted with Miss Kate Meacham. I've heard she went up to Leicestershire under an assumed name."

Henry wondered who had told him that. He still wasn't certain Delaroche knew. Perhaps it had been Bexley, who had come to take charge of their captive at the end. He had clearly known her.

"I admired her grandfather. Indeed, as a younger man, I tried to model myself on his example. Never quite came up to his standard, I fear. You've been squiring the young lady about, I believe."

If they'd been fencing, Henry would have called this a slip past his guard. But they weren't. Unless perhaps they were. "Yes, sir. She has been kind enough to introduce me to a number of people." As his uncle had promised to present Henry to his many allies in the diplomatic community, surely he could not object to this?

"At events to which she was not invited?"

"Did Delaroche tell you so?"

"As a matter of fact, he did. Among others."

A sharp retort rose to Henry's lips.

"Jerome has always been pompous," his uncle went on before the remark escaped. "Even as a small child. I doubt he'll rise very high in the ranks. A solid bureaucrat, of course." He made a dismissive gesture.

Slightly mollified, Henry sat back.

"I don't think I have met Miss Meacham. I should like to."

"So that you can reprimand her?"

His uncle examined him. "You like her then?"

Henry didn't know how to answer. *Like* seemed an inadequate word. It didn't cover incessant irritation and respect and fascination. Not to mention kisses to the edge of madness. Never mentioning those!

"She seems a young lady of abilities. If a scandal arises, of course…"

"There is no question of scandal!"

"And so no need to spring to her defense?" His uncle's scrutiny deepened. "Delaroche…"

"Is an ass."

"Not quite that. Why don't you arrange a meeting, Henry? Nothing too public. Discreet, so that we are not committed to anything."

Such as what, Henry wondered. Could his uncle mean to give Miss Meacham some diplomatic task? He knew she longed for that. "Not to scold her."

"Oh no. Nothing like that. A friendly chat."

There could be no objection to such a thing. So Henry didn't understand why he felt uneasy as he agreed.

———————

Kate arrived well ahead of the designated time, at a tea shop in a neighborhood where she was unlikely to encounter anyone she knew. Or that Henry Deeping and his uncle knew, presumably. She wished she could expect a covert exchange of information between Foreign Office peers—respectful, even comradely—but she knew this would not be that. If only she knew what it *would* be, she could be more relaxed, she thought as she took a seat and ordered a pot of tea and cakes. Was she to endure an official objection to her presence at diplomatic receptions? Delivered unofficially, as they so often were. If the meeting had been with anyone other than Brinsley Gerard, she might have thought so. But since it was him, this probably had to do with Henry Deeping.

Kate removed her gloves. She sat very straight in her chair. A young lady might be introduced to a gentleman's family as a signal that they had formed a serious attachment. But Henry Deeping must have told his uncle this was not the case for them. Mustn't he? Of course he had. There was no question of *that*. Once again the word seemed both vague and weighted with significance. There was no *that*. Mr. Deeping had not broached the subject of *that*. They had nothing of the sort to discuss. Unless she was to be warned off?

Kate's cheeks burned at the idea. She was unconventional. She admitted it. But she had done nothing irredeemable.

Except perhaps in the eyes of a pompous, hidebound, low-minded prig like Jerome. The matter of breeches intruded. But no one knew about that. Mrs. Knox would never reveal it. Unless someone else had found out? Had one of her grandfather's contacts recognized her and gossiped? Was the tale all over the Foreign Office?

Her tea arrived. Kate's hands were cold. They trembled slightly as she poured. Mr. Gerard was known as a skilled diplomat. He would not conduct an insulting conversation with Henry Deeping sitting right beside her. He would have been more oblique. Called at her house perhaps or written a letter. But why did he wish to see her? She put her hands around the cup to warm them.

She might have refused this meeting. But of course she had been too curious to do so. And too pathetically hopeful? That was a lowering reflection.

The door opened, letting in a gust of cold January air, and two men entered. Kate recognized Mr. Gerard. She'd seen him at various receptions and thought he might have visited her grandfather in times past. They'd never spoken, however. She knew nothing about him beyond his sterling reputation.

He and his nephew were not much alike. Where Henry Deeping was tall and slender, his uncle was compact and sturdy. His mane of gray hair contrasted with Mr. Deeping's dark locks. His face was lined, and his smile, though pleasant, did not light his features as his nephew's did. On the contrary, it gave nothing away. Mr. Deeping plucked at her heart; his uncle called up all its armor. He had a palpable presence. Kate stifled an impulse to stand.

"Miss Meacham," he said. "I believe we must have met, though I can't quite recall where."

He would, if they had, she thought. Was this a challenge? "We've merely attended some of the same gatherings," she said, rising to it. Might as well bring the issue to the fore at once.

Mr. Gerard simply nodded. They sat down at her small round table. More tea was requested. Refusing to be intimidated, Kate took one of the small cakes and bit into it. "Oh."

"What is it?" asked Henry Deeping.

"It's so good." She had not expected such exquisite flavors in this obscure little shop. The pastry was so luscious that it had betrayed her into an embarrassing comment.

"Yes?" Mr. Deeping tried one and looked as surprised as she'd been. "It's delicious," he said, finishing the cake off in a second bite.

Mr. Gerard looked amused, as if they were children stuffing down sweets rather than rational adults. Kate flushed and resisted having another.

"I knew your grandfather of course," the older man said. "Not well enough to call him a friend, sadly. But he gave me several pieces of good advice. He is sorely missed."

He was. And she did. But must every encounter begin with her grandfather? She was more than a remnant of his vast legacy.

"I was a little acquainted with your parents as well. We were always going off to different posts, but they were very good company when we chanced to meet."

"I have heard that about them," said Kate. It sounded more acid than she'd meant it to. But she'd had little opportunity to experience their conviviality, let alone the more unusual aspects of their characters she'd discovered later.

"I understand your ambitions run in the same direction."

For one dizzy instant, Kate imagined that he knew about the box of suggestive paintings and was accusing her of... No. Of course he wasn't! People had tattled about her recent incursions at the receptions. She braced for the reprimand. "Am I allowed to have ambitions?"

Mr. Gerard gazed at her from under his thick gray brows. His eyes were keenly intelligent. She felt thoroughly scrutinized. "Anyone may aspire," he replied mildly.

"No matter how hopelessly?" She refused to be cowed.

The new pot of tea was delivered. "Your cakes are sublime," Henry Deeping said to the neat proprietress. Kate noticed that he had eaten several when she wasn't looking.

"Perhaps another plate of them," said his uncle.

"Of course, sir." Looking gratified, the woman went to fetch them. Henry Deeping ate another, as annoyingly relaxed as he was greedy. Kate frowned at him.

"So you two met in Leicestershire when this agent was taken," said Mr. Gerard.

Kate stiffened, poised for mention of her use of a false name.

"And you have become further acquainted since. Here in London. At various receptions."

She waited for the ax to fall. Would she now be banned from diplomatic circles in truth? Officially.

"This is not an interrogation, Miss Meacham," said Brinsley Gerard.

Kate realized that his expression was neutral, not coldly critical as Jerome's had become.

"Of course it isn't," said Mr. Deeping. "Why would it be?"

"Merely a chance to have a chat," continued the older man. "My sister delegated me, as I was coming to London in any case."

Bewildered, Kate looked at Mr. Deeping. He seemed equally confused. He held a half-eaten cake as if he'd forgotten it.

"She thought it would be easier for me to say," Gerard went on. "I'm afraid this is not a suitable match for an aspiring diplomat." He gestured at her and then at Mr. Deeping. "On either side. It would be best to drop any thought of it."

"What?" said Kate.

"I mean no personal criticism, Miss Meacham," the older man went on. "Not in the least. I'm sure you are an admirable young lady. Along with your, er, charming personal attractions. And you bring your grandfather's legacy and connections with you. They've already been quite helpful to the Foreign Office, I believe. But really, one must be practical to succeed in this world. A tidy fortune is what you need. Both of you, I mean. Diplomacy can be an expensive business. And the pay is not lavish." He smiled as if he'd made a small joke.

Kate's brain seemed to have frozen. Mr. Deeping's jaw had dropped.

Brinsley Gerard looked from her to his nephew and back again. "You seem surprised. But you must know you have been rather obvious, spending so much time together.

Several people wrote to tell me about the developing connection." Mr. Gerard shrugged. "And offer their unsolicited
opinions. The gossips are so free with *those*. An old friend
contacted your mother as well, Henry. She assumed news
of an engagement was imminent." He gazed at his nephew.
"Your mother was rather hurt you hadn't informed her."

Mr. Deeping looked poleaxed, which was perhaps the
worst part of this debacle. He seemed to have nothing to say.
"Is a woman only good for marriage?" Kate burst out. "Is that
all people can think of?"

Mr. Gerard blinked at her vehemence. "Have you no such
plans? I beg your pardon. I've relied on secondhand information. Never the best course."

"I didn't," stammered Mr. Deeping. "We haven't…"

He was thinking of the kiss. Kate could see it in his eyes.
In another moment, pressured by propriety and the presence of his uncle, he might confess. And then say something
unforgivable. Whether that was a reluctant offer for her out
of duty or pity, or some other conventional stupidity, she
couldn't allow it. Words poured out of her before he could
speak. "We have spent time together because the agent we
helped apprehend has been secretly released, apparently on
orders from Carlton House."

Mr. Gerard stared at her. "What?"

Kate was appalled. Mr. Deeping was truly gaping now.
They had agreed to tell no one, and now she'd blurted the
secret out. In anger. In her own defense. To make it perfectly
clear that she thought of more than marriage and memories
of kisses that Mr. Gerard knew nothing about. She shouldn't

have. She regretted the outburst. But she *would not* be viewed as some romantic miss who wanted nothing but a husband.

"Could you repeat that?" asked Mr. Gerard. "I can't believe I heard you correctly."

She'd worried about others' discretion, but she'd been betrayed by herself. As her anger ebbed, along with her rash heedlessness, Kate nearly put her head in her hands.

Mr. Deeping carefully set down a half-eaten cake, mangled by suddenly clutching fingers. He sat straighter in his chair, cleared his throat. "My uncle was out of the country throughout the Leicestershire affair," he said, his dark eyes steady on Kate. "And out of town since he returned to England. He can have nothing to do with the escape."

Mr. Gerard watched them both with an uncomfortable intensity.

"He is trustworthy, knowledgeable, and well connected," Mr. Deeping continued, still speaking only to Kate. "Just the sort of ally we've been wishing for, actually."

He had. Kate hadn't wanted one.

"I think we must tell him everything," Mr. Deeping finished.

"Certainly you must," declared the older man. "You should have done so immediately," he said to his nephew.

There was that tone of authority. Of official position and legal sanction. Kate bowed her head. All would be taken away from her now. She was not admitted to those hallowed circles.

Mr. Deeping related the story. Kate let him, knowing that his uncle was far likelier to listen to his voice. There was a silence when he finished. "You have not reported any of this?" Mr. Gerard asked him with a frown.

That was too much. "To whom?" Kate asked. "He might tell the very person who ordered the fellow's release. And then where would we be?"

The older man's frown eased slightly.

"I did not know who to approach," agreed Mr. Deeping. "And then Abernathy came particularly to tell me that I should concentrate on my job, not my 'past glories.'"

"Oh, Abernathy." Mr. Gerard dismissed him with a gesture.

"My grandfather thought him a fool," Kate said. "But who sent him to discourage any talk of the matter?"

"You'd think he would wonder about that," said Mr. Deeping.

"Abernathy does not wonder," replied his uncle. "He doesn't seem to have a thought in his head. Other than what he will have for dinner."

"I wonder that he keeps his position," Kate said. When quite competent people would never be considered, because they were female.

"I believe he's a distant relation of the queen." The older man mulled things over. "You are very sure about Carlton House?"

"That the fellow went in there?" Mr. Deeping nodded. "He looked right at home."

"And I saw him with the prince at the Castlereaghs' ball," Kate added.

"All right." Mr. Gerard drummed his fingers on the table-top. "Our first step must be to identify him."

There it was, Kate noted. He said *our*, but clearly he was taking over. He assumed he had the right to do so. The alternative did not occur to him.

"Without rousing suspicions," he continued. "We need an exact description. Who saw this man?"

"Just the two of us," said Mr. Deeping. He looked at Kate, then his eyes shied away from hers like a startled horse.

Her heart sank.

"Do you think, between you, you could produce a sketch?"

It was a good idea. Kate hated that it was a good idea, and that she had not thought of it.

Mr. Gerard pulled a small notebook and stub of a pencil from his coat pocket and set them before his nephew.

"Now?" asked Mr. Deeping.

"What better time? You draw rather well, I think. Or perhaps Miss Meacham?"

Kate rejected the task with a wave of her hand.

Mr. Deeping picked up the pencil. "Very well. A roundish sort of face, I think?"

Kate nodded. He sketched.

"Eyes rather small," he said.

Kate nodded again. His uncle was watching them closely. They had not really dealt with the question of a romantic connection, Kate noted. She had diverted the conversation from *that* subject. Because it wasn't a subject, obviously. Whatever the gossips had concluded, *that* hadn't been in Mr. Deeping's mind. He'd looked aghast. Of course he didn't wish to marry her. Well, she didn't wish to marry him! He must have seen that in her face as clearly as she had in his. So all was well. They agreed. And the question of kisses would never arise again. There was no reason to feel bereft.

With a burst of revulsion, Kate rejected the word. She was impatient, insulted, with perhaps a touch of amused scorn. She felt no tinge of sadness. Or if she did, it was at the change in her investigation, the descent of official authority.

"Do you think so?" asked Mr. Deeping.

She hadn't been paying attention. "What?"

"Lips like this? Or thinner."

"Thinner," she replied. "But his cheeks are rounder than that."

He rubbed out lines with his thumb and made corrections. Kate did her best to show no emotion whatsoever as they worked to reconstruct the appearance of the man they'd seen. Because no matter what Brinsley Gerard had said, this had been an interrogation. The older man didn't need to speak to question her. He evaluated every move she made.

At last the drawing was complete. The tea was drunk, and the cakes eaten. Kate rejected the idea of an escort but allowed them to hail a cab for her. The journey home offered plenty of time to review the meeting just past and come up with wittier responses. Kate didn't think they would have made any difference though. Mr. Gerard had come full of preconceptions.

The cab pulled up before her house. Reaching for her reticule to pay, Kate noticed a shabby ancient couple hobbling up the walk to the front door, leaning heavily on stout canes. They had masses of untidy gray hair and drab, worn clothing.

The woman had a shawl over her head rather than a bonnet. Perhaps some friends of Mrs. Knox? Kate was certain she'd never seen them before.

"This the place, miss?" asked the cabbie.

"Yes." She found the fare and got down. The old couple were gone, inside presumably. Mrs. Knox would handle them.

Kate let herself in. There was no one in the entryway or the front parlor. She shed her cloak, pulled off her gloves, and started up the stairs.

Laughter filtered down them. It was coming from the study. As her head rose above that level, Kate saw that the door was wide open. She would be seen as she passed. There was no avoiding it. She put back her shoulders and readied a quick greeting.

But when she stepped into the upper hallway, she was surprised to discover the shabby ancients in the study. It was their laughter she'd heard. And one of them was…removing his bushy gray beard from his face?

With that, Kate realized the pair was Miss Palliser and Oliver Welden. They had been keeping watch on the escaped agent's lair today.

Miss Palliser spotted her. She pulled off a gray wig and waved it gaily. "We have been trying out a disguise. Tom helped us get ready."

That explained the lines subtly drawn on her face, making her appear much older, as well as the false hair. Perhaps the clothes as well. The theater would have all sorts of costumes.

"He taught us how to move," Miss Palliser added.

"Canes which are too short help one stay hunched over," said Welden. He set the beard aside and stretched upward. "Rather hard on the back, I must say. And the shoes!"

Kate noticed he had removed his.

"I could have hobbled perfectly well without the pinching," he added.

"You hold a pebble in your mouth as a reminder to mumble," said Miss Palliser.

"Did you speak to anyone at that house?" Kate asked. That didn't seem wise.

"Well, no."

"Nothing much happened," said Welden. "There was one visitor, a large man all muffled up in scarves so that we couldn't see his face. He stayed only half an hour."

"Like a morning call," said Miss Palliser.

Welden smiled. "Villains drinking tea together in the parlor?"

"Tea would be appropriate given its associations," replied Miss Palliser. "The merchants who push opium onto the Chinese in order to pay for their cargos of tea are villains too. But I expect our men swill down stronger brews."

"Swill," repeated Welden, clearly enjoying the word. "You put things so well."

"Speech is a kind of art, isn't it?"

"Indeed."

They exchanged a lingering glance. It was odd to see them doing so still half in the garb of ancients. "What did you tell Mrs. Knox when you went out?" Kate asked.

"That I am helping Mr. Welden hone his skills as a Bow Street Runner," Miss Palliser replied.

It was a clever excuse. *They* hadn't blurted out secrets. She couldn't bring herself to admit that she had. She would have to do so, but not now.

They didn't notice that she was more silent than usual. After a while, Kate excused herself and went up to her room.

Mrs. Knox paid her a visit later to wonder about their houseguest's choice of activities. She *did* notice Kate's mood and asked her what the matter was. Kate put her off and made suitable conversation during dinner. Since Miss Palliser was still full of her day's outing, it wasn't difficult. The day at last ambled to a close, and in the night, again, Kate dreamed.

She stood in a gilded room as ornate as Versailles. Golden light suffused the scene, slanting through gauzy draperies, gleaming in tall mirrors. Luxury was everywhere—curlicued furniture, embroidered fabric, exquisite tapestries. Kate wore an old-fashioned corset above a wild froth of petticoats trimmed with lace and ribbons. Her hair was falling down in a riot of curls. And she was laughing over her shoulder at a shirtless Henry Deeping, who was unlacing the corset strings, pulling them out one tantalizing eyelet at a time. His answering smile said that this would be a prolonged process, loosening the garment by literal inches.

In the dream, Kate knew this was a game they had played often before. Soon she would have to hold the corset to her bosom to keep it on. And a little while after that, she would let go, and it would drop away. She would wriggle out of her layers of petticoats, and they would race to the huge four-poster bed and throw themselves upon it, into each other's arms. The joy of shared desire filled her. It danced in Henry's dark eyes, the light touch of his fingers. They reveled in it together.

Kate woke up laughing. She'd never done that before. This had been entirely different from the brooding intensity of the previous dream. She remembered the bright image from her parents' collection that captured such an opulent scene. It had made her smile when she first saw it. The buoyant feeling stayed with her now for few minutes. How wonderful it must be to share that kind of connection.

And then reality descended with a thud. She shouldn't have been dreaming about Henry Deeping after that humiliating confrontation. Her brain ought to have dismissed him. Perhaps it had, commented a dry inner voice, but her body hadn't. He had brought parts of her to life that would not be quelled by cool logic.

She hadn't thought of those images in the wooden box beyond a passing curiosity until Henry Deeping entered her life. Now they unfolded in the night as alluring possibilities. Hopes even? But he had been specifically warned off by his family and his employer, in the same person, and he had not objected.

She was in trouble, Kate realized as she lay in her bed and tried to go back to sleep.

Eight

On January 29, church bells rang out in the evening across London, and when Henry went out to inquire as to the reason, he heard that King George had died at Windsor Castle. Others had come outside despite the cold and were calling the news to each other. The monarch's long, fraught reign had ended.

Henry stood in the street absorbing the news. He had known no other king. Not personally, of course, but the third George had been a fixture in his life, the figure everyone recognized as ruler. News of his doings and then of his erratic health had been a constant feature of London life. His son's ascent to the regency nine years ago had roused strong feelings and opinions. Sympathies and fears.

It felt as if some ancient monument had fallen, Henry thought, leaving a hole in the landscape. And maybe a mercy, considering the old king's recent trials.

He found his footsteps turning toward Tereford House. It was not terribly late. The duke and duchess would most likely be up.

And so they were. Henry was admitted to the blue and gold drawing room, offered a comfortable chair and a glass of wine, and joined a toast to the beleaguered old monarch.

"He was the king for as long as any of us can remember," commented the duchess.

"That is true for most of his subjects," the duke replied. "Nearly sixty years on the throne."

"Though he has not ruled for the last few," Henry said.

"And now we will have Prinny," said the duchess. "I wonder what sort of king he will be."

"He is a bad husband, friend, and son," answered the duke. "I expect he will be a bad king as well."

Henry thought of the man he'd followed to Carlton House. Was the Regent already part of some plot? Had he known his father was failing?

"I always felt sorry for King George," the duchess said. "He seemed a kindly man before he…"

"Lost his mind?" supplied her husband dryly.

"That was scarcely his fault, James."

"No, I expect it came of being father to a pack of wastrels. The Regent and York and Clarence and Cambridge. And all those girls as well." He frowned. "But if he had been a better parent…" He descended into muttering.

"James has been on a quest to meet men who seem to be exemplary fathers." The duchess appeared amused. "Looking for advice."

"I wish I'd talked more to yours when we were in Leicestershire, Henry. He seems to do very well."

Henry nodded. His father was a bulwark of their family. "You still can. He is always at home."

"I might, when I can."

Henry tried to imagine such a conversation. His father was not a great talker. He preferred action to chatter.

"He has not asked mine," the duchess said. "No, I don't blame you, James. Papa cares more for philosophy than individual people."

"Perhaps he simply does not know what to say to small children."

"They require love and care, not conversation."

"At first," he objected. "But then they begin to speak, and apparently the first word they learn is *no*. And then *why*."

The duchess laughed. "He has visited several of our friends' nurseries to make the acquaintance of their infants," she told Henry.

"They are relentless," her husband said. "When I couldn't tell a young lady of three why lemons are yellow, she declared I was very dull and stupid, and she wished I would go away."

Henry bit his lower lip.

"When I did not go at once, she hit me with a picture book," the duke added. "The one that showed the lemons."

Henry had to laugh. It was impossible to resist. Tereford gave him a rueful smile.

"That little girl is precocious," said his wife.

"Well, and our child might be," the duke replied. "There is no way to predict. But it seems very likely. Being a parent must be the most daunting task on earth."

Henry would have enjoyed his old friend's dithering even more if he had not had his own troubles. He still did enjoy the change in the formerly unflappable nonpareil. But thoughts of Miss Meacham continually intruded. Henry suppressed a shudder. The scene in the tea shop had been one of the most frustrating experiences of his life. All sorts of defenses and…wishes had sprung to mind when his uncle started in on them. And every word he conjured had felt fraught with the danger of offending her. Miss Meacham hated interference. She did not wish to be explained. He had no right to make claims. Still, he should have said *something*.

Producing the sketch under his uncle's suspicious eye had been the excruciating cap on the occasion. Miss Meacham had rushed out afterward, and he had not seen her since. It was a disaster. He'd been trying to figure out what to do ever since.

When the conversation seemed ready for a turn, he asked the duchess, "Do you write to my mother?" He had been trying to discover where Mama had gotten the idea that he and Miss Meacham had made a match of it. What he was to do about the tale was another question entirely.

"I correspond with Charlotte," his hostess replied. She smiled. "She is planning her wedding in the spring. Here in town so all her old friends can be there."

The idea of his acerbic sister deep in wedding schemes might have made Henry laugh, if he had not been preoccupied with his own concerns. "You tell her all the news from here, I suppose."

"What there is," she replied, looking puzzled.

"What's wrong, Henry?" asked the duke.

"Eh?"

"You have not twitted me on my excessive anxiety or reveled in my well-deserved comeuppance. Not even once. What has happened?"

He couldn't tell them. It was too embarrassing. On the other hand, he was badly in need of advice, and James had been his friend nearly all his life. His duchess was one of the wisest people Henry had ever met. There could be no better interpreter of the female point of view. He trusted them both. Henry took a breath and plunged in. "My uncle Gerard has arrived in town," he said.

They waited. "I hope he is well," said the duke finally.

"Yes. Quite well." Of course they would not spread the story. They despised gossip. They liked him. Henry pushed ahead. "He expressed a wish to make Miss Meacham's acquaintance. And so I arranged a meeting at a tea shop. I thought he might have some diplomatic task for her, you see. And Miss Meacham wants..." What *did* she want? That was the critical question. "But somehow my uncle had formed the idea that she and I were about to become engaged. My mother had heard rumors of that as well. And my uncle had come to tell us that he, everyone, thought the match unsuitable." The awkwardness of the occasion descended on him almost as if he was back there. "But we are not... I have not..."

"You wish to marry Miss Meacham?" asked the duke.

"No. I hadn't... We've never... It isn't... I don't know."

"You have not reached a point in your relationship," said his wife, "when you have considered the future."

She had hit on it exactly. They hadn't gone beyond one kiss. An astonishing, world-shattering kiss, admittedly. He did think of her often. He did yearn...

"So you *might* wish to marry her?" Tereford asked.

Did he? Would he? "My uncle said that one must be practical in this world. And that both of us should look to marry a fortune. Which neither of us has, obviously." He was not expressing himself well.

"What did Miss Meacham say to that?" asked the duchess.

"She looked very angry." And then she had blurted out the secret they had determined to keep. Which wasn't like her at all. She didn't make careless slips. Would she do anything, no matter how reckless, to avoid talk about marrying him? "She changed the subject. Drastically."

"To what?" asked the duchess.

He couldn't tell them that. The story had spread far enough already. "A Foreign Office concern."

"The Leicestershire matter?"

Henry nodded. It did come out of that, so it was somewhat true. "She was furious," he said. "And I don't know what to do."

"Need you do anything?" asked Tereford. "You could simply avoid her."

He didn't want to, Henry realized. And there was the investigation, of course. He would inevitably see her. And she him. That was an unsettling relief.

"Well," said the duchess. "I think you will have to have a frank talk with Miss Meacham. Clear the air."

Tereford burst out laughing. "Your expression, Henry. You looked as if Cecelia had sentenced you to the gallows. But I have to agree. It is better to have an open discussion from the beginning. I've learned that lesson in the last year."

His wife smiled at him.

"The beginning of what?" Henry asked in a strangled voice.

"Of anything," Tereford answered. "If it is to begin."

"But what can I say to her? After that dreadful occasion?"

"Was she told anything worse than that a match between you is not financially prudent?" asked the duchess. "Was your uncle rude to her?"

"Of course not." He'd never known his uncle to be rude. And he wouldn't have allowed that. He would have protested!

"No sly insults or criticisms?" asked the duke.

"No. I wouldn't have stood for that."

"And she did not seem disappointed?" asked the duchess. "As if she might have been expecting an offer?"

"She seemed irate at the very idea," Henry replied. And had she needed to be quite so angry? Was the thought of marrying him repugnant? Or had it been his uncle's forbidding the match? Had she thought of marriage? Young ladies seemed to, continually. She wasn't like that, however. What had she said? Is a woman good for nothing but marriage? That was it. She found that notion repellent. "I don't know what to say to her."

"Of course you must decide that before you speak," said the duchess. "You must be clear on how you feel about her." She gazed at him with raised brows.

He felt thoroughly muddled. Miss Kate Meacham was the definition of unexpected. "I've never known anyone else like her," Henry admitted.

"She struck me as a complicated person," said Tereford. "In Leicestershire."

"That is very discerning, James."

"Must you be so surprised? Both of you? I notice things."

"She is interesting," Henry put in. "One never knows what she'll do."

"And is that something you enjoy?" asked the duke. "Or does it fill you with creeping apprehension? A fear that at any moment you will be made to jump out of your skin?"

"James!" His wife's crystalline blue eyes twinkled. "It is not *boring* at any rate."

"You know I have sworn off that word, Cecelia."

They exchanged one of those smiles that made marriage look like an eminently desirable state.

"I kissed her," Henry heard himself say. "Accidentally."

"Accidentally?" asked both the Terefords at once.

He shouldn't have said that. It was just that the memory was uppermost in his mind, and the words had popped out.

"I am trying to imagine how that might happen," said the duke. "Did you trip and catch hold of her…mouth?"

"Perhaps they both bent over to pick up a dropped glove," said the duchess.

"And instead of knocking heads, they knocked lips?"

They were laughing at him. Henry didn't blame them. It sounded ridiculous, and he couldn't explain the actual circumstances without revealing why they had ducked into a doorway and embraced. "You won't mention it to anyone."

"Of course not," said the duchess.

Tereford nodded agreement. "Was it…pleasurable?"

The term didn't begin to describe the experience.

"Judging by his expression, I believe it was," said Tereford to his wife.

"For both of you?" she asked Henry.

"She... I think so."

"Well, a frank and open discussion is clearly in order," she replied. "Vital, in fact. You must do it as soon as you can."

"I don't know how I'll look her in the eye again," he answered.

"Cowardice, Henry?"

"Abject," he answered. Both Terefords gazed at him with gentle sympathy.

Henry stayed only a little while after that. It was growing late, and he suspected that his uncle would be looking for him at the Foreign Office tomorrow. He made his farewells rather absently, leaving the duke and duchess together in their lovely drawing room. They sat for a while in front of the crackling fire, she cozy in the circle of his arm. "More matchmaking," said James. "Do you attract it? The way flowers do bees?"

Cecelia laughed.

———

"The balance of the blade is of crucial importance," Miss Palliser said to Kate. She flicked her hand, and a small knife flew across the garden and stuck quivering in the fence at the back. It had hit the center of a circle they'd chalked there. Miss Palliser awaited Kate's reaction. "You were very eager to learn this skill, but now you don't seem to be paying attention."

"Why does everyone assume that a woman thinks of nothing but marriage?" Kate asked.

Miss Palliser looked at her, eyes large behind her spectacles. "'Everyone' and 'nothing' are exaggerations, of course."

"They don't seem to be," replied Kate bitterly. Any man she came near seemed to assume she was after a ring.

"The topic is a preoccupation." The older woman shrugged. "Many women see a wedding as their only choice in life. Many of them are correct."

"You're saying that men are right to see us as…prowling huntresses?"

Miss Palliser laughed. "I rather like that phrase. And the images it conjures."

Kate did too. But it didn't make things any better. She hunted bigger game than a wedding.

"You don't wish to be married?"

"No. I am like you. I prefer my independence." She did. She *would*.

"Oh, I would have liked a husband. And children. I have quite a few ideas about how a child should be reared. But I never attracted much notice among the gentlemen." She hesitated, then added, "Or found a congenial partner."

Kate gazed at her. Miss Palliser looked back, particularly owlish. Kate realized she had made assumptions based on the older woman's plain appearance and forthright manner. She was as bad as all the rest.

"And you know, 'independence' is often just another word for solitude. Which is all well and good, of course. I require time to myself. But true companionship is…a treasure."

Kate felt a sob trembling in her chest. She ruthlessly suppressed it.

"What is the matter, Miss Meacham? You haven't been yourself today. Is it something to do with Mr. Deeping?"

"Why do you say that?" Kate felt a flush stain her cheeks.

"Well, you have been morose since you returned from meeting him and his uncle. Was Mr. Gerard rude to you?"

"No. Yes." Was it rude to be dreadfully interfering? To make her feel like a drag on his nephew's life? Why had he stuck his nose in?

"I had thought," began Miss Palliser in a more tentative tone, "that you were partial to Mr. Deeping."

"I…" She might as well admit it, Kate thought. Silently, to herself. With the dreams. Since that kiss. Which had been like a match to dry tinder, apparently. Only she hadn't known she was so…combustible. There hadn't been the least sign until Henry Deeping, and everything that had passed between them in recent days, showed her the danger. And what about him? How did he feel? If anything in particular? They had needed time, not every emotion pulled out into the open and pawed over. She cringed when she remembered his appalled expression in the tea shop.

"You needn't confide in me," said Miss Palliser. "I certainly had no intention of prying. I know we are not…"

"His uncle—and his mother—decided that since we have been going about together, I was angling for a proposal. Because what else could a woman want?"

"Ah. And Mr. Gerard warned you off? Publicly? How insulting."

"He wasn't quite so crude. He said we should both look to marry a fortune. Consider the future *practically*."

"A diplomat with his own money has an advantage," said Miss Palliser.

"I know that!" It occurred to Kate that Jerome's intended bride was said to have a sizable dowry. Perhaps that was the real reason for his engagement, despite all his talk about sweetness and tact. He was thoroughly practical! "Mr. Deeping looked horrified at the idea of marriage. To me."

"Oh."

"Frozen," Kate added. "Like a stag surrounded by a pack of wolves." That was how she remembered it, at least. He had certainly been silent. She hadn't seen him since.

"Ah."

"Yes."

"He might have been merely surprised," Miss Palliser suggested.

"We were both *surprised*," Kate agreed. "Why must people interfere?"

"Families are organized to do so, I find. Indeed many seem to believe it is their right to dominate the next generation."

As she had none, Kate was not drawn into the topic. "I don't know what I am to say to Mr. Deeping when I see him again. If I see him again."

"Of course you will. He will not wish to give up our investigation."

"No." But his uncle would probably take it out of their hands, Kate thought. Because she was a fool and had blabbed. Mr. Gerard might be making other arrangements even now.

"You might make a joke of it?" Miss Palliser didn't sound convinced by her own suggestion. "Or pretend it never happened at all. That is what my father does with our uncomfortable conversations."

"That must be very annoying," said Kate.

"It is." The older woman considered. "He may actually forget. He doesn't devote much thought to me."

Johnny came out the back door and hurried toward them, pulling at the back of his short jacket. Their errand boy/ footman in training was outgrowing his clothes again, Kate noted. He would have to have new ones soon. He held out a folded piece of paper. "Message for you, miss."

Kate took it and read. "There will be no answer, Johnny."

The boy nodded and went back inside.

Miss Palliser waited a hopeful moment. When Kate said nothing, she went to pull the knife from the fence.

A sense of doom descended over Kate. She had to admit what she'd done. Obviously, it would all come out. There was no stopping it. She held up the note. "Mr. Deeping's uncle thinks he has identified the man who came to Russell Square," she said. "The three of us are to attend a reception tonight and confirm it, as Mr. Deeping and I are the ones who saw him there."

Miss Palliser stared at her. "But how does Mr. Gerard know about that?"

Here it was. "I told him," said Kate.

"We had agreed to keep the matter between ourselves."

"I had to make them stop talking about marriage," she blurted out. "So I told him the real reason why Mr. Deeping and I had been meeting so often."

"Ah. That diverted him."

"Yes." She gritted her teeth. "I allowed personal feelings to interfere in our investigation. Jerome was right. I am impatient and abrasive and foolhardy. I will never be a real diplomat."

Miss Palliser snorted. "I don't know who Jerome might be. But that is nonsense. Personal feelings—pride, vendettas, amours—all those sorts of things change the course of history. Even for the better, sometimes."

Kate swallowed. She'd expected disappointment, possibly a scold, complaints at the least. Indeed, she knew where those would come from. "Mr. Welden will be very angry with me." He had such a biting tongue.

"He is angry a good bit of the time," replied Miss Palliser. "But it is mostly at himself."

"What?" That didn't make sense. The man snapped at other people.

"It comes out of his childhood."

"He is angry at himself because of his childhood?" That made even less sense.

"Not because of. But as a result of."

Kate didn't understand the distinction. But her curiosity had been roused. "Was it very terrible?"

"On the contrary, he was born to older parents who had given up expecting offspring and saw him as a gift from God. They adored him and thought his every accomplishment a marvel. Particularly his academic achievements, as they were not well educated. Apparently gaining scholarships seemed like a kind of magic to them."

"And this made him angry?" Kate was more confused.

"Their attitude led him to believe he could do no wrong," Miss Palliser continued. "And that his judgment was infallible. When he discovered that was untrue, in a very painful way, over a young lady, his world collapsed. That was when he became Merlin."

"And angry," Kate said.

Miss Palliser nodded. "For a long while, he blamed everyone else for his disappointments, but lately he has turned it around and begun to put them all on himself. Which is not the whole truth either, you know. I have told him that going over and over past mistakes and becoming mired in regrets is not helpful, but he finds it difficult to stop."

"How do you know these things?" Kate asked.

Miss Palliser seemed to recall herself from a distance. She looked self-conscious. "Oh well, we have had the opportunity to talk as we stand our watches on the Judd Street house."

And apparently Mr. Welden had poured out his life story. Kate couldn't quite picture it. He'd seemed such a prickly person. "You've enjoyed that?" she ventured.

"I have," replied her older companion, meeting her eyes squarely, as if daring her to object.

Kate had no intention of doing so. Why would she? Even if she had any right. Which she didn't. However, she still thought Mr. Welden would rail at her when he learned what she'd done. "I have let the group down by speaking," she said. "And worse than that."

"What do you mean?"

"Mr. Gerard will take over the investigation now," she said.

"I suppose he will try," Miss Palliser acknowledged. "As such men do. We will not fall into line like his Foreign Office subordinates."

Kate felt a stirring of optimism. She had an ally, perhaps several.

"Because we are not obliged to follow his orders."

"Mr. Deeping is," Kate pointed out.

"It will be interesting to see what he does."

"He has to…"

Miss Palliser waved this subject aside. "Now, this reception. Clearly, you must wear something splendid. For a number of reasons."

She'd surprised Kate again. Why had she thought that Miss Palliser cared nothing for raiment? "Diplomats are asked to wear mourning whenever it is proclaimed at court," Kate replied. "With the king's death, it will be deep mourning dress." She had mourning clothes for her grandfather. It would not be pleasant to don them again.

"You are not a diplomat," Miss Palliser pointed out, raising the small knife she held for emphasis. "But I suppose you must conform in this case."

Kate took the blade from her and threw it. It struck the fence sideways and clattered to the ground.

Nine

HENRY'S PARTY ENTERED THE RECEPTION ROOM OF THE Turkish embassy near the beginning of the event. The place was already filling with black coats and somber gowns. Talk was muted. It was not considered proper to laugh too much so soon after the king's death. He was chiefly conscious of Miss Meacham on his uncle's other side. He meant to take the duchess's advice and talk with her, though tonight was probably not a good opportunity. Or perhaps this was just cowardice. He did not want to hear that she had been put off him by his family's intrusion into their affairs. Insofar as they had any, he thought. They hadn't quite got around to having any. He had devoted a good deal of time to deciding what to say, with results that could only be called mixed.

His uncle scanned the room. "I don't see any of the Carlton House set," he said. "Let us station ourselves beside the entry where we can get a good look at anyone coming in."

They did so, a silent trio in a sea of chatter. Miss Meacham had not spoken to Henry beyond a measured greeting. His uncle seemed unaware that he had complicated the matter of the foreign agent even more for Henry. Or perhaps he was simply exhibiting a diplomat's impassive manner, giving nothing away. Henry wondered if he was really cut out for his new career.

"The prince is not expected tonight," his uncle said. "King, I should say. Our new King George the Fourth. But some members of his circle are likely to attend."

They waited. People arrived. Some paused to greet Henry's uncle and talk briefly. Others passed by. Jerome Delaroche came through the door, checked slightly at seeing the three of them together, then walked on with a mere nod. Miss Meacham muttered something, inaudible but clearly not complimentary.

Servants circulated with goblets of a beverage made from oranges and spice. The Ottomans did not serve strong drink. Which was their right, Henry thought. But he would have welcomed a glass or two of wine.

"There," said Henry's uncle finally.

Several men had entered together.

"That is the man who I think resembles your portrait," he added. "The one on the right."

Henry stared. The fellow was more visible in the candlelight than he had been muffled in a topcoat and hat. His features matched the face Henry had followed from Russell Square. "It's him."

"I agree," said Miss Meacham. "His nose is distinctive."

It certainly was—reddened by drink and rather squashed looking, as if it had been flattened at some point and never fully recovered.

His uncle nodded. He said nothing until the newcomers had moved on into the room, well out of earshot. Even then he urged them into a corner before saying, "I thought so. That is Quentin Matthews. He is one of the pri…king's cronies. He has no official position, which is a relief."

"Because he will not be acting for the government," said Miss Meacham. "Whatever he does."

"Precisely."

"But then it is also a puzzle why he would be meeting with a foreign agent," Henry pointed out.

"I begin to think that 'agent' is not the correct word for this fellow," said his uncle. "He seems more like a hired blackguard."

"Didn't I say so!" Miss Meacham said to Henry.

"You did." Their eyes met and bounced off each other.

"Matthews is not political," Henry's uncle went on. "He has handled more personal…matters for our new king." The distaste in his voice was clear.

"Involving hired bravos?" Henry asked, not wanting to believe such a thing.

"No," said his uncle. "A different sort of…go-between."

Henry supposed he meant panderers. Their new monarch was notorious for his affairs.

"What can he be up to?" asked Miss Meacham.

"That is the question." Henry's uncle looked thoughtful. "And I have the feeling we had better find the answer."

"I could speak to him," she offered.

Henry and his uncle said no at the same moment, Henry with rather too much volume. "We don't want to attract his attention," his uncle said. "Not until we have a good deal more information. And perhaps not even then."

Henry managed not to say that Matthews wasn't the sort of person she should know. She would not appreciate the sentiment.

"This was our investigation before you ever arrived in town," said Miss Meacham. "You are not in charge."

There was a moment when Henry thought his uncle was angry. He braced for a cold setdown and wondered how he would mend fences between his companions. But the irritated expression faded. "We can't discuss this in so public a venue," his uncle said, obviously expecting to silence her.

"Come," said Miss Meacham. She turned and walked away, leaving them to follow perforce, and proceeded to lead them out of the main doorway, through an unobtrusive entry at the side of the stair, down a hall, and into a small empty parlor. She closed the door with a click, then turned to confront his uncle.

"How did you do that?" asked Henry.

"I know the back ways into all the embassies," she answered.

"Do you indeed?" said his uncle.

Henry looked at the closed door. "Won't we be found?"

"Not for a while. The staff is busy. And after all, why should they care?"

"These incursions of yours have been noticed," his uncle commented.

Miss Meacham looked rebellious.

Henry nearly stepped between them like the referee at a boxing match.

His uncle walked over and sat down on a small sofa. He crossed his legs and looked fully at ease. "So, the investigation. I could take over the endeavor entirely."

"You have no right…"

"I do actually. I am employed by the Foreign Office, vowed to serve Britain's interests."

"And I am not," she replied bitterly.

"Correct." Henry's uncle gazed at her. "I have the authority, and I have contacts and experience that will move matters along."

"So I am to be shoved aside, even though none of it would be known without me."

"What is more important to you? Unraveling this problem or ensuring your own involvement?"

His tone made Henry suspect this was a test. He watched Miss Meacham struggle with the question. He felt the conflict himself. He didn't want to be shunted off into obscurity. And yet...

"Solving the problem," she said through gritted teeth.

"Splendid," said his uncle. "And so I will be glad for us to work together."

"What?"

"As long as our purpose is the good of the country and not showing up others' failings or petty revenge."

Miss Meacham's jaw tightened further. "Petty..."

"Revenge nearly always is."

"I am not engaged in revenge."

"Merely showing up those who have discounted you?"

She frowned at him as if she hadn't fully taken his measure until now.

"It must be clear, however, that I am in charge," Henry's uncle continued. "No one is to go haring off on their own based on some wild theory."

"Because of course we could not have any other kind," she countered. "Not a sensible and careful plan. Or an unusual insight."

Henry's uncle smiled. "I am always ready to hear alternate views." He made the adjective sound trivial.

Miss Meacham's fingers curled into fists. What would he do if she punched his uncle, Henry wondered. What would Uncle Brinsley do? But Miss Meacham took a breath and opened her hands. His uncle nodded. "I see why you like her, Henry," he disastrously said.

She looked at Henry. Her violet eyes fumed. Was she daring him? To be daring?

"How could I not?" Henry asked. He startled them both. He had a moment to enjoy that, and then was saved from further conversation by the hand of providence. A housemaid opened the parlor door, started, and gaped at them.

"I don't feel faint any longer," said Miss Meacham with immediate, airy assurance. "I will be quite all right." She led them past the astonished maid and around a corner that was not the way they had come. Two more turnings brought them out at the place where they had left their outer garments and surprised a footman, who jumped as if they'd appeared out of thin air.

"Amazing," Henry murmured.

Miss Meacham very nearly smiled.

They retrieved capes and overcoats and went out into the February night. Here was his chance. "I will escort you home," Henry said to Miss Meacham.

His uncle looked them over. "I suppose someone must do so," he acknowledged.

"I can find a cab on my own," said Miss Meacham.

"Nonsense," Henry's uncle replied.

In the dancing light of the torches at either side of the embassy doorway, Henry wondered how Uncle Brinsley could be so obtuse. But he wasn't. He never had been. Perhaps he *wished* to provoke her, like a man trying the flex of a rapier he intended to use. The image was striking and felt apt. His uncle was subtle and clever and not very helpful for Henry just now. Encountering the older man's ironic gaze, Henry understood that his uncle didn't wish to help in this matter. Quite the opposite. He meant to divide them. Anger, always slow to ignite in Henry, stirred to life. He turned to go and find a cab.

When he returned with one, his uncle said, "We will all go."

"There's no need," Henry replied at the same moment that Miss Meacham said the words.

"There's no need for either of you," she added. She opened the door and stepped up into the cab. She would have closed it in their faces, but Henry kept hold of the handle.

"You want to take care, Henry," said his uncle.

Henry wasn't sure he did, actually. But he didn't wish to quarrel with his uncle, who had so often been kind to him. "I'm sure you have things to do. The journey isn't long." He climbed quickly into the vehicle, shut the door, and signaled the driver. They started to move off.

Henry's uncle watched them drive away.

"I don't need an escort," said Miss Meacham.

"You shouldn't be alone in the night streets."

"I have often been…"

She bit off the words, and Henry wondered what she had been about to say. The darkness was a problem. He caught glimpses of her face as they passed streetlamps, but these would grow fewer as they turned toward the less illuminated precincts around her house. "I wanted an opportunity to talk with you."

"And so you have taken it. As your uncle has taken over our search. If you think you are going to be high-handed with me…"

"I do not."

"And yet you *are*."

"No, I'm not."

"You are not escorting me against my wishes?"

"Do you want me to stop the cab and get out? I will do so."

He waited through a silence that grew more encouraging as it lengthened.

When she'd said nothing for some time, he spoke again. "I wish to remove any awkwardness caused by my uncle's remarks at the tea shop." Henry silently cursed the stiff sound of his voice. "The duchess suggested…"

"You've been talking about me to the Duchess of Tereford?"

She sounded outraged. This was going badly. The cab had been a poor choice, Henry acknowledged. He should have called to see her in broad daylight. "I asked for advice," he began. "It seemed a delicate matter."

"Nothing of the kind. We have a treaty, no more."

Her last sentence wasn't a question. But Henry thought it wasn't entirely *not* a question. Unless he'd imagined the hint of interrogation in her tone. "A treaty?"

"In the language of diplomacy. We agreed to work together. To our mutual advantage. There was no thought of anything else."

"In the beginning."

"And I do not see that anything has changed."

Henry's spirits sank. "It's true we began with a bargain. But then we kissed." Did she feel none of the fiery echoes of that embrace?

"By mistake. You took advantage."

He hated the idea. "I didn't… You grabbed me. I…"

"It was a stratagem. Anyone would have known it was a stratagem."

"I think *anyone* is an exagg—"

"Any sensible, intelligent person, in the circumstances," she interrupted.

She sounded distant and angry. Henry's mood dipped further. "So you did not like it?" he asked. That was not the main point. He had meant to talk about the scene in the tea shop. But he found this was the thing he mainly wanted to know.

There was another silence. Henry was just thinking that it was odd—Miss Meacham was most encouraging when she said nothing—when she burst out, "I have not been compromised! Such a stupid, wretched word. As if a woman was a commodity that could be… Ha!"

Her sudden scornful laugh made Henry jump.

"Adulterated," she finished. "Language is as insulting as all the rest. If this talk of matches made you think I was, you are wrong."

"I don't think so."

"Then what are we talking about? Is the *awkwardness* dispelled yet?"

"My uncle's interference was unconscionable. But it made me think... Do you feel no desire for a closer connection?" Henry found it hard to catch his breath as he waited for her answer. And waited.

"Why do you ask me? Because your uncle pushed you to it?"

"I have become fascinated with your daring spirit."

The next silence was the longest yet. Henry began to fear that she wouldn't reply at all. And then the journey would be over. He felt there was much more to say, but he couldn't seem to find the words. The ones he'd uttered so far had failed him.

"Mr. Deeping," she replied finally. "Our main purpose now is to discover what the agent is up to. I think we should keep our attention on that and avoid complications." She sniffed. "Insofar as we are *allowed* to do so."

His uncle had put him at a distinct disadvantage, Henry thought. Uncle Brinsley definitely meant to drive a wedge between them. And he was a seasoned diplomat, expert at such maneuvers. But he could be countered. "We can also further our acquaintance..."

"I suppose we cannot help but do so." The cab pulled up. Miss Meacham opened the door to step down.

"Will you give me a chance?" Henry asked as she slipped away from him.

She checked on the carriage step, made an unintelligible sound, and hurried away. The lantern next to her door lit her back as she went inside. Henry got no glimpse of her face. He hadn't been able to really see it through the whole conversation. So much had been interpretation in the dark. He hadn't really noticed until now how much one relied on seeing someone's face as they talked.

He gave the driver the address of his rooms and pulled the door shut. She'd said he had taken advantage. The idea revolted. He was not the sort of man—person—to do that. She thought his uncle was a petty tyrant. With some justification. And some wrongheadedness.

He couldn't push her. He must show her that he was a gentleman, even if it meant keeping his distance when he longed for the opposite.

———

Kate closed the front door quietly. She leaned back against it in the dim entryway, aware of the beating of her heart. In her mind, she heard Mr. Deeping's question again. "Do you feel no desire for a closer connection?" It had brought her dreams rushing back, waves of vivid longing he would be shocked to discover. So intense she could scarcely speak.

But his uncle's intervention in their affairs had inspired him to ask. He hadn't come to it on his own. Not driven by his own desires, whatever they might be. The memory of his lips on hers coursed through her. He had desires!

It had all become such a terrible muddle. If she hadn't started out so angry at his uncle, felt so patronized and belittled, she could have been clearer. Probably. Perhaps. But she'd been itching for a fight, and Mr. Deeping had...reaped the benefit of that irritation. All in all, a wholly *dis*satisfying conversation. She was still jumpy and agitated.

Kate gathered her skirts and started up the stairs. Low voices filtered down to her as she climbed. She moved softly, not ready to encounter anyone else and possibly vent more annoyance on undeserving heads.

Oliver Welden was here, she discovered when she reached the next level. He was talking with Miss Palliser in the study, the door slightly ajar. This was not proper, of course—a lady and a gentleman visitor alone together at this time of night. Kate found she didn't care in the least.

She couldn't help but be curious, however. Especially after the details Miss Palliser had shared about the man. Were these two courting? She paused on the landing and heard Miss Palliser say, "We are all subjected to an entrenched hierarchy."

"The gradations of power in society are obvious once one's eyes are opened," replied Mr. Welden. "Most are victims of its oppression."

"I don't care for that label."

"Is it not the truth?"

It was odd, Kate thought. Their remarks were measured and abstract, but they spoke in warm, almost caressing tones.

"I will not admit to being a victim," said Miss Palliser. "The word suggests there is no recourse."

"Well, is there?" Mr. Welden's voice vibrated with affectionate admiration. Kate had never heard him speak so. She had not imagined he could.

"I believe there is, working together."

She gave the final word a soft emphasis that made Kate blink.

"And what is that?" He was encouraging, intent.

"Power is not given but taken," Miss Palliser answered.

The declaration struck Kate like a clapper hitting a great bell. It felt like a revelation and a call to action.

"My dear," said Mr. Welden.

She'd been eavesdropping too long, Kate noted. She slipped silently past the door and up to her room.

Not given but taken, she repeated silently as she undressed and prepared for bed. Just how might that be done? She realized that she had a few ideas. And with that her lingering anger faded into amused anticipation. She lay down in a much different mood.

In the depths of the night, once more Kate dreamed.

She was in a room decorated with murals in deep reds and blues. Marble columns punctuated scenes of myths and ancient gods. She reclined on a padded couch, raised on one bent elbow, draped in the robes of classical antiquity. Her hair was caught up in golden bands, a few curls falling to one shoulder. Jeweled brooches fastened the shoulders of her tunic. Other gems gleamed in her ears.

Henry Deeping lay on a similar couch beside her. He

wore the toga of a Roman noble, a wreath of laurel leaves on his head perhaps a prize or other accolade.

They were alone. A laden table spread out before them, heaped with countless exotic delicacies.

Kate plucked a ruddy grape from a great bunch on a platter. She held it out. Mr. Deeping leaned a little forward to take it with his mouth. He licked her fingertips as he did so. She ran one along his lower lip.

She was aware in this dream that he would do whatever she wished. He longed to. She need only speak a desire, and it would be fulfilled.

But they never talked in these dreams, some separate part of her noted. Was it possible? Could she say all that she wanted?

She opened her mouth to try, and with that she woke. "Blast," said Kate Meacham to her empty bedchamber.

Ten

"WHAT NEWS?" CALLED MISS PALLISER'S VOICE AS KATE came down rather later than usual the next morning. She paused in the doorway of the study, surprised to find the older woman in place at the desk at this hour. "Did you recognize the man?"

The only man in Kate's thoughts was Henry Deeping. Of course she'd recognized him. What did that mean? Then she recalled the purpose of their outing yesterday evening. "Oh. Yes."

"Come in and tell me everything."

Briefly Kate was sorry that she no longer lived alone. But when she joined Miss Palliser in the book-cluttered room, she was surprised by a feeling of relief and comradeship. Kate had never had women friends. She'd been given tutors rather than going to school. She hadn't participated in the social round of calls and parties. So she hadn't really learned how to make them. But now here was Daphne Palliser, just when she wanted someone to talk to, someone she could trust.

"Is something wrong? Did the conspirator suspect you?"

"No," Kate replied to the second question. The first was too complicated. She sat down.

"You look distressed."

Because she was a mass of conflicting impulses, Kate thought. "We identified the fellow as soon as he entered the reception," she replied. "Mr. Gerard knew him as one of the prince's—the new king's—cronies. His name is Quentin Matthews. He has no official position."

"That's good, I suppose?"

"I don't think it is actually." She had thought this over after their meeting. "If the government was involved, we could find information eventually and trust that there was some sort of plan. Even if a bad one. From the way Mr. Gerard spoke of this Matthews, I suspect he's a…procurer."

"For the Regent?"

Kate nodded. Their new monarch had an unsavory reputation. He'd had a string of mistresses over the years as well as many more fleeting liaisons.

"But what would the agent have to do with…that?" asked Miss Palliser.

"I don't know. Perhaps nothing. It likely means the king trusts this Matthews's discretion."

"Knows he will keep his mouth shut," the older woman suggested.

"Yes."

"Although we have no proof that His Majesty is connected to this matter."

"True. Although a hanger-on like Matthews usually acts under orders."

Miss Palliser nodded. "Well, we have made some small progress. Why do you look so morose?"

"Do I?" Is that what she was?

"Rather."

"I'm tired. I didn't sleep well." Should she speak about how she felt? After what she'd overheard last night, Kate thought Miss Palliser might know more about matters of the heart than she'd imagined. But Kate had never had a confidant. It was difficult to begin.

"Did Mr. Deeping and Mr. Gerard escort you home?"

"Mr. Deeping."

"The two of you in a cab."

"What? Yes." How else would they have traveled under the circumstances?

"Did he apologize?" Miss Palliser asked.

"For what?"

"Indeed."

Kate was confused. That state was becoming wearisome.

"What did he talk about on your short journey?" When Kate didn't answer at once, she added, "Our investigation? The hospitality of the Turks?"

"He wished to remove any awkwardness caused by his uncle's remarks at the tea shop."

"Remove it? Like a bit of fluff from his coat sleeve?"

Kate laughed. Daphne Palliser was a most refreshing person.

"And is it removed?"

"No," she replied. The awkwardness had expanded like one of those balloons aeronauts filled to make their flights, rising and billowing until it loomed over them.

"You know, Miss Meacham…"

"Don't you think you should call me Kate? We must be more than acquaintances by this time."

Her companion looked touched. "And I am Daphne."

"Daphne. Mr. Deeping said he was fascinated by my daring spirit."

"Ah." The older woman eyed her. "And you didn't care for it? That sounds like admiration."

"Does it? If you really consider the phrase? What does 'fascination' mean? It could refer to appalled astonishment. Or the helpless horror one feels when watching a…a cliff-side collapse into rubble."

Her housemate smiled. "Really, Kate, I don't think he can have meant anything like that. Perhaps he was trying to offer something more substantial than praise of your appearance."

The collapsing cliff was more a personal sensation, Kate realized. Henry Deeping's…incursion was rearranging her internal landscape. And he wasn't even doing it on purpose. She was fleetingly conscious of a wish that he *did* mean to do it. "How does anyone ever make a match?"

Daphne seemed to ponder this question for a moment. "Families often push matters along."

"Or the opposite. Like his uncle."

"They are usually more subtle. From what I have observed. Is a match what you want in this case?"

Kate started to answer, then fell silent. The question had layers. Did she want marriage after all? Like all the other females? Did she want Mr. Deeping? Did she actually have that choice?

"It is best to know exactly what you want," the older woman went on. "And then you can set about getting it."

It made Kate think of what she'd overheard last night.

Power was to be taken, not given. "Is that what you do?" she asked.

Daphne straightened her quill pen on the desk. "I haven't very often, in the past. I intend to, from now on. Living here has inspired me."

"Here?" Kate was startled.

"Why yes. We are managing extremely well. Pursuing a serious investigation, earning the respect of…intelligent individuals."

"Like Mr. Welden," Kate couldn't help but say.

Her companion looked a little self-conscious, but not embarrassed. "Him, and others. How did you leave things with Mr. Deeping?"

"Nowhere."

"So you put him off."

"Probably."

"I mean, you deferred the issue to a later date," Daphne said.

A choked laugh escaped Kate. "You make it sound like a matter for the courts."

"Well, if you are courting…"

"An entirely different use of the word," Kate pointed out.

"I know. It's odd, isn't it? And in the courts one sues but is not a suitor."

"Very interesting."

Daphne acknowledged her ironic tone with a smile. "It seems to me that nothing disastrous has happened, Kate. You had an uncomfortable conversation with Mr. Deeping.

He probably felt as uneasy as you did. Or more so, since his uncle was the cause of the original 'awkwardness.' You will be seeing Mr. Deeping as we continue our work, and you can speak to him again whenever you like. Clarify."

"Like butter?" Kate joked. She was cheered by Daphne's calm determination. She would take it as inspiration, she decided, glad to feel that she had a friend.

———————

That evening, dressed to go out, her cloak over her arm, Kate found Oliver Welden waiting with Daphne in the parlor. They stood in front of the fireplace, their heads bent together like a living arch. She had not known he was coming to escort them. Or accompany Daphne, really, she supposed. They straightened when she came in. Not guiltily but with an air that made her feel she was interrupting.

"We should not have agreed to hold our regular meeting elsewhere," Welden said. His acerbic tone showed that he had not given up his habit of complaint.

"Surely it is more private here," Daphne replied.

"This Gerard fellow wants to flex his muscle, bring us into line."

"Official and officious."

"Well put," said Welden. He and Daphne did not smile at each other. They exchanged a look that was more complicated than that.

Kate said nothing, though she agreed. They'd all been *informed* of this gathering, which felt much the same as being ordered. And they were to come to Mr. Gerard, not a house that was hers, at a time and place he set.

"If we had all insisted on meeting here, he might have given in," said Daphne.

"Or refused and excluded us from whatever he plans," said Kate. That was far more likely. She was certain of it, in fact.

"It is a great pity he has been brought into this," said Welden. "Mr. Deeping is in his uncle's power, I suppose. He owes his position to him."

He assumed that Henry Deeping had shared their secret. Kate avoided Daphne's eyes. She ought to admit her fault, but she could not explain the circumstances to Welden. Henry Deeping probably would have informed his uncle, she told herself, now that the older man was in London and taking an interest in his work. He was, in a sense, in his power. She had only hastened the inevitable. Perhaps. "We should go," she said. Welden took up the cane he still used, and they departed.

They arrived at the Golden Lion pub a few minutes before the appointed hour. When they asked for Mr. Gerard, they were directed to a private parlor on an upper floor, a comfortable room with refreshments on a sideboard and a large round table in the middle. Mr. Gerard sat there, a note-book open before him, his attention on Tom in one of the other chairs. "So you have no knowledge of your parentage?" he asked the lad.

Tom shook his head. "I've been on my own since I was small. First thing I remember is scrounging about in the garbage on the streets of Bristol. I've thought I might have wandered off a ship at the docks. But I never heard of sailors searching for a lost kiddie. Maybe I was born in the workhouse and m'mother died."

Gerard gestured at the empty chairs, signaling that the rest of them should sit. Kate gritted her teeth as she removed her cloak and hung it on a peg by the door. "Go on," Gerard said to Tom.

"I was in an orphanage for a bit. I spent a year at a dame school, doing odd jobs and seeing to the fires and all. The missus taught me to read, and my numbers. But in the end, I got tired of Bristol. Seems I've a natural yen to move. So one day I just set off walking south."

"And came under the patronage of the Earl of Macklin."

Tom grinned. "That's a bit of a tale, that is. It'd take a deal of time to tell it."

"He got you taken on as an actor at the Drury Lane Theater," Gerard continued. They were less questions than verifications of data he already had, Kate realized.

"That was more Mrs. Thorpe," Tom said.

"The toast of the London stage?" Kate asked. She hadn't meant to join Gerard's interrogation, but it slipped out.

"That's her," said Tom amiably.

Mr. Gerard wrote something in his notebook. He turned a page and addressed Welden, who had taken the chair next to Tom. "You have recently been engaged as a Bow Street Runner." Again, it was not a question.

Oliver Welden frowned at him, looked at the notebook, and glared. "You've been snooping into our histories?"

The older man looked unmoved. "Of course. I must know who I'm associating with. You were employed as a private tutor and a schoolmaster, and then there is a blank space in your history."

Welden gazed stonily across the table.

"Several years long," Gerard added. "Before the Leicestershire matter."

Welden said nothing.

"I will find out about it, with a bit more time. There are no doubt people who know."

She was one of them, Kate thought. But she wasn't going to admit it. Meeting Daphne's steady gaze, she saw the same determination there, and approval of her silence.

"I assume there was no criminal enterprise involved," Mr. Gerard said. "The Runners wouldn't stand for that."

"You may take your notebook and stick it…"

The door opened, and Henry Deeping walked in.

Kate's pulse accelerated. She'd been wondering where he was. An image from one of her dreams surfaced, and she flushed.

He paused in the doorway, conscious that everyone was looking at him. "Good evening," he said.

His voice sent shivers across Kate's skin. That mustn't happen under his uncle's critical scrutiny. She wouldn't give him the satisfaction.

Mr. Gerard indicated a chair. His nephew shed his coat and took it. No one had touched the offered refreshments, Kate noted. Despite appearances, this was not a convivial gathering.

"So, to begin," Gerard said.

"Who put you in charge?" Welden objected.

"His Majesty's government and many years of experience," the older man replied calmly. Gerard looked around as if ready to counter any other protests. When none came, he went on. "We have two men to keep in our sights. The one taken in Leceistershire, who eventually gave the name Richard Rankin."

It annoyed Kate that he'd been able to find that information when none of them could. She saw a similar resentment in Welden's expression. "It might be a false name," she said.

Gerard nodded. "And Quentin Matthews," he continued. "We must watch them both until we can discover what they are plotting."

"We all knew that," muttered Welden. "We have been *doing* that."

Mr. Deeping's uncle ignored this comment with a bland carelessness that made Kate grit her teeth. "Rankin will be naturally suspicious," he went on. "We must keep our distance from him. But Quentin Matthews is another matter. He is no great intellect by all reports. Quite stupid, in fact. I think we can risk having someone approach him. Not the ladies obviously."

Kate started to protest.

"Given his unsavory reputation," Gerard added before she could speak. "He would think of nothing but, er, rousing their interest. And it can't be Henry or me, since we are known at the Foreign Office. And busy with our work there."

"I'll do it," said Welden.

Mr. Gerard shook his head. "You haven't the temperament."

"What is that supposed to mean?"

"Your…irascible manner argues against a confiding role."

"There is nothing wrong with my *manner*." Welden spoke the final word in a growl, rather negating his point.

"No," replied Gerard with quiet authority. He clearly did not expect opposition. Kate wondered what he would do if they all stood and walked out. Continue happily without them, she supposed. He clearly didn't put much value on their abilities. "Tom is the obvious choice," the man declared. "As an actor, he is the type of person Quentin Matthews might approach on his own." He looked at Tom. "Because you have access to young actresses."

Tom grimaced. "I won't be providing any *access* to the likes of him."

"There will be no need to actually do so. You will just dangle the possibility."

The lad looked reluctant, but he nodded.

"Rankin is a problem," Mr. Gerard went on then. "He had contact with all of you in Leicestershire and will recognize you."

"Not me," said Welden.

"Indeed?"

"I was laid up with a broken leg all that time."

"Ah yes. But you are recovered?"

"Completely."

It was very nearly true, Kate thought. And she didn't blame him for exaggerating.

"You could take the lead with Rankin then," said Gerard.

He was luring the men over to his side, Kate decided. And bringing them under his authority in the process. Didn't they see it?

"He could manage Ned Gardener's lads," Tom said. "They need a bit of overseeing."

Mr. Gerard raised an eyebrow. The apprentice's cronies were explained to him. "A clever idea," he said. He turned to Daphne. "Miss Palliser, could you bring together all the information gathered and produce comprehensive reports? I think you would be good at that."

"I am," Daphne replied. There was a tinge of irony in her tone, but she also looked pleased by the commendation. Difficult to resist, Kate thought. Mr. Gerard was a skilled diplomat. And it was the sort of job Daphne liked best.

"Good. This gives us a beginning then." Mr. Gerard gestured toward the array of bottles on the sideboard. "Shall we toast our endeavor?"

People rose, helped themselves to drinks. Only Daphne seemed to notice that Kate had been given nothing to do in the plan. For her part, Kate was not surprised. It was the way of the world. Females were expected to be obedient and often invisible. And Mr. Gerard had a personal motive in this case. He would prefer her to simply disappear, taking any connection she'd formed with his nephew along with her. He'd begun to separate her from the group by handing out tasks like gifts. That would continue, with dollops of judicious praise. After a while, they probably wouldn't notice if she faded out of the picture. Well, Daphne would. But the others? She thought not.

And through it all, Henry Deeping had been silent. He'd made no suggestions, no protests. There'd been no mention of fascination with her daring *tonight*. He was under his uncle's thumb, as Oliver Welden had said. Perhaps he'd been ordered to stand back. And he had done so! Kate seethed with anger and frustration and disappointment. Mr. Gerard was an expert manipulator, but she wouldn't be pushed from center to periphery. She wouldn't stand for it! He was foolish if he imagined she would.

She nearly told him so. Until she caught sidelong glances that seemed...anticipatory? It appeared that Mr. Gerard expected her to begin an argument before the others. No doubt he was ready to respond. He would try to make her look silly or difficult—the cool, rational male tolerating emotional feminine outbursts. It was such a common scenario that the others would probably be swayed.

Kate clamped her lips. She wouldn't give him the satisfaction. She could be as sly as he was. She would take steps of her own. He had no authority over her. He wasn't *her* uncle. With that thought, Kate realized that she particularly didn't want to see Mr. Deeping fail to support her. His silence was bad enough.

———

Henry stayed on in the inn parlor after the others left. He waited while his uncle wrote in his ubiquitous notebook and then said, "You didn't give Miss Meacham any part in the action." She'd been furious. Henry knew it, though she hadn't said so. He was convinced now that his uncle set out to make her furious. To put her in a bad light or drive her away? To quell his interest in her? It was underhanded, not what he expected from his august relative. And it had failed, on every level. She had not lost her temper. Henry had not brought up the omission before the others so that his uncle could goad her further.

"I didn't see what she could usefully do," his uncle replied. He showed no sign of regretting his behavior.

"But she has been the most useful of us all. She began this whole endeavor."

"She is rash and impulsive, likely to expose us before we are ready."

"I don't think that's fair, Uncle. She has been very careful." She'd been rather amazing, Henry thought.

"Invading receptions uninvited? Making up tales for embassy servants? Loitering in the street? A young lady? I think you are too inclined in her favor."

His expression might have been called avuncular, but Henry thought it a bit patronizing. He had looked forward to deepening his connection with his mother's brother in his new position. It was not going as he'd expected. "Is that why you also gave me nothing to do? Because you believe my judgment is clouded?"

"Now, Henry, I never said anything of the kind. You need to concentrate on your work. It is important, especially at the beginning, to demonstrate diligence and keenness and compliance."

"Not go haring off after rogue agents." Or become

fascinated with daring young ladies. That went without saying.

"Precisely."

"That's what you did?" Henry couldn't quite see his uncle arranging appointments and copying reports day after day.

"I was sent abroad from the first. But those were different times." He looked down at his notebook. "Now what do you think of this lad Tom? Is he trustworthy? His background is unfortunate."

"I don't know him well."

"So you think we should be wary of him?"

"I don't... He seems solid to me." Henry felt uncomfortable being asked to be an informer.

His uncle gazed at him. "A diplomat provides evaluations of all the people he meets, you know. That is part of his job."

The more Henry learned about his new post, the greater his doubts. "My sister and her friends would vouch for Tom. Also the Earl of Macklin."

"Yes. There is that." His uncle rubbed his chin. "I wish I might have a quiet word with the earl. But he is not in town." He shrugged. "Well, I wouldn't have chosen to confide in the lad. But then I might say the same about everyone in this group. Apart from you, of course. An actor, a prickly eccentric, some street urchins, and two...unconventional ladies."

Henry had stiffened at bit more with each characterization. "I'm sorry you are disappointed, Uncle."

If he expected a denial, he didn't get it. His uncle said, "It just shows you should stick to your assigned position, eh?"

Henry could hear Miss Meacham's scornful rejection of

that idea. Welden's too. Miss Palliser would just smile iron-ically as if it was scarcely worth objecting in the circum-stances. His sympathies lay on their side, Henry realized.

His uncle closed his notebook and rose. "We should be on our way."

They should be, Henry thought as he followed the older man out of the pub. But what way was that?

Eleven

KATE EXAMINED HER REFLECTION IN THE MIRROR ON THE door of her wardrobe. In the dim streets of nighttime London she would easily be taken for a fresh-faced young man. A tight cotton band wrapped her chest. She wore old clothing of her grandfather's—stockings and knee breeches, a full-skirted coat. He had been a small wiry man so the garments fit well enough. They were a bit loose, but that was to be preferred in the circumstances. Her hair was tightly braided and wrapped around her head. It would be hidden under a close-fitting cap that came down low on her forehead and was at no risk of falling off. Grandfather's shoes were always the greatest challenge. She had to stuff the toes with wadding to keep them on.

The garments were top quality but quite out of fashion. People would take her for a lowly clerk or shop assistant who had purchased them from secondhand dealers. She put a finger under the top of her neckcloth and eased the pressure a little. She didn't see why men deigned to wear such ridiculous things. It felt like a bandage wrapped around her neck, poised to choke her. She poked at it. The folds were more like creases than any established mode. But that didn't matter.

A pink of the *ton* would sneer at her ensemble, or perhaps laugh himself sick, if he lowered himself so far as to notice her at all. But she wasn't going among the fashionable fribbles. They would be no use to her. Her grandfather's old contacts were her target. Some already knew her as his youthful "assistant." Others she might reach tonight.

Kate shrugged into a warm overcoat. This disguise was simpler in the winter, when everyone was muffled up to the eyes. Her figure was wholly obscured. And people kept their coats on in the places she would go, where heating was meager and thieves common.

She put on the cap and adjusted the angle. Mr. Brinsley Gerard might think she would sit back with meekly folded hands while he shut her out of the search she had initiated. He was mistaken. "Woefully mistaken," Kate murmured to the mirror, pitching her voice low and rough.

She picked up her grandfather's old sword stick, gave her image a cocky salute, and went to listen at the door of her bedchamber. The house was quiet. The servants would be downstairs, sitting together, their tasks mainly done for the day. Daphne was in the study as usual, engrossed in her work. None of them must see her leave. Mrs. Knox would try to stop her, and Daphne would, at the least, delay her, wanting explanations. Kate checked her coat pocket to make certain the latchkey and gloves were there and eased the door open.

The stairwell was dimly lit. Kate started carefully down. She knew every creaking board and concealing shadow in the place. She moved with only a whisper of sound, keeping the stick down at her side so that it didn't rattle against the wall.

On the floor below, the study door was half-open. Daphne generally left it that way to show that she welcomed visitors. Pausing outside the shaft of light streaming from the room, Kate listened. Daphne's quill pen was scratching quickly over a page. She would be looking down, engrossed. One sometimes had to speak to her more than once to get her attention. Kate stepped swiftly and silently past the doorway and onto the stair going down. There was no reaction.

On the ground floor, she could hear voices and movement from below. Mrs. Knox might choose to make the rounds of the house at any moment. Johnny's cackling laugh rang out. The sound seemed to be moving toward the stair. Kate stepped quickly to the front door, unlocked it, and slipped out. On the stoop she paused, listened, then quietly relocked the door. Grandfather had made a point of keeping the mechanism and the hinges well oiled. Retrieving a small lantern she kept hidden in a shrub—but not lighting it as yet—Kate strode off down the street.

It was important to walk differently in this guise, but the clothing itself encouraged it. A person felt quite different in breeches than in trailing skirts. Legs could swing freely. Sturdy shoes pounded the cobbles. Kate's chin came up, her shoulders squared, her expression pugnacious. She felt a surge of elation. No one looking down the street and spotting her would see a vulnerable young lady and think to accost her. She swung the sword stick as if ready to defend herself, which she was. She wished Mr. Gerard could see her now. And did not wish it, of course. The fuss wouldn't be worth it. He'd think even worse of her than he already did, if that was possible.

Kate paused to light the lantern. She held it low to illuminate the cobbles and, more importantly, the spots where they were missing or ended and could trip her up. Then she made her way to one of the pubs her grandfather had frequented when he was in search of information. Dim and smoky, the place suited her disguise. Many of the men who came here didn't care to be recognized by just anyone.

She'd been here before, and she was aware of her persona being accepted as she ordered a mug of ale. If it hadn't been, she'd have been in trouble. But she'd used the signs her grandfather had let fall—as part of an entertaining tale, not instruction. He would not like to see her here, she acknowledged. Yet she also thought he'd be proud of her skills. She hoped so, at any rate.

She sat with her back to a wall, sipped very slowly, listened, and occasionally talked. Direct questions were no way to find out things in a place like this. One dropped a nugget of information like bait, trolling it through the crowd. Other bits were let fall in return, and as the evening unfolded—here and in several other watering holes she would visit—she would weave details together into a story. People like these kept careful track of the territories they inhabited. Their survival depended on it. Someone would have heard about a house rented on Judd Street, and the stranger who stayed there. There would be theories about what sort of no good he was up to, observations or guesses about who else might be involved. Hearing them all, Kate would sift for truth. Tonight, or on some other night, she would discover things.

This sort of fishing was a slow process. Time passed as Kate focused all her faculties in stuffy, noisy rooms. She was alert to every phrase, every quirk of eyebrow and shift of expression, categorizing, analyzing, storing it all away for later. One didn't dare take notes in places like this. She'd begun to develop a headache by the time she'd made her planned round, and she was very glad to finish and head outside into the clear, cold air. She breathed deep to cleanse her lungs.

Kate turned toward home, only to be struck by an errant impulse. That would be rash. Daring indeed. Possibly foolhardy. She paused, considered. One corner of her mouth turned up in a sly smile. She couldn't resist. She pivoted and walked swiftly in another direction.

She knew the street where Henry Deeping's lodgings lay, and the building. In a few minutes, she was gazing up at it. There were lights in several windows. She didn't know which was his. If she had, she might have thrown a pebble and startled him. She lingered a while, toyed with the idea of knocking. Not seriously. It was growing very late. She turned away.

And there he was, striding down the street, heading for the door she stood beside. Unable to resist, her heart pounding, Kate stepped out of the shadow and walked toward him. "Good evening, Mr. Deeping," she growled as they passed each other. She stifled a laugh as she hurried on.

Only to hear rapid footsteps following. Most people, greeted by a stranger, stood puzzled for a moment or two, trying to work out who it was. This made it easy to slip away from them. But Mr. Deeping, Kate now learned, was *not* most people.

"Hello," he called out. "Who is that?" His steps quickened.

She looked for a place to duck out of sight, but this neighborhood was not part of her familiar territory. She didn't know its nooks and crannies and found no bolt-hole or obscure alley. It wouldn't do to run. For one thing, she would be too clumsy in her grandfather's ill-fitting shoes. Mr. Deeping would catch her. She might even fall on her face at his feet. Kate stopped and turned, head down to keep her countenance shadowed.

Henry Deeping came up to her. "Who are you?" he asked. "How do you know me? Why were you lurking at my door?"

Her voice a careful, raspy murmur, Kate said, "Friend of Tom Jesperson's." She was, in a sense. And actors were out late at night. Nothing suspect there. Except her location, of course.

"From the theater?" He looked over her dowdy clothes as if doubting this assertion.

"Where else?"

"Did he send you with a message for me?" The skepticism in his tone was stronger.

Kate started to raise a hand, and her overlarge glove pulled off inside her overcoat pocket. The dismissive wave she'd planned—and could not now hide—was made with a small, delicate white hand. She shoved it back into her pocket, groped for the glove, and fatally, her gaze met his.

Seeing the youth's face in the light of the lantern he held, and discovering a pair of flashing violet eyes, Henry

Deeping was seized by a wild surmise. His mind boggling, he hustled the youth over to a gaslight and bent to examine him more closely. "Good God! Miss…" He broke off before bandying her name in the street. "What the devil are you doing?"

She actually grinned at him. "I've been out gathering information." She turned away from the gaslight so that her face was shaded.

"Gathering…"

"It's much easier this way." She indicated her clothes. "As you may imagine. I can venture into places my grandfather frequented without attracting undue attention."

"Attention!"

"Yes, Mr. Deeping. As a young lady so often does. The number of places they…we are not able to go is legion. Practically everywhere, really."

She was enveloped in a voluminous greatcoat. Nothing of her shape showed. This masquerade wasn't openly improper. Except in its very inception. Certainly all of society would think it scandalous and condemn her. "Is this what Delaroche suspected?"

"Him!" She made a disgusted sound. "No, his ideas were much more vulgar. And insulting."

"If anyone discovered the disguise, you might be…"

"No one does discover it."

"I did."

"Because I indulged in a fit of whimsy and greeted you."

"Whimsy." Henry's surprise had faded, and fascination was rising, as it inevitably did in this young lady's presence.

"Will you stop repeating my words? I've been doing this for ages."

"Your grandfather allowed it?" When she didn't reply, he said, "You didn't do it when he was alive. So not really ages then."

"There was no need. He conducted the inquiries himself."

"And so you divert my question rather than answering it. You make a habit of that."

"If a person *will* stick his nose in when he has no right, I don't owe him any answers."

He had no rights over her, Henry acknowledged. Only the fascination that was threatening to take over his life and burning, contradictory desires—to shield and protect her, and to sweep her into his arms and carry her up to his chamber. But that would be taking advantage. A point occurred to him. "Why did you come here then?"

"What?"

"I didn't stick my nose in. You were waiting outside my lodgings. Why?"

She looked down so that the brim of her cap hid her face.

"To taunt me," Henry concluded. Oddly, this didn't offend him. In fact, he was buoyed up by the idea. She'd been thinking of him. She'd taken some trouble to unsettle him. Far more than she'd needed to. He was thoroughly off-balance already.

"It was only a joke," said the irrepressible Miss Meacham.

It wasn't. She'd wanted to show him that she would not be excluded from their quest, that she would take steps—outrageous steps—to be sure she was not. Henry didn't blame her for the impulse. Her methods though…

She wrapped her arms around her chest. "May I come upstairs to get warm?"

"To my rooms?"

"I suppose you have a fire."

Certainly there would be a fire. His landlady would have seen to it. The street was empty and icy cold. He noticed that Miss Meacham was shivering. Actually? Or was it a pretense? Of course he shouldn't under any circumstances... "All right," Henry said.

He turned and led her to the door, the stair, and up to his comfortable parlor, where a cozy fire indeed burned. Henry stepped quickly across to shut the bedroom door. When he turned back, his scandalous guest had tossed her greatcoat and cap over a chair. She stood near the hearth, her hands held out to the flames.

Henry took off his own gloves and overcoat and hat as he noted that she'd braided her honey-colored hair tight around her head. Her outmoded garments were loose, though not so much that her form was hidden by her breeches. His eyes were irresistibly drawn. He looked away, bent to throw on an additional log.

"It's a pleasant room," she said, as if her presence here was commonplace.

"I find it so. Would you like, er, a glass of wine?" It was what he would offer a male friend. A female...even his sister had never visited him here.

"No, thank you."

Inspiration struck Henry. "Hot chocolate?"

She blinked. "Can you...? I don't wish to see anyone."

"No need. I have a spirit lamp. I can make it here."

"You make yourself hot chocolate?"

"Occasionally. Or rack punch. But I am fond of hot chocolate."

"So am I."

Their eyes met. Henry lost himself in those violet depths and grew even more conscious of the bed behind the closed door. Had a woman ever been so beguiling? Or so bewildering?

He tore his eyes away and busied himself with lighting the spirit lamp, getting the tins of sugar and cocoa from a shelf, pouring out water from a carafe into a small saucepan he kept. He blended and stirred, glad to have something to do with his hands. "The cups are there," he said after a while, pointing.

She fetched them. He poured carefully. "Do sit down," he said then.

They settled in the armchairs that flanked the fire. She cradled her cup in both hands, warming them. They sipped. He should speak, Henry thought, and then was rendered speechless when she crossed her stocking-clad legs. "It's good," she said.

Spectacular would be a better description, Henry thought. And realized she meant the drink. "Ah. Uh." He cleared his throat. "So was your…mission tonight successful?"

"I did find useful information," she replied with a touch of defiance.

"What?"

"I shan't tell you. You would just hand it to your uncle, and he would…appropriate it. You must have seen that he cares nothing for my efforts. Despises them, in fact. It was obvious." She frowned as if daring him to deny this.

He could not. "I wouldn't tell," Henry began. And stopped. If it was something vital to their goal, wasn't he obliged to do so?

"You would," she said. "And one can't blame you, I suppose. You are employed by the Foreign Office and thus your uncle, indirectly. You have pledged yourself to them." Despite what she said, she looked disappointed.

"I wouldn't say *pledged.*"

"You did not take the oath?"

He hadn't raised a hand and sworn, but his superiors had emphasized that he was now in service to king and country and expected to put them first.

Miss Meacham nodded at the look on his face. "Well, *I* did not." She drank her hot chocolate, stared at the fire.

"What do you intend to do with what you've found?" Henry asked.

"I shan't tell you that either."

"Because you don't know?"

"You are an annoying man."

"Then we are even."

A smile touched her lips. "I am an annoying man as well, you mean?"

"*You* are no kind of man at all."

She smiled at him over her cup, her eyes sparkling with mischief, and Henry's heart seemed to skip a beat. "I shall analyze and think what to do," she said. "But I *won't* be made to disappear."

"What do you mean?"

"Exactly what I said. Your uncle would be happiest if I simply dropped out of the investigation and you never saw me again."

Henry started to protest. But thinking over recent events, he realized she was right. His uncle preferred things to happen without any fuss, as if they had been natural events instead of interference. But in this case, he was clearly meddling. That was why he wanted Miss Meacham furious and Henry set apart at his desk copying reports. "I shall see you as long as you wish me to," he declared with more force than strictly necessary. "No one but you can prevent it."

Miss Meacham's cup rattled against its saucer. She looked down as if startled by the sound. The air in the room seemed to thin, as Henry tried to catch his breath. She was fearless and lovely and unique in his experience. She sat here with him in his rooms as if she belonged. She wore her unconventional costume with defiant ease. She was an amazement.

"I am warm now." She flushed as if the words were suggestive.

"It's hot," replied Henry, and reddened as well. The fire in the grate was much as usual. The blaze in his veins came from another source. It seared in the gaze that locked their eyes. As time stretched out in aching pulses, it threatened to consume him.

Miss Meacham made a small soft sound. She turned her head like a shying thoroughbred. For a moment, she was very still. Then she set aside the dregs of her hot chocolate and stood. "I should go."

She should, Henry acknowledged, before his control broke and he closed the distance between them with a wild embrace. She hadn't come here for that. She trusted him not to insult her.

She went to pick up her greatcoat and put it on. Henry did the same. "I'll go with you. It's late."

"That's not necessary."

"Please allow me to do so."

She paused in the act of pulling on her cloth cap and considered him. Henry held *his* hat in his hand, a suppliant. "All right," she finally said. She relit her small lantern at one of the candles and turned toward the door. Henry followed.

Outside, the February night was even colder. Their breath puffed out in steaming clouds. The streets were empty, and Henry knew they wouldn't find a cab. People were asleep. The half-frozen drivers would have headed home by now. They walked rapidly, harmoniously in step along the pavement.

"It's so different, being out in the darkness," she said after a while. "The daylight world is distant as a dream. We are shrouded in shadows. We must rely on our ears and our intuition to sense any threat, be always aware of which way to run."

Henry looked around. The darkness felt uninhabited. "I hadn't thought of it that way."

"You have never had to decide whether you dare go out at night," she replied. "A man will not be taken for a light-skirt and mauled. Look at the very word. There are no lightbreeches."

"Wouldn't it be 'heavybreeches'?" Henry said. "Falling down?" Even as he choked on a mortified laugh, heat suffused his skin. His mind filled with a whirl of skirts flying up and breeches sliding down in lascivious farce.

His intrepid companion made a gurgling sound. "What a very improper conversation."

"I beg your…"

"So much more…stimulating than society chitchat. Don't you think?"

He nodded, realized she couldn't see it with only the splash of lantern light at their feet, and said, "Yes."

They passed the silent bulk of Montagu House where the relics of the ages slumbered in the museum, and turned the corners that led to her house. When they stopped before it, she set down the lantern and looked up at him. "So you have escorted me home," she said quietly. "And now you are left to walk back alone. How is that different from me doing the same?"

"It…it just is," said Henry.

"In fact, your case is worse, because you are better dressed than I am. A much more tempting target for footpads."

"I can defend myself."

"As I cannot?"

There was a whisper of sound, and she held up a blade before his eyes. Her cane was a sword stick, Henry realized. Still, it was not so easy to unsheathe those in the face of attackers. She might easily fumble. Particularly with a lantern in her other hand. He didn't think she'd ever tried to use the weapon.

"Also, I know every alley and doorway in this part of London," she added. "I can slip away before anyone gets near me."

She was too cocky. Henry feared for her. "Can you?"

They stood nose to nose. The steam of their breath mingled in the meager light of the little lantern.

"I would not let anyone...else get so close to me," she said. And then she rose on tiptoe and kissed him.

Henry's lips parted in astonishment. Hers were cold, and then hot as desire flamed between them. She threw an arm around his neck. As his arms tightened around her, Henry thought overcoats the most annoying garments on earth. The bulky cloth kept her far from his hands. He heard the sword stick drop with a muted thump, and then he was pulled into a throbbing sea of arousal and longing. She kissed as she lived, with wholehearted daring. She held nothing back, and in an instant he was lost.

The embrace seemed endless—dizzying, overwhelming —and far too short. Henry reached for her when she pulled away, but let his arms drop when she took a step back. "I did not take advantage," he gasped.

"No, I did." She laughed shakily, took another step away. "There's a freedom in breeches, isn't there? I hadn't realized. You imagine you can do whatever you like." She looked down. "It's silly that a pair of trousers should feel like liberation. But there it is."

"What?" Henry's mind was still drowning in desire. It was hard to put two thoughts together.

Bending, she picked up the sword stick, sheathed it, and slapped the hilt into his hand. "You can borrow this."

His gloved fingers closed around it automatically. "Miss Meacham. Kate."

She moved away from him. She must have had the latch-key ready, because she unlocked the house door and slipped silently inside before Henry could form a coherent sentence. He heard the quiet snick of the lock restored, and then he was alone in the empty street.

She'd left him the lantern too. Henry stood in its dim light, in the depths of the icy night, and wondered if a man could go mad from desire.

His breath streamed out, clouds of heat. His heart still pounded. Other parts of him signaled their frustration. But silence and solitude and biting damp eventually cooled his ardor. He gripped the sword stick, picked up the lantern, and departed, almost hoping a footpad would accost him. He felt like punching something.

Inside the house, Kate leaned on the front door and struggled with her reeling senses. Her body tingled and ached for more of Henry Deeping's touch. Wild laughter still bubbled in her throat. She wanted to throw propriety to the four winds and dance with wild abandon. She didn't feel a single scrap of regret.

The tap of a footstep and light flooding down the stair-well interrupted her. "Kate?" Daphne Palliser called softly. "Is that you? Are you there?"

"Yes." Kate stepped away from the door and found she wasn't too dizzy to walk. She put a hand to the railing none-theless as she went upstairs. Daphne held up a branch of candles to light her way. "You're still awake," said Kate.

"I went to your room some hours ago to ask a question and found you gone," Daphne replied.

"Did you think I had an assignation?" The laughter was still there in her voice. She didn't care.

"Not until I looked out the window just now."

"Oh." That was…inconvenient.

With a gesture Daphne indicated that they should go into the study. Kate led the way. Coming into the warmth of the bright fire, she took off her gloves, scarf, overcoat, and cap.

Daphne looked her up and down. "Ingenious," she said, setting the candles aside. She closed the study door.

Kate appreciated her matter-of-fact manner. Even Daphne might have been scandalized. "Male dress opens up the world," she said.

"If one can carry it off."

"I can."

"In order to go out with Mr. Deeping?" Daphne sounded more puzzled than shocked. Or perhaps she was a bit shocked.

Kate threw herself into a seat. One could do that in breeches, collapse in a tumble of limbs with no thought for decorum, hook a knee over the chair arm. "No, I met him by…chance." No need to mention going by his lodgings. "I went out dressed like this to speak with informants known to my grandfather."

"I see."

"They wouldn't talk to Miss Meacham. Even if I could meet them as myself. They know me as a lad who worked for Grandfather."

Daphne nodded. She still looked dubious.

"I discovered some things."

"What?"

Kate raised her chin. "I won't tell you unless you promise not to share them with Mr. Gerard."

"But he is…"

"In charge? The voice of authority from on high?"

"No." Daphne shifted uncomfortably from foot to foot. "I know he pushed his way into our group. But he does have resources that we do not. Look how he found the agent's name."

"And that gives him the right to exclude me? You *did* notice that he had no use for me as he was handing out tasks?"

"Yes," her friend admitted. "That was not right."

"That's how it's done. As you know very well. The woman is left in ignorance, belittled or even bullied, and finally shut out completely. *You* have been relegated to writing reports."

Daphne shrugged ruefully. "It's true. I do enjoy doing that, however."

"I'm happy for you. But I won't be shoved off into irrelevance. If you wish to side with Mr. Gerard…" Kate broke off, finding that the idea hurt much more than she'd expected.

"I don't." Daphne went to sit down at the desk. "Though I do wish there weren't any sides in this matter. In Leicestershire…"

"They thought to leave us out of the capture, and we took matters into our own hands."

"That's true." Daphne smiled reminiscently.

"So you promise?" Kate wanted to discuss what she'd discovered with an ally. It was too bad Henry Deeping couldn't be that person. She set aside the flash of heat that came with complicated thoughts of him.

"I do. Shall I raise my hand and swear?"

"I'll take your word." Kate sat straighter. "Richard Rankin's arrival in the Judd Street house was noted. He doesn't really fit in the neighborhood. He used another name to take rooms there. Liam Fallow. Everyone assumes it's false."

Daphne laughed. "I should think so!" When Kate looked inquiring, she added, "Liam Fallow? Lying fallow. Like a field between crops."

"I didn't think of that."

"Because you're not an impudent jackanapes."

"I nearly am." Kate gestured at her garb.

"True," replied Daphne with a smile.

"Whatever the fellow's, fallow's, name, he seems to have plenty of money. He is being grossly overcharged for his refuge and never bothers to bargain."

"Money from Carlton House?"

"That seems a likely source, given what we have seen. And our new king has always spent freely."

"For what, in this case?"

"That was not clear. Rankin has dropped hints in some low alehouses that he's looking for men who aren't 'overparticular.'"

"Ready to bash heads on command, in other words?"

"So I imagine. And if he can pay…"

Daphne nodded. "He will find them. But who is he going after? And why?"

"Indeed. I let on that I would like to know more, as if I might be interested in such employment."

"They accepted *you* as a potential head basher?"

"No. As a youth who was getting so far above himself he couldn't see his own feet. I provided a good deal of amusement. One grizzled ruffian nearly fell out of his chair laughing. But better that than to be too inquisitive. Questions draw attention, make people suspicious."

"And word might get back to this Rankin. Or Quentin Matthews."

"Right."

"That would annoy Mr. Gerard."

Kate made a rude noise.

"Nearly as much as you kissing Mr. Deeping in the shrubbery," Daphne added.

"We weren't in the shrubbery," Kate replied automatically.

"That is true. You were right out in full view. With a lantern at your feet for illumination. It was almost like a play."

Kate felt both embarrassed and defiant. "I wanted to kiss him, so I did."

"I see."

"Men do as much all the time."

"So I have heard." Daphne gazed at her. "Did you like it?" she asked, her tone almost wistful.

"Exceedingly." Kate flushed at the memory.

"Well, we did say you needed to know exactly what you wanted, and then set about getting it. But what next?"

"Perhaps I'll do it again," Kate declared.

"And then?"

"Whenever I like," she answered, though she knew that was not reasonable.

"And then?"

"Will you stop?"

Daphne bowed her head. "But you must consider…"

"Must, must, must. Hateful word." Kate sprang up and gathered her discarded outer garments. "If Mrs. Knox hears us and comes up, she'll give me a thundering scold. I'm going to bed."

"Sleep well."

A low laugh escaped Kate. She didn't think peaceful rest was anywhere in her future. And walking up the stairs, she realized she didn't want it. She wanted one of her sensuous dreams. She was ready to lose herself in another realm where anything was possible and desires were always fulfilled.

Partly, she got her wish. But the dream that came when she finally slept was different from those previous ones. She found herself outdoors, hovering before a towering cliff of seamed, cracked stone, with wilderness spreading out all around her. Wind bent small water-starved trees. The orange light of the sinking sun threw long shadows. The place looked harsh and unforgiving.

Kate saw that two people were climbing down the nearly vertical precipice. As soon as she noticed, she was closer to them. A man and a woman wearing male clothes, as she had been tonight, were struggling from tiny ledge to precarious handhold, making the descent. Clearly, they were not skilled mountaineers. Strain and anxiety showed in their faces. Which Kate abruptly recognized. It was her parents.

Even as she realized this, her father's foot slipped off a crumbling lip of rock. Kate cried out in fear. She was surprised that they didn't. He teetered, caught himself with his fingers jammed into crevices, and hung by them until he found a new foothold. For a few moments they leaned against the rock, panting. Then they looked up, scanning the top of the cliff, before resuming the descent.

They were running from something, Kate understood. They had to reach level ground so that they could flee. But they couldn't climb too fast or they would fall. And night was coming. They wouldn't be able to continue in the dark.

Her mother freed a hand long enough to make an emphatic gesture. Then she stepped sideways instead of down, moving across the cliff toward a pool of shadow.

Not a cave, Kate noted. But there was an indentation in the cliff with a bulge of rock overhanging it. It created a ledge perhaps three feet wide and almost as high in the middle. The sides slanted away to nothing.

Her mother made it to one edge. She had to lean outward a bit to ease along the lip. Kate saw her hands trembling. The moment when she had to let go and bend to crawl into the space made Kate's heart pound. She suspected her mother felt the same because when she was at last safe she collapsed into a boneless pile on the rock.

Her father followed the same route in the failing light. When he made it to the refuge, Kate's mother reached for him and pulled him in. They curled around each other and lay still.

There were shouts in the distance. Kate realized she'd

been hearing them for a while, but she'd been too intent on her parents' progress to pay attention. Now, they grew louder. A troop of fierce-looking men appeared at the top of the cliff. They peered over, shook rifles and sabers at the darkening sky, and shouted to each other in an unknown tongue. Kate didn't need to translate to know what they were hunting. Her parents had only just escaped.

And then it was Kate lying on the rock ledge with Henry Deeping's arms around her. They pressed against each other, trembling with fatigue and relief and…mutual excitement. She saw it in his dark eyes. They danced with the knowledge that they'd pulled off a coup, as daring as Prometheus stealing fire. He kissed her tenderly, passionately, and she responded with all her heart.

Kate woke up.

She was embracing one of her pillows, she found. And her pulse raced. The scene had been so vivid. It was not one from the images in the wooden box. This was something different.

She released the pillow and sat up, breathing in the air of her dark chilly bedchamber. She lit the candle sitting on the side table.

There was a story she'd heard—not from her grandfather but someone else. Jerome? Perhaps. When they were much younger and he was not so pompous. Whoever had told her that her parents had strayed into wild country on one of their trips abroad. A wrong turning or a misdirection. And they'd stumbled on the lair of a bandit chieftain who had been terrorizing the farmers and travelers in that stretch of country.

It had been a perilous accident that nearly got them killed. But they had managed to bring back the news to the area's authorities, who had been after these bandits for years. With this new information, they were able to root out the killers.

It had been Jerome who told her, Kate remembered. He'd claimed he overheard his parents talking about it. She hadn't really believed him. It was the sort of tale they liked to read in adventure books and memoirs. She'd assumed he invented it.

Perhaps not?

She threw back the covers and went over to her dressing table to fetch two miniatures that always sat there, hinged together like an oversized locket. Her grandfather had commissioned the portraits a few years after her parents' marriage. She'd sometimes wondered if he'd had a premonition they would die young.

Kate returned to the warmth of her bed and gazed at their faces in the dim candlelight. She knew them from these paintings more than memory. They'd been away so much. She gazed at her mother's half smile, the twinkle in her father's eyes. It was a great sorrow not to know them better. But Kate decided she would see this dream as an omen that she was on the right track.

Twelve

WHAT WAS HE TO DO ABOUT KATE MEACHAM? HENRY wondered as he hurried along the street to a meeting with his uncle. He hadn't had a moment to call on her since that extraordinary night in the icy darkness two days ago. He was being kept very busy at the Foreign Office, asked to stay into the evenings and take on extra tasks. He was fairly sure his uncle was behind this onslaught. But it might be a test of the new man, inflicted on everyone, to measure one's dedication. Whatever it was, work was filling his days. So, though he thought of Miss Meacham constantly, he hadn't seen her. He'd thought of writing a note, but what could he say on paper? It was vastly frustrating.

But tonight that would be remedied. He'd been summoned to the Golden Lion, where they'd gathered before. The place seemed to be a favorite haunt of Uncle Brinsley's. When the session was over, he would get Kate to himself, one way or another. And ask her...ask her where the deuce she thought they were headed.

But when Henry entered the private parlor upstairs, he found only his uncle and Tom Jesperson present. "Where are the others?"

"What others?" asked his uncle.

"The rest of our group."

Uncle Brinsley looked blank.

"I was wondering," said Tom.

"We are merely taking a report," said Uncle Brinsley. "We don't require anyone else."

Henry realized that his uncle didn't think of the people who'd begun this investigation as a unit. There was the project, his now, and individuals he might find useful in pursuing it. He didn't see that a separate meeting like this would divide them because he didn't see them as together. Or perhaps it was more convoluted than that? *Did* he want them dispersed? Miss Palliser had been asked to write reports, he remembered. How could she do so if she wasn't here? Henry and Tom could pass along news, but it wasn't the same. Henry looked at his uncle, who had his eyes on Tom. "So," the older man said, "report."

Tom looked at Henry, shrugged, and began. "I watched this Quentin Matthews and found he liked a certain tavern, the Sheaves. So I got two of my friends—opera dancers—to help out, and we 'happened on' him there when he was well along in drink." Tom frowned. "He's the sort of fellow who paws at a lady when she don't want him to."

Most of the new king's cronies were, Henry had heard.

"We gave him more brandy and led him on to talk about himself," Tom continued. "Which he seems very fond of doing. He likes to puff off his consequence. How at home he is at Carlton House and all. Good as a brother of the new king, according to him."

"He'll be caught out at that," muttered Henry's uncle.

Tom paused to see if there was more, then went on. "And from what he said, it seems the king spends a deal of his time these days raging about the queen."

"She died two years ago," said Henry.

"Not the old queen. His wife, Queen Caroline. Only our new King George says she ain't going to be crowned. He won't have it. He purely hates her. Says she's a disgrace, a slut, and a terrible harpy, according to Matthews. She's to be thrown out, divorced, kept from England for all eternity." Tom looked as if he relished the phrase. "Matthews says he talks of little else."

"To him at any rate," said Henry's uncle.

"Right. And that's because Matthews knows all about females, he says. A regular expert." Tom shook his head. "My dancer friends said he's the greatest nodcock they've ever come across."

Henry choked back a laugh.

"Anyhow, the king wants to be rid of his wife, divorce her and all. And Matthews thinks he's just the man for the job. He's already been spreading rumors about the lady, whispering to members of Parliament about her scandalous life."

"Our new king is hardly one to talk of scandals," Henry said. The man had created a string of them since his youth.

"His life has been rife with them," murmured Henry's uncle.

Tom nodded. "That's the problem, seemingly. A divorce case would kick up all those old stories, and the government doesn't want that. Not right at the start of a new reign."

"Or ever," said Henry's uncle.

"Wouldn't go over well, I expect," Tom agreed. "But they ain't giving up. Matthews was crowing that they got the pope to refuse Queen Caroline an audience, insisting she was just Duchess of Brunswick, not a queen."

"Petty spite," said Henry.

"Or policy," replied his uncle. "It strengthens her position if foreign leaders recognize her."

Tom nodded as if this answered a question for him. "The king's crazed over the idea that she'll come back to England to claim her rightful place. Claims she's planning on it as revenge. Makes him foam with rage, Matthews said."

"That must be a pretty sight," Henry's uncle remarked.

"Matthews says it ain't," Tom replied dryly. "But he's going to save the day."

"How?" asked Henry.

"Well, he wasn't very clear about that. He muttered about plans he has and how she'd be sorry. That sort of thing. We couldn't coax any details out of him."

"Perhaps he hasn't any," Henry suggested. "Just boasts."

"That is what we must discover." Uncle Brinsley tapped his chin with one finger. "You must keep after him, Tom. Become his friend. Find out more."

Tom grimaced. "He's not the sort of company I care to keep."

Henry's uncle made a dismissive gesture. "This is not a social engagement. You agreed to help." His tone was schoolmaster stern.

Henry saw Tom's lips tighten. The lad's eyes held a frosty look he'd never seen there before. It seemed Tom was not *always* easygoing. But he nodded and said, "So I will."

"Perhaps ask him where he finds helpers for his plans," the older man went on. "You could suggest that you are willing to help spread rumors about the queen. For a fee. He would expect that."

"I don't want his money."

"You could hand it along to a charity." Henry's uncle gathered up his notebook and rose to leave. As he was putting on his greatcoat, he noticed that Henry hadn't moved. "Are you coming?" he asked him.

"I'll stay a bit longer, Uncle. I haven't seen my friend Tom for a while." Henry endured several moments of scrutiny, but Uncle Brinsley said nothing more. He merely put on his scarf, hat, and gloves, and departed.

Silence fell over the room. Henry rose and poured himself a small brandy at the sideboard. "Would you like something?" he asked Tom.

"No, thanks."

Henry returned to his chair, sipped.

"Mr. Gerard likes things his own way," commented Tom then.

"I think he has become accustomed to it, as he rose in his profession." Henry hadn't known this about his mother's brother before now. He'd only encountered a genial relative at family gatherings.

"The others are going to wonder why I've told him and not them."

Miss Meacham in particular, Henry thought. Or no, she wouldn't wonder. She'd declare her predictions fulfilled. And it seemed she was probably right.

"I expect they'd be annoyed," Tom added, as if reading his mind. "Only I'm going to give them the same report as soon as may be." He raised his eyebrows.

Henry nodded to show he had no objection.

"I reckon you're stuck between."

With the irate Scylla of Miss Meacham on one side and the whirlpool Charybdis of his uncle on the other, Henry thought with bitter amusement. She might pluck him right out of his current life, like one of Odysseus's sailors taken from the deck. Or the spinning waters might pull his nascent career down to oblivion. And he was exaggerating. It wasn't as bad as all that. "Of course you will tell them," he answered. "You made no promise not to."

"Mr. Gerard didn't ask me," Tom said. "I was a little surprised at that."

"He wasn't thinking of the others at all," Henry replied. "His mind is focused on the problem."

"And not on a bunch of amateur investigators with no influence. Unless we should happen to be useful to him, that is."

Henry acknowledged it with a nod. "Would you have promised?"

Tom shook his head, looking older than his years. "No. We started out together. I say we keep on that way."

"So do I."

"That's good then."

"I certainly hope so."

As Kate walked down the stairs from her bedchamber the following evening, she heard voices in the study. Their group was due to gather there tonight. Someone must have arrived early. Thinking of Henry Deeping, Kate felt simultaneous impulses to rush in and hang back. She had to hold on to the banister as her feet actually tangled with opposite commands and she nearly stumbled.

Mr. Deeping had requested this meeting, stating that his uncle would not be attending, or even told of it. Kate felt this was a good sign. At the least she could enjoy the fact that *he* was being excluded this time.

She stood still and listened. She couldn't tell who was speaking. Slowly she continued down.

The study door was slightly ajar, as if someone had meant to shut it and not pushed quite hard enough. "I do not see why we could not try kissing," said Daphne's voice from inside. "Purely in the spirit of experimentation."

Kate stopped. Her hand, which had been raised to open the door, dropped to her side of its own accord.

"I have had enough trouble in my life because of that sort of thing," replied Oliver Welden.

"But that trouble arose out of a mistaken impression."

"It *arose* because a careless young lady thought only of herself."

"And perhaps you were a trifle heedless."

"Yes," said Welden grudgingly. "More than a trifle. I was a young idiot."

Kate knew she ought to slip away, but she couldn't make herself go. She was a reprehensible person, she decided. And stayed.

"*I* am not careless," said Daphne.

"No."

"And to avoid any misunderstanding, we are engaging in a full and frank discussion of the issue."

"Which rather takes the thrill out of it," muttered Welden.

Kate bit her lip on a smile.

"I do not think only of myself," Daphne added.

"You do not," her companion replied in a much softer tone.

The was a silence, followed by the sound of footsteps. Kate eased back, but they didn't reach the door.

"There," said Daphne after a little while. She sounded breathless.

"Miss Palliser." Welden was practically gasping.

"Didn't we agree?"

"Daphne!"

"Yes, Oliver?"

Kate decided that the experiment had been made. It was a temptation to peek in and see their faces. But she wasn't *that* reprehensible.

"You should not have done that," Welden said.

"You found it unpleasant?"

"No."

"Nor did I. *Quite* the contrary."

There was another, longer silence. Kate imagined an embrace that she would *not* observe. Indeed, it was time for her to retreat. Yet she stayed where she was, thinking—just a bit longer.

"Oh my," said Daphne.

"I am not an experiment," said Welden in an uneven voice. "Not some disposable person you can use to further your own ends."

"As if I would ever do such a thing! I did not mean the word that way."

"What did you mean?" he demanded. "If you go about kissing…"

"I've never kissed a man before in my life," interrupted Daphne.

"Indeed? You're rather good at it."

"Really?" She sounded inordinately pleased. "You are… masterful. You've quite disordered my senses."

Welden made a low sound. "But…to what end?"

That was the thorny question, Kate noted, thinking of Henry Deeping. Again.

"Where kisses lead?" asked Daphne. "I would like to experience that as well."

Kate backed up. This was getting too intrusive. A board creaked under her foot, and she went still.

"You cannot say such things," Welden answered in a strained tone.

"We are not youngsters. Can't we do as we like?"

"No! If life has taught me anything, it is that."

"But, Oliver…"

"I have next to nothing to offer you, Daphne. In fact 'next to' is an exaggeration."

"I don't agree," said Daphne.

"Well, you will be the only person to hold that opinion," he replied harshly. "And I will not subject you to the…flood of opprobrium that would break over your head at any alliance with me."

The brief silence that followed did not have the same quality as the earlier ones. It felt heavy to Kate.

"Do you wish to end our patrols together?" asked Daphne. "Have I ruined everything?"

"No! I don't want that. But…you must see there can be nothing more."

At the pain in his voice, Kate backed silently away. She slipped upstairs and waited. When she heard the knocker sound at the front door, she tramped noisily down and entered the study. Daphne sat behind the desk with folded hands. Welden was very straight in a chair before it. They looked emotionless, only a little flushed. "Good evening, Mr. Welden," Kate said.

"Evening," he muttered.

Sally ushered in Henry Deeping and Tom. They sat. Kate found she was staring at the lips she'd kissed the last time they met. Their owner was gazing at her, his dark eyes questioning. She tore herself away and offered refreshment, which was declined. The maid left them.

Mr. Deeping leaned forward. "Tom and I met with my uncle last night," he said.

"What?" said Welden. "Without us?"

"He don't see any of *us*," said Tom. "There's just him and what he wants to know."

"That's…"

"Not acceptable," interrupted Mr. Deeping. "Thus, we are here tonight, so that Tom can repeat what he's learned."

"You will oppose your uncle?" asked Kate.

"I don't wish to do that," he admitted. "But I believe we should pool all our information."

"And then you'll give it to him," said Welden.

"If a point comes when only his authority and connections will solve the problem we face, then I will. Up to that, I won't."

"You've thought about this," said Daphne.

Mr. Deeping nodded.

"It seems fair," she added.

Kate had to agree, though she refused to say it aloud. Truly she couldn't let her personal resentments stand in the way of a crime.

"But we'll stick together no matter what," said Tom.

"Some of us will," muttered Welden.

Tom told the group about his talk with Quentin Matthews. The man sounded dreadful. Kate repeated what she'd learned. Daphne kept notes on the discussion.

"Liam Fallow," said Tom. "Amusing himself."

Daphne nodded.

"I've since heard that he's bought pistols," Kate finished. "And is interested in more."

"But how did you discover these things?" asked Welden. He looked envious.

"I contacted people my grandfather knew." Kate intercepted sidelong looks from Daphne and Mr. Deeping. She evaded them. She would tell all she'd heard, but she wasn't going to explain how she'd reached those sources.

Daphne gestured at Welden. "We and Ned Gardener's

friends have seen several thuggish men go into the house on Judd Street."

"Ugly customers," agreed Welden. "They didn't stay long."

"Long enough to be hired for whatever mischief he's planning?" asked Kate.

"Very likely. There was another man too, a different sort. Roughly dressed, but he had an air of authority. We set the boys following him to see where he goes, maybe hear his name."

"They're quite good at it," said Daphne. "There are enough of them so that they can trade off, not draw attention to any one lad. And people tend not to notice children."

"Unless they try to pick their pockets," said Welden.

"They're not doing that."

"Anymore."

Daphne acknowledged this with a shrug. The group turned to Mr. Deeping. "I have nothing to add," he said. "I'm being kept too busy to look into this matter. Purposely, I think."

Kate thought he looked tired. "Your uncle hasn't said anything?"

"Only that it would be best if I keep my mind on my job."

Curious, Kate turned to Welden. "Has he asked what you've discovered?"

"No."

She considered this fact. "He must think Quentin Matthews is the key to this mystery."

"The royal connection," said Daphne.

"Because what could a commoner matter?" asked Welden bitterly.

Mr. Deeping frowned as if he disagreed, but he said nothing.

"I suspect it is more that he believes the…content of this matter lies with Matthews," said Kate. "The reason for it. And we did see Matthews meet with this Richard Rankin, or whatever his real name might be, so the connection is established." She let her thoughts run on. "Rankin is for hire. I suspect he has no personal interests except money. And Matthews has access to funds." An idea occurred to her. "I wouldn't be surprised if Mr. Gerard had watchers of his own around Judd Street."

"What?" said Welden.

"He could order that done," said Kate, still following her train of thought. "It is more difficult to approach Quentin Matthews without rousing suspicions. So he wished to hear from Tom."

"Indeed," said Mr. Deeping. He looked impressed.

Welden looked intensely irritated. "You are imagining he posted others to duplicate our efforts? As if we were incompetent or untrustworthy? The idea is profoundly insulting."

"We would have noticed other watchers," declared Daphne.

"Even if they were stationed inside nearby houses?" That was something to inquire about, Kate noted. "He could probably arrange that."

Welden scowled.

"My uncle is accustomed to working within certain

guidelines," said Mr. Deeping. "And with the employees of a large organization. I suppose it is natural that he would turn to them."

"Somebody in that 'organization' let Rankin loose," replied Welden.

"My uncle must have allies he trusts." Mr. Deeping sounded uneasy.

Silence descended on the room. There was no controlling Mr. Gerard.

"Kate has offered an astute analysis," said Daphne then.

"My grandfather taught me."

"He was a canny one, I reckon," said Tom.

Kate nodded. "I think we go on as we have been. Unless anyone has another idea?"

No one did.

"I will prepare a summary of what has been said tonight," said Daphne. "Adding it to the information we already had. And see that everyone has a copy."

With murmurs of appreciation, the meeting began to break up. Tom and Welden went out together. Henry lingered behind as Miss Meacham showed them out. When she shut the front door behind them, he took her hands and pulled her into the front parlor.

They faced each other before the dying coals of a fire. The room was chilly.

"Yes, Mr. Deeping?"

The place was too dim. Henry took a candle from its holder, lit it at the fire, and ignited several others before replacing it. Now he could see her face properly. She looked…amused?

"I don't know what to say to you," Henry admitted. "But I know I must say something."

She shrugged as if disappointed by this remark. "I don't require it."

"We can't simply ignore what is happening between us."

"We could. People do such things."

"Ignore the fact that every time we meet now, we end up in each other's arms? I don't think people do that, actually." Henry examined her expression. "Do you wish to?"

Miss Meacham bent and added a log to the fire. It crackled as flames enveloped the dry wood. "All right, I won't be cowardly," she said. "I like kissing you. But I do not expect you to do anything about that. You have no obligation. Please feel none."

Easier said than done, Henry thought. He had been raised a gentleman. But obligation wasn't all he felt. In fact, it was a small part in a welter of much stronger emotions. "You are like no one else I know. I want to…grow closer."

"Your uncle has made it clear that a connection to me is risking your career."

"And I have told you that I take risks," Henry replied.

Miss Meacham shook her head. "I don't care to be responsible for damaging your prospects."

"That is not your decision."

"It is, in a way. I choose whether to see you."

"Yes."

"Perhaps I won't. Perhaps it is best if we keep our distance."

Yet even as she spoke the word, she was moving closer,

as if it had been a taunt or—he dared to hope—she couldn't resist. She put a hand on his arm, and they drew together like iron to lodestone. Irresistibly, inevitably.

This time there was no overcoat in the way of the kiss. When she pressed up against him, he let his hands roam over the gentle curves of her body. They were learning each other's lips, Henry thought. The taste of her was both familiar and new, sweet and intoxicating. She twined her arms around his neck. He pulled her closer still as they fell over the edge of passion. The wild, tender exploration drove him frantic with desire. He was pounding dizzily with it when she pushed at his chest and stepped away. "Our...meeting is over, I think." She appeared to be panting.

Henry grabbed for the scraps of his spinning senses. "You can't keep doing this. Kiss me that way and then dismiss me. I'll go mad."

"I think you kissed me that time."

"Mad," Henry repeated, with emphasis.

"I don't think we will, actually. That is hyperbole."

"We?"

"You, I meant. Of course. You." The final word came out on a sigh.

Henry gazed at her. Her breath did seem to be fast. Her violet eyes were wide and her luscious lips parted. She had one hand on a chairback as if she required support. "Because nothing like that could happen to you?"

"It was a slip of the tongue."

Mention of tongues was inflammatory. "Has anyone ever called you a liar, Miss Meacham?"

"I suppose everyone has been accused of…prevarication."

She made the innocent word sound provocative. Henry closed his hands into fists to restrain them. They were desperate to reach for her. "You talk of keeping distance. And then you…don't."

"It is odd how one's mind and body…"

Henry waited for the end of this very interesting sentence. "Yes?" he asked when it did not come. "One's mind and body?"

"Can drive one in different directions," she said.

This was halfway hopeful. Thrillingly more than he'd had before. And Henry was delighted at the part that seemed to be on his side.

"But of course the mind must win out," she added. "Anything else would be…"

"A risk?" Henry asked. "I thought you admired daring."

"But I am not reckless. No matter what some people may say."

"I didn't."

"Not you," she acknowledged softly.

"Minds can change. They often do."

"Not when all the weight of logic and responsibility are guiding them." She moved a bit farther away. "It is time…"

"Are you going out in breeches again?" Henry asked to forestall her.

"Of course. That is how I have gathered the best information."

"I would like to go with you." He would like to go anywhere with her, Henry realized. The "with" being the key element.

Miss Meacham shook her head. "You would hinder my efforts. Indeed, wreck them."

"I could stay in the background, unnoticed."

"No, Mr. Deeping, you could not. You'd stand out like a goat in a sheepfold."

"Goat!"

One corner of her lips twitched. Something in Henry twitched in response. "I meant no insult," she said. "Merely that you would be noticeable and rouse suspicion in the people I need to question."

"While you…"

"Know how to appear innocuous."

"Because you are slippery as an eel wriggling out of one's hands."

"Eel!" she said in the same tone he'd used for goat. But she was looking at his hands. The hands that had caressed her. Heat rushed through Henry. He took a step forward.

"Kate?" Miss Palliser's voice sounded down the stairwell. "Has everyone gone? Where are you?"

"Just coming up," Miss Meacham called back. She moved away. "You must go."

"This is not settled between us."

She started to shake her head, then shrugged. "No. Unless we are going to be sensible."

"I don't think I am."

She looked him up and down, a smile lurking in her violet eyes. "Perhaps I will have to decide for us both then."

Henry decided to take this as progress. Miss Palliser called again.

"My coat? And hat."

She pointed. They were draped over the sofa, in plain sight. Had they been...eels, they might have bitten him. "Tomorrow," Henry began. But he was occupied into the evening at the office. Damn Abernathy and his briefings.

"'Creeps in this petty pace to the last syllable of recorded time'?"

"It seems so, now and then, at the Foreign Office. One often wishes for a dagger."

Miss Meacham laughed.

It was a free, musical laugh. Henry reveled in it. "Sunday?"

"Very well. You may call on Sunday afternoon." She made a prim face. "Daphne and I will give you tea. Or no, *I* will. Daphne will give you a lecture on the political evils of same." Her eyes sparkled as she teased.

And so Henry was able to feel a spike of triumph as he pulled on his coat and took his leave.

Thirteen

OUT IN THE FREEZING FEBRUARY NIGHT, HENRY REALIZED that it wasn't particularly late. It would be hours before he slept. He was restless and in need of…several things. Which he would not be getting tonight. If ever. He would not think of that.

Friends might be a comfort. He turned his steps toward Tereford House. There were lights in the windows. He rang and was admitted almost like a family member. That was warming. He found the duke and duchess together in their blue and gold drawing room seated before a cozy fire. She smiled and held out a hand. Tereford stood to greet him, setting a newspaper aside.

When they were settled again, Henry provided with a glass of good wine, Tereford said, "We were reading about the old king's funeral." He picked up the newssheet. "Apparently it was tumultuous."

"You were not there?" asked Henry.

"I used Cecelia's condition as an excuse to stay home."

"I've become extremely convenient," said the duchess with a smile. "In high good health if James wishes to venture out, rather poorly if not."

"You are and ever will be far more than convenient," the duke replied. "Pah, a paltry word."

"I hope you are feeling well," said Henry.

"Perfectly," she replied with a serenely happy smile.

"Except for the…"

"I am assured by ladies who know that my digestion will return to normal quite soon." She placed a confident hand on her stomach.

"It had better," muttered Tereford. "It makes no sense for the child to starve you. And I shall be seriously at odds with him if he does. Or she."

Henry had never seen his old friend so anxious. His handsome face was creased with worry. Intercepting a look from the duchess, Henry said, "So the funeral was tumultuous?"

The duke drew a breath, nodded, looked down at the newspaper. "Our new king took the time to plan a grand rite for the father he mistreated in life. Thousands of people crowded Windsor, wishing to pay their respects, and things became somewhat chaotic, it seems." He read aloud. "'Men and women of all ages pressed against each other so closely that there was risk to life. The guards who were stationed at the gates did their best to control the masses, but in vain. The shrieks of women and children could be heard in all directions, with several women fainting and having to be saved from being trodden underfoot.' I wonder how Prinny—which I still find it difficult not to call him—enjoyed that?"

"He loves spectacle," said the duchess.

"But not a riot," said Henry.

"Oh, that might amuse him, as long as they weren't protesting his excesses," answered Tereford.

"It's not what old King George would have wanted," said his wife. "He was quite a humble man."

"When in his senses."

They all paused a moment to contemplate the former king's difficult life.

"How are you, Henry?" Tereford asked then.

"You look a bit tired," said the duchess.

"This new position is more taxing than I expected."

"I certainly understand *that*," replied the duke.

"James spent the afternoon on another father training visit," the duchess explained with twinkling eyes.

"A what?" Henry looked from one to the other of the most fashionable couple in London.

"He visited the Smythes. They have three children under five years of age."

The duke groaned softly.

"Very charming and well-behaved children, I understand," she added.

"Cecelia! I told you, they swarmed over me like a Mongol horde. You saw the sticky handprints all over my coat."

"Your valet must have loved that," Henry couldn't help but say.

"He nearly fainted when he saw them."

"You shouldn't have given them candy," said the duchess.

"I thought one did that with children. It seems...almost canonical."

"Only for rare treats. In small doses."

"How do you know these things?" Tereford shook his head. "There is a secret arcane network to which men are not admitted, Henry. We have to sneak in."

"Or you can have three younger brothers and a little sister and learn by observation," Henry replied.

"Ah, yes. You knew some of your siblings when they were very small."

"Bertram was a terror in the nursery. I was often away at school, but I heard tales. And endured his pranks when I was home."

"How did you manage him?"

"Through an eldest brother's natural position of authority," Henry teased.

The duke shook his head. "I don't think I believe you. I'm finding that infants cannot be reasoned with. They don't listen. The ones who can even talk. The others…slobber."

"You could think of them as puppies," Henry suggested. Tereford was very fond of dogs. He treated them with firm affection.

"You cannot rap a child on the nose in reprimand. Or order it to heel." He paused thoughtfully. "Though I suppose the nursery is rather like a kennel."

"No, it is not, James," said the duchess. "And you are exaggerating for effect. You told me that you threw little Amelia into gales of laughter."

Tereford's smile was unexpectedly tender. "I pulled a coin from behind her ear. Over and over. And over. She didn't seem to tire of it."

Henry tried to picture this scene. He found it difficult to see his aristocratic friend behaving this way. "Most men of your class just leave their children to their wives and servants," he pointed out, as he thought perhaps he had before.

"As mine did, and we had a wretched relationship. And as yours did not."

"He did when we were very young," Henry said.

"You've told me you were running through the breeding stables by the time you were three."

"Well, yes."

"And I suppose your father was present on those occasions?"

"That's where he was." Henry smiled when he remembered those childhood days. He, and then his younger brothers, bolted their breakfast in their hurry to get outside.

"And I imagine he spoke to you now and then," Tereford added.

"He taught me how to deal with the horses."

"In a friendly manner."

"He is a good teacher."

"One can see that he would be," said the duchess.

Tereford frowned. "How does one learn to be *that*, I wonder. Rather than a jumped-up martinet." He sighed. "At any rate, my point is, you spent a good deal of time with your father. Pleasantly."

"But it was just part…" Henry searched for words. "My family works together in the breeding business."

"And mine will…" The duke grimaced. "My family. Good lord."

"Really, James, you are making too much of this." The duchess put a hand over one of his. "I know you are partly joking, but…"

"Indeed you are," agreed Henry. "You will do very well." He thought it was true, surprisingly.

His friend turned to him. "Are you saying you won't feel a weight of responsibility when you have children?"

Immediately, startlingly, Henry thought of Miss Meacham and what a child of hers might be like. Wild and adventurous probably. Almost certainly. He imagined three of them crawling over him like a Mongol horde. The idea filled him with a mixture of consternation and delight.

"You see?"

"You had such a strange expression just then," said the duchess. "What were you thinking of?"

Henry made no answer.

When it became clear that he did not intend to, Tereford said, "Speaking of a weight of responsibility, you seem much changed since you began your new work."

"For the worse?" Henry asked. He'd wondered that himself.

"I wouldn't say so. We are neither of us what we once were."

"And you are happy with your transformation." It was not a question.

"Extremely." Tereford smiled at his wife. "Gratefully. Are you not?"

Henry didn't know what to say. His life had changed, partly due to his new position. But there was also the secret pursuit of Richard Rankin and the advent of Miss Kate Meacham. The three added up to a virtual revolution.

"I am a little tired," said the duchess. She waved away

Tereford's immediate concern. "As I often am in the evening now, James. You know that. I am going to bed." They rose with her. "Do stay, Mr. Deeping. You and James can reminisce about your carefree bachelor days."

She was tactfully leaving them alone, Henry realized. The Duchess of Tereford was perceptive, and very kind.

Her husband walked with her to the door, kissed her hand, and returned to his chair. He refilled their wineglasses. "Those days were more heedless than carefree," he said. "At least on my part. Not yours." He sipped. "So, Henry, what is it?"

It occurred to Henry that James, the duke, was a power in society, with many friends in high places. He didn't think of that often, and it was not why he had come to visit, but now that he was here, it couldn't hurt to consult him. If he could just decide what he wished to ask. "My new position seems to require many hours of…somewhat insignificant labor," he began, feeling his way. "Copying reports and so on. Far more than is asked of others in the same rank, it seems to me." He was often the last person left in the offices as the evening came on.

"Testing the new boy, perhaps?"

"I did think of that. And of course I am willing to prove myself. But it shows no signs of stopping."

"You would prefer a posting abroad?"

At one time Henry would have jumped at the idea. Now, as he realized that Tereford might be able to pull strings and get him sent overseas, he hesitated.

"Or something else?" asked the duke with his newly developed intuition.

Someone else, Henry thought. "I believe my uncle has told my superiors to keep me fully occupied. Until he decides how he wishes to employ me." Patronage in the foreign service was more complicated than Henry had understood. To the internal hierarchy, he was, in a sense, his uncle's creature. They would do as his relative asked.

"And to keep you away from Miss Meacham?"

Henry nodded glumly.

Tereford turned his wineglass in his hand. Firelight made the red liquid glow. "The last time we talked, you were, ah, assigned to speak with the young lady."

"I tried," Henry said. "I didn't get very far."

"So no more kisses then."

"Oh yes, plenty of *those*. They've become...almost inevitable when we're alone together. And you needn't raise your eyebrows at me, James. She is as much the...instigator as I am. I might even say more so. I do say it."

Tereford started to speak.

"If you say, 'Indeed,' in that superior way you have, I swear I will come over there and punch you."

One corner of the duke's mouth turned up. "But what *am* I to say, if not, 'Indeed'?"

"She told me she liked it, but I was to feel no obligation," Henry continued. "What is a man to make of *that*?"

"You wish to feel an obligation?"

"Coercion isn't necessary, when I feel so much more."

"So you *are* thinking of marriage?"

Henry faced the fact that had been tugging at his attention for some time. He loved Miss Kate Meacham. He wanted to spend the rest of his life being astonished by her intrepidity and set aflame by her ardent kisses. And more than kisses, of course. He wanted to see what life would be like with that amazing woman by his side. And he by hers, naturally. She was not an appendage. "My family is against it. Which would not signify. I could bring them around. But she says she will not ruin my prospects. She refuses to discuss it."

"If it is a matter of money…"

"I can't be your pensioner, James." Every feeling revolted. "And I want something important to *do*."

Tereford nodded. "I don't know what to say except that I would be glad to help you, Henry, if you tell me how."

"Thank you." Henry didn't see any way. Sending Tereford to talk to his uncle would be a disaster. As for Kate Meacham—she despised interference. No, this was his life. It was up to him to make a success of it.

"You are my best friend," Tereford replied. "Or, well…"

"Second best, these days. After the duchess."

The duke nodded.

"And I couldn't be more pleased about that." Henry held up his glass in a toast.

The following morning, Oliver Welden arrived at Kate's house at the fashionable hour for morning calls, though Kate doubted that he knew this. He might or might not know, by this time, that he really came here to see Daphne. Their investigation continued, of course, and he always had the excuse of some tidbit of news or a question he wished to hash over. But it was obvious to Kate that he really just wanted to be with her friend. And Daphne was very pleased to receive him, in her quiet, self-contained way.

As Kate saw it, the two of them were kindred spirits. Both were acerbic, Mr. Welden more than Daphne. Both were pedantic, Daphne more than Mr. Welden. Both were rebellious, perhaps equally so. They had eccentric ambitions. And their enthusiasm for the investigation had spilled over into a more intimate connection. Kate often came upon them with heads together, deep in a conversation that was cut off, red-faced, as soon as she appeared. They were a good match as individuals, yet nothing seemed to come of it. Rather as nothing did, or could, with her and Henry Deeping, Kate thought glumly.

Society—that damnable, insubstantial, yet relentless thing—put thorny obstacles in all their ways. An alliance with her would ruin Mr. Deeping's career. His uncle had been clear about that. A marriage to Welden would destroy Daphne's social status. The daughter of a baronet, even one who was a bluestocking and quite on the shelf, did not wed a penniless Bow Street Runner. A grubby thief taker with no pedigree! The thought of the dropped jaws, the utter consternation, in drawing rooms all over London would have made Kate laugh if it hadn't involved her friend's future happiness. Society was like a—what was that thing she'd read about?—a juggernaut, crushing all before it into a pulp of conformity.

A person might rebel, kick over the traces, and do as

they pleased. She did. And she would face the consequences head-on. Society could go hang! But she couldn't inflict disaster on someone she loved.

Yes, Kate thought with a rush of emotion, she loved Henry Deeping. She might as well admit it. The sentiment had been growing for weeks as she'd come to know him—his dry wit, his open mind, his kind heart. His kisses! He was just the man for her.

Only he wasn't. She would be his ruin. She'd been a fool to let things go so far. But looking back, she didn't see how she could have resisted him.

Daphne and Welden had been talking softly. Kate was about to leave them alone when he said, "Our street patrol followed Richard Rankin to three different apothecary shops. Young Sam managed to slip in at one place and over-heard him asking for something to rid his rooms of rats."

Kate moved closer. "Poison?"

Welden nodded. "Quite a store, if he bought it at three places."

"That house on Judd Street *could* have rats," said Daphne, suppressing a shudder.

"He would order someone to take care of them," Kate replied, remembering the arrogant man who had taunted them in Leicestershire. "He wouldn't stoop to do it himself."

"He might not wish to draw any attention," replied Daphne.

"Perhaps," said Kate. They needed to examine all possi-bilities. But this didn't feel right. She shook her head. "He wouldn't need such a quantity."

"He's going to kill somebody," said Welden.

They turned to look at him. Daphne put a hand on his arm, confirming Kate's conclusions about their bond.

"Miss Meacham is right," he went on. "A man like Rankin doesn't deal with vermin. He hires himself out to 'solve' problems. By any means necessary. Including violence."

"But who is he after?" Daphne frowned. "And what does it have to do with Carlton House? Perhaps that's another matter entirely. He met with some other men."

"Thugs and ruffians," said Welden. "Not the sort who could pay him what he wants. It has to be Matthews."

A knock sounded on the front door. Kate's pulse speeded up, but it couldn't be Henry Deeping. He was occupied at the Foreign Office at this hour. They were keeping him constantly busy.

A few minutes later, Sally brought Tom Jesperson up to the study. The lad threw himself into a chair, his expression uncharacteristically sour. "I've had all I can take of this Matthews feller," he said. "He's a right blackguard. The girls at the theater won't come out with me anymore. He paws at them right there in the tavern, pulls their clothes half off. Acts like I'm offering them to him. People are going to start wondering if he's right. I can't do it no…any longer. I very nearly punched him last night."

"And you haven't learned anything new?" Kate asked.

Tom grimaced and shook his head. "He just rants about Queen Caroline." Tom used her title defiantly. "The things he says about her. I wouldn't repeat them. He has a vile tongue. And he claims our new king is practically foaming at the mouth because they don't know where she is just now. Maybe she's coming here to 'bedevil' him. Wishes he could send her to the tower and cut off her head like old Henry the Eighth. What's wrong with these people?"

"They are spoiled and petty and monstrously selfish," said Oliver Welden.

"But he's the *king*," replied Tom.

"And that is the problem." The older man scowled. "I share a name with a famous republican, you know. Oliver Cromwell had some good ideas."

Daphne looked torn between shock and admiration.

"Was he the one who chopped off King Charles's head?" asked Tom.

"Not personally. But he was involved in Parliament's rebellion."

Tom frowned. "I wouldn't go so far as that."

"There is no question of regicide," said Daphne. Her eyes went wide. "Unless... No, of course it's not for him. Matthews is his minion."

"What isn't?" asked Tom.

Welden explained about the rat poison.

"I don't like the sound of that," said Tom.

Kate didn't either, and she had the feeling that this plot was moving toward its conclusion. If they didn't work out the details soon, events were likely to get away from them.

So that evening she donned her breeches again and set off to make the rounds of her grandfather's old haunts. They would be busy on a Saturday night, offering more chances to glean bits of information to piece together into a whole.

She heard nothing useful in the first or the second spot. In the third she learned that two notoriously hard men had hired on with Rankin for amounts that roused bitter envy in thuggish ranks. They were thought to have taken advantage in some unspecified way. Her informant, who would have gladly taken their place, wished them the worst of bad luck.

In the fourth and lowest alehouse, Kate spent a long and unprofitable time listening to unsavory mutterings and pretending to sip sour ale from a dirty mug. She couldn't quite make herself touch her lips to the greasy rim. But she was adept at seeming to do so, and no one was paying any particular attention to the shabby lad in the corner.

She was about to give up and go when her luck turned. Rankin himself entered the place. He stood near the door and looked around at the battered furnishings and disreputable patrons with sour disapproval. Careful not to show that she'd been startled, Kate stayed slouched in her corner and bent her head a bit more so that her cap totally shadowed her face. She watched from under the brim as Rankin scanned the taproom, blinking in the smoky air. She made no sign when his eyes passed over her, though she had a moment of anxiety when his scan seemed to pause. But it soon moved on.

Then he found what he was searching for and went to join a bulky figure on the other side of the room. They were too far away for her to overhear. But from the way they leaned close and spoke in each other's ears, she doubted that she could have from any spot. They didn't want their conversation known.

The conference went on for some minutes. Kate was careful to not to stare. She observed them in casual glances, letting her gaze wander as if she was in an alcoholic stupor, disguising her looks with a raised mug. She only barely caught Rankin slipping a purse under the sticky table. The pouch disappeared into the stranger's overcoat pocket with one quick swipe.

This appeared to conclude their business. They leaned back and said no more. Rankin bought the fellow another glass of the swill they called whiskey here. They sat at ease to give the appearance of casual comrades. After a time, Rankin rose and departed. The other man sipped his drink, his free hand spread over his laden pocket to make sure the purse stayed undisturbed. Finally, he also stood and made his way out.

Kate wished she could follow and see where he went. But with a fat purse on him, the man would be particularly vigilant. He would notice a "lad" behind him and ask what he wanted. Too, he might be simply relieving himself against a wall outside. She couldn't afford to encounter him at that. Minutes ticked past. He didn't return. Aware that he was out of reach, she began to inquire about his identity.

She had to ask too often and grew afraid her questions would rouse dangerous notice. She might not be able to come back here after this, but she felt it was vital to keep on. The exchange of the purse implied some imminent action. They needed to know what it was, especially considering the poison Rankin had acquired. And so she took the risk and kept on.

At last she found someone who knew the stranger. "Ship's captain," said a drink-sodden old man who smelled of sweat and dirt and worse things. "Goes back and forth to Calais. Or thereabouts." He attempted a wink. "Claims he's a trader, but what does he 'trade,' eh? Things as might be taxed? Ha! Not taxed is the idea belike." His gurgling laugh sounded as if it came from the bottom of a well.

"Do you know his name?" Kate had to persist.

The ancient tapped his empty mug. Kate ordered him another. Only when it was before him and he had slurped up a good mouthful, did the old man say, "Miller, was it? Somethin' like that."

Kate felt a flash of anger. He'd cozened her to get more drink. As such fellows always tried to do.

But then he went on. "No, Murphy, that's it. Cass Murphy. Sounds Irish, don't it? He ain't on land very much. Likes to keep out of the way of...most everybody." He laughed thickly again.

"Do you know what his ship is called?"

"Ship? Why would I know that?" A spark of suspicion swam in the old man's bleary eyes. "You're mighty nosy, ain't you? What's it to you?"

"I've a fancy to go to sea."

"You?" He swayed on his stool as he stared at her. His leer was a mass of wrinkles. "A pretty lad like you'd be right popular on shipboard. But why would you be wantin' to do that?"

Kate knew she'd gone as far as she could with her questions. Perhaps too far. She'd sparked curiosity even in his addled brain. "Will you have another glass?" she asked to divert him.

He accepted eagerly. Kate provided the drink and left him to it. She certainly could not return to this alehouse any time soon. Gradually, as if she had nothing much on her mind, she moved to the door. She did not stagger about though. She didn't want this crowd to think she was drunk and thus an easy mark. On the contrary, she held her stick in a visible, firm grasp.

She lit her small lantern at a candle by the door and took care to check the street outside before she departed. The dark lane was empty, still, and damply cold.

Walking toward home, Kate made herself move with her usual wariness, hand on her sword stick, though her brain was buzzing.

It seemed that Rankin was leaving England. Why else give a ship's captain a substantial amount? That purse had been fat. And she didn't think he would pay in advance for smuggled goods. He was not the trusting sort.

Facts combined and reshuffled in her head. And then, all at once, a possible sequence fell into place. The idea was outrageous, but it fit.

She'd stopped walking. That was unwise. She moved on, watching her footing on the uneven cobbles.

It was very late when she reached her house. Even Daphne was asleep. All was quiet and serene, the opposite of the places she'd visited tonight. In her bedchamber, Kate shed her men's clothes, which smelled of tobacco smoke and damp and the cheapest sort of liquor. She stuffed them into an old valise, to be aired out later. Her hair, when she unbraided it, held the same scents. She brushed it until they faded, her mind racing all the while. What was she going to do?

Because of course she was going to do something. She was determined to see this matter through. If it weren't for her, nobody would know anything about it. The difficulty was—just about everything.

She got into bed and tossed restlessly through the wee hours, forming and rejecting wild plans. Her agitation left no room for dreams. The sky was graying toward dawn when she acknowledged that she would prefer not to be quite alone on this venture.

———

Henry called at Miss Meacham's house as early as was reasonable on Sunday. Indeed, he feared he was rather *too* early. But she opened the door herself when he knocked and practically dragged him into the front parlor, shutting the door behind him. Henry's gratification at this welcome died as he noticed the fatigue in her face and the wild glitter in her violet eyes. "Is something wrong?" he asked.

"Richard Rankin is going abroad with poison and hired thugs. I believe he means to track down Queen Caroline and assassinate her. At the behest of Carlton House."

Sheer astonishment jumbled these words in Henry's mind. His confusion grew as she poured out the story of rat poison from apothecaries, the new king's rage at his wife and wish to have her executed, and a purse passed to an unsavory ship's captain. "Wait," he said when she paused. "Say that again."

"Which part?"

"All of it," Henry replied. "Slowly."

Miss Meacham looked impatient, but she complied. "They could be sailing right now," she finished, wringing her hands.

"The boys are still watching the house on Judd Street," Henry pointed out.

"That's right." Some of the tension went out of her expression. "They will send word if he goes to the docks. But we… I must be ready to move."

"Move where?"

"I'm going to stow away on that boat," she replied. She put a hand to her head. "I'll have to cut off my hair," she added with obvious regret.

"No," said Henry, his whole being revolting.

"I can't keep my hat on all the time."

"You can't get on that ship. The crew know each other. You will be discovered at once. And Rankin will recognize you." At which point he would slit her throat and toss her into the channel. "That is an idiotic idea."

"I shall lurk in the… What is it called? The bilges."

If he had not been so worried, Henry might have laughed. "In pitch-darkness, with filthy water up to your knees, at least, and a host of rats?"

She looked daunted.

"We must tell my uncle what you've discovered and let him take steps."

"And what would those be?"

"He could send a navy vessel to stop them," Henry said.

"From sailing to Calais? That is not a crime."

"Rankin is a wanted man."

"He was. Apparently Carlton House has got him off. Have you heard any word of his escape? Or pursuit of him?"

Henry shook his head. The man, and the Leicestershire affair, were no longer mentioned. They might have gone up in smoke.

"Also, your uncle is unlikely to accept any idea of mine," she added. "He will call it a wild theory. By a hysterical female probably."

This was probably true.

"And if he does believe me, I expect he'll be glad to hear Rankin is leaving England. And good riddance to him."

Henry also knew that his uncle preferred not to oppose the new king openly. If Rankin departed, he might drop this matter. "What you propose. It *is* just a theory."

"Which explains all of our observations."

"But murder. Surely that is out of the question."

"For Rankin? I think not."

"For our monarch and our country," Henry said.

"But it isn't him, is it?" replied Miss Meacham. "All will be done by this agent, at arm's length. Prinny would deny any connection, of course. Having muttered to Matthews, 'Will no one rid me of this troublesome queen?'"

"This is not ancient times. And she is not Thomas à Becket."

"The principle is the same."

Henry was fixed on one thought. "If you get on that ship, you will never arrive...anywhere. They will discover you and throw you in the sea."

Some of the fire seemed to go out of Miss Meacham. She

sank into a chair and sighed. "So I just give up? Stand back and bow to your uncle's authority? Allow him to decide to let a villain go? Because I think he will. Admit that I can do nothing, no matter how clearly I see the threat."

Henry understood that this referred to more than Richard Rankin. She was speaking of her life, her wish to do something important with it, her frustration at a host of limits. He had felt the same, in his youth and lately. The sorrow in her eyes cut at him. But she could *not* set foot on that ship. That was certain catastrophe.

A wild thought popped into Henry's head. Reckless. Beyond reckless. Unthinkable. Only he *had* thought it. And it was…possible? "I might have an idea," he said slowly.

She looked up dully. "Something you can do, because you are a man with an official position."

"No. The opposite of official, actually. And it would be both of us." Henry's mind reeled at the risk he was considering. If it went wrong…well, a great many other things would fall to pieces with it. But he found he was ready to take that chance, to restore the fire to this beloved woman's eyes.

Miss Meacham sprang up. She took his hands and searched his face. "What?"

"I must find out first if it will…"

"No! Tell me now."

He would do anything for her, Henry acknowledged. He cared more for her than for anything else in his life. "I might be able to get us a ship of our own," he said.

The look she gave him was reward enough. But then she threw her arms around him and held on as if she would never let go.

Fourteen

HENRY SLIPPED AWAY TO CALL ON THE DUKE OF TEREFORD at midday the next day. He received some sidelong looks from other clerks as he left the office, but no one questioned him. This was an advantage of his uncle's patronage. He might be on some errand for him.

He found James at a large desk in the library of Tereford House writing a letter. "Do you know that we have dealt with all the correspondence my predecessor left behind?" he said when Henry was ushered in and sat down. "Some of it exceedingly odd. I call that a triumph."

Remembering the mountain of unanswered letters the former duke had accumulated, Henry was impressed. "You wanted to consign them all to the fire," he recalled.

"Which I couldn't light without risking a general conflagration. But Cecelia convinced me otherwise."

"As she does."

The duke's smile was tender. "As she does."

Full of his mission, Henry burst out, "You said you would be glad to help me if you were told how."

The duke's gaze went sharp. "Indeed."

"I would like to borrow your yacht. You still keep it here on the Thames, don't you? Not in Southampton?"

"Yes. But what do you want with the *Sea Nymph*?"

"I can't tell you."

Tereford examined him. "Some Foreign Office matter?"

Henry almost said it was. A case might be made. Barely. But he didn't want to lie to his friend.

"You wouldn't need my boat for that," the duke added before he could speak. "You'd have other choices. But not just a pleasure cruise?"

He might have said it was only that, Henry realized too late. But James probably would have seen through the story. "It is confidential."

"Are you eloping?"

"What? No."

The duke continued to examine him. Henry was trying to find further arguments that would not sound completely daft when the duke said, "When do you wish to sail?"

Relief, and perhaps just a touch of regret, ran through Henry. "I'm not entirely certain. Soon probably. The next few days. We..." Henry bit off the sentence.

"So you are not going out alone?"

He couldn't mention Miss Meacham after that question about eloping. Or even without it.

"You must know you are driving me wild with curiosity, Henry." The duke's blue gaze was acute.

"I can't say more just now." The fewer people who knew what they planned, the better. For their sake as well as his if a great dust was kicked up over this. Henry shied away from thinking about that.

"Perhaps you will tell you when you return. Unless you are fleeing the country permanently?"

"What?" Henry shook his head. "No."

"I didn't think you could be." Tereford's dark brows drew together. "Not wishing to quibble. Of course you may have the boat whenever you like. But you are not an experienced sailor. Perhaps your companion, companions may be?"

How could he have forgotten about that? He couldn't manage a seagoing yacht, and he was fairly certain Miss Meacham couldn't either.

Responding to his expression, Tereford said, "May I ask that you take my crew along? The *Nymph* is rather large for…one or two men to handle."

Henry nodded. There was no choice. But the sailors wouldn't have to know the purpose of the trip.

"That's settled then." The duke surveyed him with a rueful smile. "In the old days, I would have insisted on coming along."

In the old days, this might have been a lark, or a prank, Henry thought. Now it was something darker. He felt that twinge of regret again. If James had refused, they wouldn't have been able to attempt this mad venture. But Miss Meacham would have been wretchedly disappointed.

Tereford took out a sheet of notepaper and dipped his pen to write a few lines. He used his signet ring to affix a seal at the end and held it out. "Give this to Bailes, who takes care of the boat for me, and he will be at your disposal. I'll send him word directly as well."

Henry took the page. "Thank you."

The duke gazed at him, then opened another drawer in the desk. "Here's this as well." He held out a fat roll of banknotes.

Henry started to reject it, reflexively. But he might need money, he realized. Perhaps a large sum, depending on what happened. He didn't know where they might have to go, or what they would have to do. He could raise the requisite amount, but it would take time. Which he probably did not have. He accepted the bills, putting them in his pocket. "I will repay you."

Tereford nodded cordially. "Partly by telling me every detail of the adventure you are clearly about to have, Henry. And since you are so closemouthed, I hope it involves a touch of seasickness. And cold rain and mud at the other end perhaps. Though ending successfully, of course."

"Thank you, James," Henry repeated.

"Of course, my second-best friend."

As if on cue, the door opened, and the duchess came in. "I've eaten an enormous breakfast, James, and I feel perfectly well. Oh, hello, Henry. I didn't know you were here."

"He's come to tell us he is going out of town for a…few days?" The duke cocked an eyebrow at Henry, who did not rise to the bait.

"Where are you off to?" she asked.

"We are not to know *that*," replied her husband.

The duchess smiled. "Has the Foreign Office given you a secret mission?"

"Cecelia! You mustn't ask."

James might have changed over the last year, but he still liked to tease. Henry shook his head in a general negative.

"I beg your pardon," said the duchess. "I was joking." She looked from one man to the other.

"But were you?" asked Tereford.

Henry rose. "I must get back." They would be wondering where he'd gotten to, and he didn't want to tell any more half-truths. Also, he had arrangements to make.

"Bon voyage," said the duke with a grin.

Henry departed in the face of the duchess's quizzical glance.

———

Two days later, word came that Rankin was on the move. One of the boys who took turns watching the house on Judd Street brought the news to Kate. Another had gone to alert Henry Deeping, and a third was following Rankin to see where he went. "He were heading for the docks," the boy told Kate.

Kate was ready. Indeed, she'd been vibrating with readiness since she learned the ship captain's identity. They had been able to find his ship on the waterfront through seemingly careless wandering and artless questions by their urchins, who were developing into a very effective surveillance force. Tereford's yacht had been readied, and Kate had sent a bundle of her things aboard. Now she quickly changed into her coat and breeches, braided up her hair, pulled on her cap, and muffled all in a thick cloak. Evading Mrs. Knox was one of her biggest challenges. She crept down to the study to ask Daphne to divert the staff while she slipped away.

"Yes, all right." Daphne rose. "You will go off adventuring, and I will stay here to make excuses."

"You may have the harder job."

"I am well aware." Daphne shrugged. "Actually, I don't mind so much. I prefer my perils on the pages of a book. But Ol…Mr. Welden is still brooding. I don't know when he will forgive you. If he ever does."

It had been decided that Welden would stay to oversee the boys, in case Rankin had left unpleasant surprises behind. There might be more than one part of this plan. They couldn't be sure. Welden had admitted this necessity with sullen bad grace. Only Daphne could coax a pleasant word from him just now. Tom had to remain in London. His role in a new play was beginning.

"You will have trials to face," Kate observed. "Mr. Gerard will be furious."

"At you. And his nephew. Particularly you, I suppose."

Kate nodded. "I'm sorry to leave you to his wrath."

"We intend to be shocked and mystified and rather hurt." Daphne put a hand to her breast and widened her eyes in mock astonishment. "Whatever could have happened? Oh, I hope they are all right. You don't suppose they've been kidnapped as Rankin did in Leicestershire?" She let her hand drop. "Mr. Welden wanted to say that he suspected you'd eloped, send Mr. Gerard haring off to Gretna Green."

"What? That would not…"

Daphne waved away her concern. "I dissuaded him."

"Thank you."

"Gratitude is in order and will be expected for the foreseeable future." Daphne smiled. "You'd best be going."

"It's two hours until the tide turns." Kate had become an expert on the tide tables recently. "They won't sail till then. They wait for an outgoing current. But I should go."

"Best of luck. Do take care, Kate. Promise you will."

"I promise." Though how she was to keep that vow, Kate did not know. Anything might happen.

Daphne went down to occupy Mrs. Knox and the others in the kitchen.

Now that the moment had come, Kate felt a whisper of doubt. Was she doing the right thing? Should she step back and leave this matter to others? What would she do if she had to confront Rankin and his henchmen? Her knife throwing had not progressed very far.

A wave of rebellion swept her. She'd spotted Rankin in London. His plotting was known because of her. She *would* see this through. Moving silently down the stairs, she pulled her cap tighter, slipped out of the house, and walked rapidly away.

She reached the *Sea Nymph* twenty minutes later and was welcomed aboard by Captain Roger Bailes and two young crew members, all of them sun-bronzed and muscular. Tereford's lovely yacht was nearly forty feet long, and they'd been assured she could navigate all but the stormiest seas. "Today's the day then?" asked Bailes.

"Seems so," replied Kate, keeping her voice low and gravelly and her head down. The crew thought her a lad, and she wanted to keep up the masquerade.

"Wind and weather's good for a Channel crossing. If that's what we're doing?" Bailes exuded competence. He'd been courteous and steady throughout their preparations but also clearly curious. One could see him biting back direct questions.

"We'll be following the *Kestrel*," Kate replied. They hadn't told him this before, not wanting to risk word leaking out. He needed to know now. "Without appearing to do so."

Bailes gave her a long, measuring look. His pale blue eyes seemed to see right through her. An illusion, Kate told herself. "*Kestrel*," he repeated.

Kate hadn't realized it was a query, but one of the young crew members responded at once. "Trader," he said. "So they sez at any rate. I've heard they're not picky about what they carry long as there's money in it. Bigger than the *Nymph*. Two masts, but she ain't well kept. Wallows. They ought to scrape her down and recaulk. We can outrun *her*." He sounded contemptuous.

"Captain?" asked Bailes.

"Fella name of Cass Murphy. A bad lot."

Bailes frowned. In general, and then at Kate.

Fortunately, Mr. Deeping arrived at the dock just then and came aboard. Kate retreated to the far rail, leaving the conversation to him. He was the duke's friend, after all. Tereford's employee was more likely to listen to him.

There wasn't much talk. Kate thought that Bailes was confirming her instructions. Mr. Deeping shrugged at one point. Then Bailes joined the crew in preparing the boat to sail.

Deeping came to join Kate. He too was bundled in a heavy cloak. The late February day was not freezing cold, but a biting damp rose from the water, carried on a brisk wind. The breeze was required, of course, to fill the sails. It also chilled fingers and cheeks. She pulled her woolen cloak closer.

"We're really doing it," he said. His face was shaded by the hood of his cloak.

"Did you think we might not?"

"It didn't seem quite real until now."

"And you are...sorry?"

He shook his head. "I'm excited. As much as I've ever been perhaps. Or nearly."

Kate felt a thrill at the gleam in his dark eyes and the emphasis he put on that final word. She thought she knew what other excitement he meant. The lips she'd kissed more than once were a little parted. She had to resist an impulse to throw her arms around him. That would never do.

"It should go without saying, but I will say it anyway," he went on. "Though we are traveling alone together, of course I would never..."

"Take advantage," finished Kate, echoing a phrase that had passed back and forth between them. The embraces that had occurred at those times were a palpable, arousing presence.

"P-precisely."

"I'll try to be as scrupulous," Kate joked. "If I can."

"Miss Meacham!"

"Shh. I am Rob Jones. A quiet lad along to assist you in

your…endeavors." They were facing the water. Kate didn't think he could have been overheard.

"Sorry." Mr. Deeping gazed at her. "It is difficult to see you as anything other than…"

"Provocative?" A word with more than one meaning, and she dared to say it.

"Enchanting."

Kate was left speechless.

"Tide's begun to turn," Bailes said. He was looking at them.

Sam, one of their young watchers, appeared on the dock and gave the signal they'd agreed on. Kate saw Bailes notice the interplay. "The *Kestrel* is on the move," said Mr. Deeping.

"Watch for it," Bailes told his crew.

After a time, a ship appeared out on the wide river. Compared with the *Sea Nymph,* it looked shabby and disreputable. "That's her," said the crew member who had described it earlier.

"Loose ropes," said Bailes. And then a moment later, "Push off."

The *Sea Nymph* turned to catch the outgoing tide and ride it down the river. As the gap from the dock widened, Kate murmured, "The die is cast."

"It is indeed," her companion replied.

Once they were well away from the docks, the crew raised the mainsail partway. It caught the wind and increased their speed. They kept the *Kestrel* in sight as they traveled down the Thames and out toward the Channel. Henry noted other ships departing on the ebbing tide. There was no reason for the men on the *Kestrel* to notice them particularly. He pulled his cloak closer against the cold wind and watched. There was a cabin below where Miss Meacham might have sheltered, but he didn't think she'd want that any more than he did. Not with the pursuit beginning and their quarry right there in sight.

The estuary widened. The sails were fully raised, and the *Sea Nymph* heeled over a bit and speeded up. The *Kestrel* had done the same, as had other vessels that dotted the wide expanse. They scudded east over moderate waves, headed toward France.

The English coast retreated behind them. The rigging creaked, and the water hissed along the hull. Gulls called. The deck heaved gently under Henry's feet. Gradually, the sameness of the scene—sky, sea, ship—grew monotonous. Henry felt chilled. He paced the deck to warm his muscles and wished he had some task to occupy him. Sailing was a slow and steady means of travel, he saw. It wasn't the least like hurtling over the countryside on a spirited mount. A rider could feel he was urging things on, though the horse did most of the work. Here, he was more of a package.

"I almost want to row," said Miss Meacham one of the times he passed by her. She stood near the bow leaning in the direction of their travel.

Henry nodded his understanding of her impatience and paced on.

Some hours had passed when Bailes said, "The *Kestrel*'s bearing south toward Calais." He gave orders to adjust their sails. "We'll drop back till we can just see the top of their mast," he told Henry.

"We mustn't lose them."

"We won't do that. I thought you didn't wish to draw attention to the fact that we're following."

"Right."

"Then we won't."

Tereford's men knew their business. Henry nodded and watched the outline of the *Kestrel* sink mostly below the horizon.

"It's none of my affair," Bailes went on then. "But I've remembered a thing or two about this Cass Murphy. He's a right blackguard."

Henry wasn't surprised. Rankin would look for his own sort of villain. "I don't expect to meet him," he replied. "I imagine he'll be staying with his ship."

"Aye. But the men he keeps around him are no better. Some of them are worse. Whoever it is you're chasing…"

"We mean to take care."

Bailes nodded. "That's always the idea, isn't it? And then the troubles come along."

This was all too true. They intended only to observe Rankin and see where he went, calling in the authorities when his criminal purpose was revealed. Henry was concerned about the last part. He'd assembled all the credentials he could gather to convince French officials of their bona fides. But they weren't especially weighty. It was the weak point in their plan. And then there were the two London toughs Rankin had hired to accompany him.

"I know some stout fellows in Calais who can be trusted," Bailes went on. "They've worked for the duke before, and they know their way around France. And how to keep their mouths shut as well."

"Tereford isn't involved in this venture," Henry felt bound to say.

Bailes shrugged. "He lent you the *Sea Nymph*. And told me to aid you. That's enough for me."

Local expertise would be welcome, Henry acknowledged. He spoke fair French. It was required for an aspiring diplomat. But the rapid patter of the streets and local accents would tax his abilities. And Kate Meacham had told him that her French was limited. "Their help would be welcome," he replied. "Thank you."

"I don't want to have to tell His Grace that I've lost his friend," said Bailes with a half smile.

"Nor do I wish you to," answered Henry with feeling. "How long will the crossing take?"

"With this wind, a full day. Bit more or less if it shifts. The journey's much quicker from Dover."

"So not until tomorrow morning?"

Bailes nodded. "You and your comrade should go below. We'll keep the *Kestrel* in our sights."

"But when it grows dark?"

"We'll move a bit closer. There's a half-moon. She won't slip away from us."

"I suppose we can't do anything," Henry said.

"No, sir, you cannot. There's food in the cupboards below. And a chamber pot for those who don't care to hang over the stern." His smile was a little broader this time.

Henry understood what the captain didn't say. He'd

prefer his passengers out of the way. He went to join Miss Meacham at the front of the yacht. "We should go down to the cabin," he said. "You must be cold."

"I want to keep watch."

"It's going to be many hours before we reach Calais."

She turned to look at him. The tip of her nose was red with cold.

"And we have matters to discuss. Come."

She hesitated a moment longer, then turned to follow him to the open hatch.

They went down the short steep stair into the space below-decks. It was warmer out of the wind. The cabin was fitted with narrow bunks on either side and a host of latched wooden cupboards. Henry opened some of the larger ones, revealing bread and cheese and apples. Jugs of ale and cups were cleverly strapped in another. And in one at floor level he found the chamber pot. He pointed it out. "The crew make use of the sea," he told her. "In…certain cases, they hang out over the side."

Miss Meacham looked daunted. "What if they fall in?"

"I expect they learn not to. It must be a…prerequisite to a seagoing life."

She smiled. "Well, I am glad to see there is another choice. What did you wish to discuss?"

Even dressed as a lad and huddled in a bulky cloak, she was lovely, Henry thought. She also seemed quite unafraid. He told her what Bailes had said. "I judged that local help would be a good idea."

"I agree. They needn't know everything we are doing," she replied.

"Apparently they are accustomed to discretion."

She looked intrigued. "I wonder what they've done for Tereford?"

"He has far-flung interests."

"Which require stout fellows who can keep their mouths shut." She raised her eyebrows.

Henry admitted it was interesting. "I don't know. I'll have to ask him when we return." Because of course they would, safe and sound. "Are you hungry?"

She appeared to consult her inner state. "Yes."

He found a knife in a drawer and a neat shelf that pulled out of the wall. Henry cut the loaf and handed her a slice with a chunk of cheddar. He helped himself as well. They ate and then sampled the ale. When they'd finished and tidied all away, she said, "I need to use the chamberpot," in a matter-of-fact voice.

Henry rose at once and went up on deck. He stood at the rail to relieve himself, then loitered about for a while. When he judged sufficient time had passed, he went to the hatch and called down, "All well, Rob?"

"Yes," she answered in her gruff lad voice.

Henry asked Bailes if the crew needed food or rest. Bailes told him they'd be stationed on deck for the night. Henry saw mounds of blankets in the prow, amidships, and at the tiller. One of the sailors came with him below to fetch rations, and then left them alone again.

The day began to darken. Henry lit a small lantern fastened to the wall by an iron bracket. It gave a dim light with dancing shadows. Miss Meacham seemed to recede into them, becoming a less visible presence. Yet he was more intensely aware of her. So many of their closest encounters had taken place in the dark. He remembered each minute of every one.

"Have you ever done anything like this before in your life?" she asked after a while.

"Just like this? No."

"What is the rashest thing you've ever done?"

Henry thought about it. "My brothers and I got into various sorts of mischief, mostly involving horses. I tried to stand on my hands in the saddle once. But that was more…"

"Playful than this," she suggested. "Though dangerous, I suppose."

"Yes."

"Did you manage it?"

"No." Henry laughed. "Astra, my mount, took strong exception to the flapping stirrups and the change in my balance. He stopped short and looked around with stark incredulity. When he saw I was upside down, he tried to bite me. I nearly fell off."

"Nearly! I would have thought a fall inevitable."

"Sticking to the saddle like a burr is a Deeping family tradition."

"And if one can't manage that?"

Henry had never thought about it. "We all do."

"Your mother as well?"

"She's a fine rider. My father proposed to her after she beat him in a race." Miss Meacham laughed softly. Henry loved the sound of it in the dim lantern light. "I suppose going out in breeches must be your answer to the original question," he said.

"I wouldn't call that rash," she replied. "It was a carefully considered decision. The only way I could gather information that..."

Nobody had asked her to find, Henry finished silently. He didn't say it. But he knew how it rankled. That was why they were here, partly. Mostly, perhaps. As a kind of gift. He hoped it would end well. "And this journey. Did we consider carefully?"

"Rather than fling ourselves into it with wild abandon?" she asked, amusement still in her voice.

And now Henry regretted another conversation where he couldn't see her expression. His thoughts fixing on the phrase *wild abandon*, he wished for more light.

"As for rash, let me count the ways." She gestured broadly. "I ran away from home when I was eight years old."

"A disagreement with your parents?" Henry asked, remembering times when he had stomped off into the countryside to cool down.

"Not exactly *with* them. I was hardly ever with them as they were hardly ever home. Because of them, rather. They'd gone off on another diplomatic mission, leaving me to the servants and my governess. Again. I was heartily sick of that arrangement and decided to go to my grandfather. I judged I could walk the twenty miles to London, given time."

"That does seem rash," Henry said. The thought of that determined little girl marching along the road was poignant. And frightening.

"I had a knapsack of food and clean linen. Sturdy boots too. A good coat and a stout walking stick. No money. They never gave me any money."

Something in her tone made his heart ache. "It sounds as if you were prepared." Though not for the perils that could befall an unprotected child.

"I wanted a pistol. But there was none in the house. My grandfather had told me never to go out adventuring without ample supplies, as you could never know what might happen."

"I wish I had met him."

She made a small affirmative sound. "It was rash, of course. I might have met the wrong sort of person and… regretted it."

"Did you reach your grandfather's house?"

"Oh no. They caught up with me the next day. I slept too long in a hayrick and was discovered."

Henry had to be glad of it.

"I was confined to the house for weeks after that, like a naughty pet."

"I'm sure your parents didn't think of you as…"

"They didn't think of me at all, Mr. Deeping. I was much happier later with Grandfather."

"It's too bad they didn't send you to school," said Henry. "That seems a better solution."

"I agree. I don't know why they didn't."

"Charlotte loved her school, and you would have liked her and her friends."

"But would your sister have liked me?"

"She does. She said so."

"She did?" Miss Meacham leaned forward so that the lantern light fell over her face. She looked eager.

"Yes," replied Henry. Indeed, his sister had taken to this unique young lady—Miss Brown as she was thought to be then—before he did.

"We parted rather...abruptly."

Henry wondered at the unease in her voice.

"Do you think, if I wrote to her...?"

"She would reply, of course."

"Even though I wouldn't tell her my real name? I thought I would never see her again," she added in excuse.

"I'm sure she would answer. Charlotte always wants to know everything."

Miss Meacham drew back into the shadows. "I hope we can tell her how this chase turns out."

"She would be delighted to hear the tale. Though eaten up with envy, of course."

This earned Henry another soft laugh.

Silence descended on the cabin. The deck rocked beneath them. Water hissed and gurgled on the other side of the wooden hull. "I don't want to be simply rash," Miss Meacham said quietly then. "I want to be *effective*. In more than a petty way."

"Yes."

"I don't suppose you can understand how dispiriting it is to long for action and be denied any outlet."

She'd said similar things before, but here and now it seemed more plaintive. "Oh, I can," replied Henry.

Clothing rustled in the dimness. She'd turned to gaze at him.

Moved to his depths, Henry told her the story of his youthful military ambitions, his injury, and the collapse of his plans into months of pain. He never talked about that to anyone. Yet he found it natural to tell her. As if it was something she needed to know.

"I'm sorry you had to endure that," she said into the silence when he'd finished.

"You don't think it was my own fault for riding recklessly?"

"I? That is the last thing I would ever say. Do you imagine you were riding any differently than you always had?"

"No." He had considered it, of course. Even believed it in his lowest moments. But he didn't now.

"That is what they do. Those who want to keep us from wanting, trying. They blame us for any setback. It is always our inadequacy—rather than purposeful obstacles or unavoidable circumstances or mere bad luck—that stops us. And that is a lie." She reached out. Her hand was slender and white in the wavering lantern light.

Henry took it. Her fingers were chilly. So were his. But they warmed each other. He held on. So did she. And in that moment, Henry knew that he wanted to shape his future with this intrepid young lady and no one else. Whatever that required, he would give.

The urge to pull her across the cabin and into his arms was nearly irresistible. But footsteps across the deck over their heads emphasized what Henry already knew. This was not the time or place, even if she wanted what he did. He had to let go.

Reluctantly, he did so.

He sat back. So did she. He couldn't see her violet eyes, but he thought she was staring at him. The small cabin held them like a giant guardian's cupped hands. Henry breathed in the intoxicating scent of her. There was much to do before the future could be considered. And no guarantee of how the next few days would go. "We should get some rest," he said.

They lay down on the bunks, adding blankets to their cloaks for warmth. The boat would rock them toward slumber. "Sweet dreams," said Henry.

The low throaty laugh that came in response set him aflame. What was she thinking of, to laugh like that?

With only a few feet separating them, Henry could hear her breathing slow into sleep. They would be alone together for days—a responsibility and an honor and a sore temptation. He would ignore the latter, naturally, fighting his longing like the gentleman he was.

Fifteen

WAKING WITH FIRST LIGHT, KATE WAS SURPRISED BY THE movement of the bed under her. She needed a moment to remember where she was—in the cabin of the Duke of Tereford's yacht on the way to Calais. It was not a dream. She had actually done it. They had.

Henry Deeping lay on the opposite bunk, his face smoothed in sleep. Their conversation in the dimness last night came back to her as she gazed at him. At times, that talk had seemed more intimate than caresses. She didn't think she'd ever felt closer to another person in her life.

In the growing brightness, she could look her fill at his face. Not stunningly handsome, like his friend the duke. Better than that, Kate thought, with her knowledge of the admirable character behind that high forehead and narrow chin, those strong cheekbones. His long dark eyelashes brushed the top of them. His lips were a little parted. Those lips! She'd dreamed of him last night, but the memory was jumbled—not as clear as those earlier elaborate scenes. She wondered why, since he was so much nearer to her here.

It occurred to Kate that this was what he would look like if one woke beside him after a night of passion—sleeping in the sated aftermath. And then she noted that they would be traveling together for the next little while and might find themselves even closer than they were now. Close enough to reach out and touch, to rouse drowsiness into desire. A wave of heat passed over her body at the idea, like a sudden plunge into steaming water. She had never woken next to any man, of course, still less one she loved. What would one say? Then she realized that in those circumstances there would be no need to *say* anything. Lips, and hands, would convey all.

Henry Deeping's dark eyes opened, looking directly into hers. Light reflected off the sea sparkled golden in their depths. Kate felt a sort of glorious pain in the region of her heart. He blinked once, and then again, as if he didn't quite believe what he saw. Then memory flowed back into his gaze. "Good morning, Mi…Rob," he said.

"Good morning," Kate whispered.

They stared at each other, in bed but not quite together. Yet more so than they would ever have imagined a few weeks ago. Kate trembled with longing. How she wanted to reach out to him! How easy it would be. And how impossible!

He looked away, pushed back the blankets, sat up, and ran a hand through his dark hair, tousling it further. "We must be nearly to France," he said, strain evident in his voice.

With a villain to pursue and a mystery to solve. Practical concerns descended on Kate. She put a hand to her head. The cap had slipped half off in the night, and her braids had loosened a little. She needed to redo them. She felt grubby after sleeping in her clothes, but of course that had been the only choice. She wondered if the crew had looked in on them during the night, and if any of them suspected her true identity. She could only rely on Tereford's trust of his men.

Henry Deeping rose, pulled on his cloak, and went up on deck, tactfully leaving her to make ready for the day. Kate set about renewing her appearance as young Rob. She refused to bemoan the absence of a basin of hot water or a cup of tea. She was not such a poor creature.

After a while, Mr. Deeping called down, "Captain Bailes says another hour or so to the Calais harbor. The *Kestrel* is still up ahead of us."

Kate gathered the remaining provisions and carried them up to be shared out among passengers and crew.

The sun climbed higher. It was a bracing late February day, clouds scudding in from the north. Bailes said he was glad that they wouldn't be sailing in the rain that was clearly on the way. "Tereford hoped there'd be mud," murmured Henry Deeping. Oddly.

The *Sea Nymph* maneuvered in toward the Calais docks, moving more nimbly than their quarry. They tied up well away from the *Kestrel*'s berth, and Kate and Henry Deeping prepared to disembark.

Bailes worked with brisk efficiency, sending one of his crew to watch the *Kestrel* and see where her passengers went and the other to fetch the helpers he'd mentioned.

The latter returned first, bringing two sturdy young men with him—one blond and blue-eyed, and the other darker of skin and hair. Henry took in the rough neatness of their clothes, the intelligence in their expressions, and their air of casual physical competence. He wouldn't want to exchange blows with this pair. They'd likely put him on the ground in short order. He found he was relieved to have them. He would have discovered how to hire transport or whatever they needed from here. He had the funds to pay. But things would go much more easily with local knowledge and fluent French speakers.

"This is Rene Henderson," said Captain Bailes. The stockier blond nodded a greeting. "And Etienne Jordaine." The darker young man did the same. "The duke has employed them on a number of matters. I know them to be reliable. They will help you as needed."

"Thank you for coming," Henry said.

"His Grace asks, and we arrive," said Henderson. He had a slight Continental accent, hardly noticeable, but his gesture was very French. "We are glad to do whatever he needs." Jordaine nodded amiably.

Henry knew he should say this wasn't really Tereford's venture, but he didn't. He introduced "Rob Jones" instead.

Henderson looked at Miss Meacham, paused, and then looked carefully away. Henry suspected that he'd penetrated her disguise and was perhaps slightly shocked. But he didn't intend to say anything about it. Neither did the *Sea Nymph's* crew, if they had guessed. That was the important thing. His friend the duke really had done them a great service by providing them with these trustworthy fellows, Henry thought.

The other crew member returned just then with his report. Three men had left the *Kestrel*—a small "gentlemanly" fellow and two bruisers. Rankin and his thugs, Henry supplied silently. It had to be. "The biggest one don't care much for sailing," the young crewman added. "Puked his guts out on the crossing, seemingly. He were complaining about it for all the street to hear. Cursing at the sea."

This amused everyone.

"The smaller one told him to shut his face and stop drawing attention," the sailor continued. "I figured the big 'un would cut up stiff at that. But he didn't."

"The little man is the boss," said Rene Henderson.

"I reckon."

"Did you catch any names?" asked Miss Meacham in her rasping voice.

She was right, Henry thought. They should not assume.

"When they got to an inn," replied the young sailor. "I heard them say Rankin."

Henry met Miss Meacham's triumphant gaze.

"Which inn was it?" asked Henderson.

"Le Lapin Noir," answered the crewman, his French pronunciation very English.

"That's a rum place." Henderson gave Miss Meacham a quick sidelong glance. "Wouldn't want to be going in there if we don't have to."

"I don't believe we do," Henry replied. "I don't think these men will be staying in Calais. We want to see where they go and what they do."

"Right." Henderson nodded to his companion. Etienne Jordaine gave them a salute and left the yacht, presumably to keep watch on the inn.

"We'll wait here for a bit in case you want to sail back to England," said Captain Bailes.

"I don't know how long we may be." With that statement, the enormity of what they were doing descended on Henry. How long would Rankin travel? Where did he intend to go? They couldn't follow him indefinitely. He glanced at Miss Meacham and saw the same realization in her face.

Bailes shrugged. "We've no other task unless the duke should send for us."

Henry knew he wouldn't while they were gone.

"I'd appreciate word if we're not needed," Bailes added.

"Of course," said Henry. With that, they picked up the bundles they had brought and left the *Sea Nymph*.

"I can recommend a decent place to stay," said Henderson on the dock. "Depending on your purse…"

"The best place you know where we will not attract undue attention," said Henry.

This answer clearly pleased their helper. One would prefer employers to be plump in the pocket, Henry acknowledged, even with Tereford's resources in the background. They started walking, Henderson leading the way.

"You live in Calais?" asked Miss Meacham in her grumbly lad's voice.

"Always have," said Henderson. "My dad was English, and my mother is French, which didn't make for an easy life while the war was going on. As it did for half my life."

"We are all glad to have it over," she answered.

Henderson nodded. He indicated a turn down a narrower lane with a gesture. His ease of manner and sure sense of direction made them unobtrusive—three plainly dressed people walking with a clear goal in mind. This was much better than two obvious foreigners wandering an unknown town, Henry thought. Tereford had done them a greater service than he knew. Or perhaps he did.

After fifteen minutes, they came to a hostelry called La Belle Dame. Inside, the premises were clean and well kept. A tall Frenchman approached, wiping his hands on a rag. "Etienne will find us here when he has news," Henderson told them in a low voice. "Better not to speak English before the staff. If you do not wish to draw attention."

Henry nodded. "We require two rooms," he said in French. He didn't look at Miss Meacham.

Henderson's nod was bland. He left them to speak to the landlord. His French was rapid and fluent, Henry noticed as they walked off together.

"I don't suppose I could have a bath," Miss Meacham murmured very quietly.

"Well…"

"No, of course I can't. That would shatter the illusion. I think Mr. Henderson already suspects me."

She was quick to have seen the signs. "He may."

"I suppose we must be glad he is discerning. And trustworthy. I must be more careful." She sighed. "Well, at least I will have a room to myself."

"I hope you know I would never…"

"I just want to loose my braids," she interrupted with an impatience he didn't understand. And a little too loud. "They are so tight they give me a headache."

A few minutes later they were conducted to side-by-side rooms on an upper floor. Kate found the accommodations spare but neat and comfortable. Mr. Henderson seemed to know what he was doing. She shot the bolt on the door and unfastened her braids, which was a great relief. Running her fingers through her hair, she rubbed her scalp vigorously. She'd never remained in her lad's persona for such a long time. The ruse was tiring—to remember every moment, in every way, that she was Rob, not Kate.

She lay down for a bit and thought over the journey so far, wondering how they would have managed without the Duke of Tereford's help. They would have found a way, she told herself. They were resourceful. But she had to admit that this was easier. She dozed briefly on the thin mattress that did not rock beneath her and woke to find that she missed the sight of Henry Deeping's face across from her.

Jordaine returned that evening with the news that Rankin had secured horses for an early morning departure. Speaking French in the inn's common room, even though there was no one seated near them, he said he had left a watcher at Le Lapin Noir. "I spoke to Dubois," he told Henderson, who seemed to be the leader of the pair.

"He has decent hired mounts," the blond man added. He glanced at Kate. "Unless you prefer a carriage? It would be more awkward to follow riders, but…"

Understanding that the question was addressed to her skills, Kate searched for a French verb and then said, "I ride fairly well." Her grandfather had seen that she learned, though she hadn't had much opportunity to practice. She *was* apprehensive about remaining in the saddle for whole days at a time, but she pushed this worry aside. "Mr. Deeping is very good. His family"—she looked for a word again and settled for—"makes fine horses."

"Breeds them," Mr. Deeping supplied.

Kate supposed the Deepings would know how to speak of their business in different languages. Their horses were renowned beyond England. With some amusement, she wondered what he would think of the hired mounts. His taste in horseflesh was refined.

When she asked him the next day, he characterized the animals as adequate. "Not slugs, but a bit dull and plodding. Hired horses tend to be. I understand they're better than the ones Rankin procured."

For her part, Kate was thankful not to be put on a prancing, spirited horse that would constantly challenge her skills.

They set off right after breakfast. Rene Henderson rode with them, while Jordaine went off on his own. "We sent several men out along the main roads leaving Calais," Henderson told them. "They'll watch for your party and bring word which way they've gone."

Kate had seen Mr. Deeping hand over a sum of money to their guide. This would pay the observers as well, she assumed.

"They are taking care not to be noticed," Mr. Deeping said.

"Right. The ones from the routes the travelers haven't used will come back, and we will substitute them for those who could have been seen."

"And so, we won't have to go too close to them. Well done."

Kate had to agree. Tereford had chosen his helpers well.

"You seem very good at this," Mr. Deeping added. He

sounded curious, and Kate understood. She too wondered why the duke would need expert lurkers.

"I try to be good at whatever is required," Henderson replied repressively.

Following the information brought to them through the day, they rode south and east. Kate was all right for the first two hours, but after that her body began to protest. The saddle seemed to grow wider, the horse's gait more jolting. Muscles she wasn't accustomed to using started to ache.

"They're not heading to Paris," Henderson observed as one of his troop reported in. "They've turned off the main road. More southerly." He rode a little ahead with his watcher, who spoke rapidly in French and pointed.

"Where can Rankin be going?" Kate asked Henry Deeping quietly. "And why?"

He shrugged, controlling his mount with mere touches of his knees, she noted enviously, and sitting in the saddle as if it was a cushioned armchair. "How long do we intend to follow?" he asked more practically. "Two days? Three? More?"

Kate nearly groaned at the idea of many days on horseback. Yet she had no intention of giving up. "Could one of Henderson's men speak to them? Strike up a casual conversation and see if they would reveal their destination?"

"We can inquire."

But Henderson preferred to wait before trying this ploy. "My fellows know how to fade into the background," he said. "But they are not subtle in conversation, and they don't have much English."

The rode on through the afternoon. Kate's legs were screaming with pain when word came that Rankin and his men had stopped for the night. "Either they're going a much greater distance, or they're not in a hurry," Henderson observed. "Otherwise they'd push on and not worry about their dinner."

"The Londoners may not be great riders," Kate murmured.

"Or ready to deprive themselves when they think they have a cushy job," said Henry Deeping.

Henderson took this in, as he did every detail they let drop, then went to confer with his informant. "Marais will watch their inn," he told them as the man rode off again. "They've chosen the best one along this route, I'm afraid. Indeed the only established place. But Marais says there is a village nearby with a small sort of…tavern. With perhaps a room or two." His glance at Kate was dubious.

Ready to lie in a hayrick if it would get her out of the saddle, Kate said, "I'm sure it will be fine."

It wasn't, really. The nameless establishment was a low ramshackle building, really just a village dwelling that sold liquor in its front room. Kate hoped it wasn't too dirty and resigned herself to the fact if it was.

"We could go on," Mr. Deeping said.

"No." Kate managed not to moan the word.

"I'll go and speak to them," Henderson said. "We will contrive something."

Henry Deeping dismounted with maddening grace. Kate hauled one leg over the saddle, suppressing a groan.

She turned and slid down, clinging to the stirrup with both hands. Her feet reached the ground. Her legs gave way. She sank into a heap on the earth.

In an instant Mr. Deeping was beside her. "What is it? What's wrong?"

Kate would have thought it obvious, but he was so completely at home on horseback that it was not, to him. "I'm not accustomed to riding for so long," she replied. She rose slowly, painfully, to her hands and knees. Her muscles protested. "I don't know if I can get up," she had to admit.

He bent and put an arm around her waist, raising her with easy strength.

Kate rested against his side. "Don't let go."

Holding her, he looked down, his dark eyes concerned. "I'm sorry. I should have thought… You should have said you needed a rest."

"We were pursuing villains."

Henderson came out. "The landlady is a trifle put out. She's a widow who earns a living selling drink, and this is just her home. But she was swayed by the coin I offered, and there is one room you can have. The place looks clean enough."

"Splendid," said Kate as both the men hesitated. It was better than a hayrick. She tried to move. Her thighs offered strong objections. She put an arm around Henry Deeping, to join his around her, and limped painfully inside.

The few men drinking in the front room looked amazed to see them. A thin, anxious-looking woman bustled forward and led them to a room at the back of the small place. Kate suspected it was her own bedchamber. She'd see that they paid her very well, Kate thought. She let her cloak drop and collapsed on the bed.

"Is the young man hurt?" the landlady asked in French. She picked up the cloak, assessing its quality with quick fingers.

"Merely worn out," Mr. Deeping responded in the same language. "He will be well after a rest."

"I will bring wine," she answered and went out.

"I don't want any wine," Kate murmured.

"No, that's not what you need. Wait here."

As if she could go anywhere, Kate thought as he departed. As if she wanted to so much as twitch. She only wanted to lie still and not encourage her body to hurt any more than it already did.

Their hostess returned with a mug, a plate of stew, and a hunk of bread. She said something in rapid accented French. Kate had no idea what. She tried a smile and a brief, "*Bon.*"

This seemed to suffice. The woman nodded and disappeared.

Kate looked at the food. She was hungry, but the thought of moving, even to feed herself, was not appealing. How was she going to ride tomorrow? She could hardly stand up. She'd become a drag on their expedition. What sort of adventurer was this? A tear escaped and ran down the side of her cheek.

After what seemed like a very long time, Henry Deeping returned. "I had to ask around the village," he said. "The blacksmith had some of this." He held up a small jar.

"What is it?"

"Liniment. You will feel better once you rub it in."

"Isn't that for horses?"

"It is good for any creature with strained muscles."

Kate supposed he would know. Without sitting up, she took the jar and unscrewed the cap. Even her fingers hurt. A pungent herbal scent escaped into the room—sharp but not unpleasant.

Mr. Deeping sniffed. "That smells right. It will help."

Kate put down the jar and slowly sat up. Her back twinged, but not nearly as much as her legs. "I don't think I can take off my breeches."

"I'll get the landlady to…"

"Reveal my imposture to one and all," Kate finished. "We can't ask her. In fact, can the door be latched? We don't want anyone coming in."

He went, found a fastening, and attached it.

"You must help me undress," said Kate then.

Henry Deeping whirled to stare at her. "I can't do that!"

"You would leave me to suffer instead?"

He put a hand on the latch as if to go. "Surely you can get out of your clothes." His gaze was reticent and hungry at the same time.

Kate experienced a moment of disorientation. This was like the beginning of one of her dreams about him—the start of a passionate interlude that would leave her wildly frustrated. Only this was reality. He was here. She was. Within touching distance. And there was no one to care what they did.

She *could* remove her clothes. It would be painful but not

of course impossible. But she wanted... She wanted him to undress her. The idea flamed through her, making her aches less noticeable. She pushed at the lapels of her coat, groaned a bit artistically. "Come pull this off."

He took a step closer, looking like a man resisting the irresistible. His dark eyes had gone a little blurred. Kate beckoned. He approached the bed, reached out, drew back, reached out again. She poked at the coat.

Carefully, he eased it over her shoulders and down her back. Kate pulled her arms out of the sleeves. She was sitting on the tails. She put her arms around his waist. "You will have to lift me," she murmured into his chest.

His breath caught. She felt it in his body and enjoyed the sensation. He smelled of horse and healthy male.

He lifted her, jerked the coat free, and tossed it to the end of the bed. Then he let her go as if she'd burned him. Kate bounced a little on the coarse bedding.

"Shoes and stockings," she said, moving her feet back and forth.

"You do not know what you are..."

"I do know," she interrupted. She held his gaze, commanding him to continue. He stared at her like a starving creature. "Go on," she said.

He removed her low boots and set them aside as if they were precious and not her grandfather's aged footgear. Turning to the stockings, he eased them down. His hands on her calves were tantalizing caresses.

Kate untied her neckcloth and flung it away. Her aches were nearly forgotten in a welter of arousal. "Breeches," she breathed.

"I can't."

She undid the fastenings and pushed the breeches over her hips. She wore a brief singlet under them. She wriggled, and her strained muscles made their presence felt more sharply. Her moan was echoed by a tortured sound from Henry Deeping. "You rub the liniment in?" she asked him. It was half question, half demand.

"I can't," he repeated.

Kate took his hand, dipped the tips of his fingers into the open jar, and ran them down her thigh. "I need you," she said.

"No gentleman would…"

She guided his hand over her skin. "I'm a free-spirited adventurer on an important quest, not a wilting debutante. And I want you." Releasing his hand, she reached up and pulled him down to a kiss that matched the searing embraces of her dreams.

His resistance seemed to crumble after that. He drew her close and joined her in a round of increasingly dizzying kisses. Kate still felt her aches, but they seemed a much more distant thing, overtaken by a torrent of longing. One of his knees slid between hers, and she welcomed it.

She began to undo and push at his clothes. He joined in with jerks and panting fumbles until finally they were both naked, skin to burning skin. His hands were so much more skillful than the vague caresses of her dreams. He found all the places that had been enflamed by those fantasies and tended to them, triggering the release she had longed for all those nights.

At the ultimate moment, he said, "If you would prefer not…"

"I would prefer *to*," Kate said, capturing his lips once again.

They came together in a rush. She was so aroused that the small pain was nothing. She moved with him in a sort of wonder. And exultation. This was the thing her dreams had tried to grasp. This was the reality behind all those suggestive images in her parents' collection.

He reached his own peak with a muffled cry. Kate savored the sound. They panted together. He gathered her close to his side.

After a while, when their pulses had slowed and breathing grown even, he massaged the liniment into all her sore muscles. These prolonged tender attentions led to a repeat of their lovemaking, and it was late when Kate felt into a sated sleep.

Sixteen

HENRY WOKE TO THE RAP OF KNUCKLES ON A WOODEN door. He opened his eyes and discovered an unfamiliar rustic bedchamber. When he turned his head, he found Kate Meacham beside him, her naked limbs tossed in lovely abandon. The pleasures of the night rushed back into his consciousness.

"Monsieur Deeping?" It was Henderson's voice outside the door. He spoke in French. "Our friends are on the move. We'd best be going."

Her eyes opened. Kate's. Henry really couldn't think of her as Miss Meacham any longer. He searched their violet depths for remorse, embarrassment, accusation. He found only warmth. And perhaps—delight? The thrill of that was glorious, even though another part of him wondered what they thought they were doing.

He searched for words that fit the situation and found not a one.

"Good morning," she murmured.

His lips parted to respond with some tender endearment, and his stomach growled, loud, emphatically unromantic. He'd had no dinner the previous night, and judging from the plate of congealed stew on the table beside the bed, neither had she.

"Monsieur?" Henderson said.

"We will be with you momentarily," he called out in French.

His companion, his exquisite love, made a small disappointed sound.

It made Henry shiver. He'd never felt so aroused and tender and uncertain all at once. "Rankin is leaving," he said quietly. Of course she had heard, but what else should he say?

"And thus so must we."

"Unless we wish to abandon this impulsive pursuit and… turn our minds to other matters."

She gazed at him, actually seeming to consider it. Then she shook her head and sat up. "Ha. The liniment helped."

"Movement and stretching are good for the muscles as well."

She met his eyes with a smile that fired Henry's blood even more, which he had not thought possible. She extended her arms above her head, arcing her spine in a way that made her breasts rise in invitation. He reached for her. Her smile broadened. "Tonight perhaps," she said and turned away to rise, giving him a view of another shapely part of her anatomy.

He gazed and longed, and then tore his eyes away. If he watched her dress, he could not answer for the consequences. Fighting down his intense arousal with thoughts of icy waters and the strangers waiting on the other side of the door, he donned his own clothes. Kate rebraided her hair with deft fingers and pulled on her cap. She gave him a nod as she went to the door and unlatched it. Henry walked out on her heels, thinking he would follow her anywhere in the world. She need only lift a finger, and he would... She was Rob, he reminded himself, a stalwart lad, not the glorious woman of his dreams.

Jordaine was in the front room along with Henderson. Bowls of porridge also awaited them, along with small mugs of weak ale. There was no tea or coffee in a place such as this. They devoured them, took bread and cheese along to eat in the saddle, and went to mount up. Kate made no complaint as he helped her onto her horse, though he imagined her muscles protested.

"Our friends are heading for Saint-Omer," Henderson said when they were under way. "It is the first place of consequence on this road they have taken." He waited a moment as if expecting Henry to comment, then went on. "Jordaine has been asking questions of travelers coming from that direction. You are aware that the new English queen has arrived in the town?"

"What?" exclaimed Henry and Kate in unison.

Henderson examined them. "I wondered if perhaps you knew this?"

"We did not." Ideas tumbled through Henry's mind. "But it might explain..."

"I think we must go faster," Kate said in a wavering version of her lad's voice.

Henry nodded.

"It is time to catch up with these people?" their guide asked.

"Yes."

"And you fear trouble?"

"Now that you have told me this news, I do." All that Henry had been told about the new king's hatred of his wife ran through him mind. This was a perilous development.

Henderson looked at Jordaine. The latter made a gesture of acknowledgment and urged his horse into a gallop. In a few minutes, he had disappeared around a curve in the road. "He will meet us at the edge of Saint-Omer," Henderson said. "And tell us where these men have gone to roost."

They increased their pace. Henry caught a grimace on Kate's face, but she made no complaint. She never would, he thought. She was indomitable.

"Perhaps you will inform me now of our goal?" Henderson asked. "I wish to be as helpful as possible. This is easier if I know what is going on."

Henry exchanged a long glance with Kate. He saw the same apprehension and resolve he was feeling in her eyes. "We think these men may be planning to harm the queen," Henry said.

Henderson gaped at him.

"We have…reason to believe that the new King George would like her…"

"Eliminated," rasped Kate.

"What?" Henderson looked back and forth as if he hoped one of them would say they were joking.

"Perhaps simply intimidated," said Henry.

Kate merely growled.

"Will there be English authorities in Saint-Omer?" Henry asked.

"Authorities?" Henderson frowned at him and shrugged eloquently. "Of what sort? It is not Calais or Paris. Not a place for ambassadors. There might be an English merchant or two. But also perhaps not."

"It's up to us to save her," said Kate.

Henry was afraid she was right. Henderson was clearly appalled.

―――――

For the rest of their ride to Saint-Omer, Kate's mind worked furiously. She scarcely noticed the pains of riding astride. Rankin's intentions obsessed her. She knew the man was capable of villainy. Indeed, it was, in a manner of speaking, his profession. He hired himself out for ill deeds, not to carry messages or negotiate agreements. He had no benign reason to travel to the town where Queen Caroline was. He'd procured poison. He'd brought two thugs, fellows primed for violence. It seemed he could have only one object.

Kate didn't believe the new king had openly ordered the assassination of his despised wife. She didn't admire George IV. Her grandfather had thought him spoiled and fickle and monstrously selfish. But she couldn't imagine George would sink that low. The toadeaters and office-seekers who surrounded him were another matter. He associated with dubious characters, and they had even more ruthless connections. George's incessant complaints, his peevishly wishing his wife away, might well have encouraged others—such as Quentin Matthews—to think of removing her by force and to search out someone to do so. Once Queen Caroline was dead, the king would deny all knowledge of the attack, of course. He would probably mourn ostentatiously, while feeling relief and even triumph. "He is a pig," she muttered.

"What?"

Kate turned and found Henry gazing at her. The warmth in his dark eyes sent tenderness and desire prickling through her, along with a spike of elation. Her thoughts veered back to their night together. When people spoke of dreams coming true, they did not usually mean something so…lusciously specific, she thought with a small smile. She'd reached for what she wanted, savored the result, and was not the least bit sorry about that. Not the least bit.

Her mind caught on one concern. She did not wish to have a child—a son or daughter who would bring a weight of responsibility. She had been that to her parents, Kate supposed. She did not intend to do as they had.

She would not have conceived last night. She knew her body's timing, explained by unauthorized reading in her grandfather's library. But if she and Henry continued… Kate's smile returned. Her parents' collection had shown that there were other paths to pleasure that they could enjoy.

"What are we going to do?" Henry asked.

Henderson was riding a bit ahead, out of earshot. "Repeat, with variations?" Kate dared.

"What?"

Would she show him her parents' collection? Would he

be scandalized or intrigued? Probably both, as she had been, and still sometimes was, to be honest.

"Variations?" He looked confused. "To deal with Rankin, you mean?"

He'd meant their current mission, not their night together. Kate didn't blush. She was through with blushing, she thought. It was a waste of…warmth. But she did bring her thoughts back to the present. "Would you agree, putting together all we have learned, that he means to poison the queen?"

Henry nodded. "To try, at any rate. I don't know how he expects to manage it. It's an insane idea."

"She is not in the royal court surrounded by servants and guards."

"But she will have people around her."

Kate nodded. "We must go to them, and to her, in Saint-Omer and warn them. At once."

"If she will see us."

"From what people say, she is not terribly high in the instep." Kate grinned. Despite the ominous situation, she couldn't help but be happy. "You can tell her you are the best friend of the Duke of Tereford."

Henry responded with a wry grimace. "Second best. The duchess has taken my place."

"Good for her. It is still a noble…reference, however. And you are an official English diplomat, of course."

"Traveling with a master of distraction and exaggeration."

Kate laughed. "There is my proper profession! Perhaps I will have cards made up."

"You are in a fine mood."

She held his gaze. "Yes. I am."

Henry's dark eyes lit. She never found out what he might have said, however, as Henderson fell back to join them and point out the town of Saint-Omer just ahead.

Jordaine met them as promised with the name of the inn where Rankin had gone. He had also discovered where Queen Caroline and her attendants were staying. "She has only a few people with her," he told them. "Her arrival caused a sensation in this provincial place. The gossips say she is preparing to return to England to assert her claim to the throne."

"Assert?" asked Henderson. "Is she not the king's wife?"

Jordaine shrugged.

"They are at odds," replied Kate. "The new king was dissatisfied with the marriage from the very beginning. It has been a scandal for years."

Henderson shook his head.

Jordaine led them through narrow lanes to a small clean hostelry well away from where Rankin had gone. "So we will try to see the queen as soon as possible," Henry said when they had approved the rooms.

Kate nodded. "We don't know when Rankin might make a move."

"Surely he will need a little time to set his plans in motion."

"Yes. I suppose I will have to return to skirts."

"If the queen noticed your disguise…"

"From what I have heard of her, she would probably laugh."

"Perhaps. We cannot know."

Kate couldn't resist a small test. "And if I insist on going as Rob Jones? In my comfortable breeches?"

"I will argue with you," Henry replied. "Pointing out the drawbacks of that and the advantages of your normal dress."

"Such as?" She was teasing him, mostly. She also wanted to see how he would take her opposition.

"If they see through your disguise, they might conclude we are deceptive persons and be less likely to believe us. Also, a woman's viewpoint and opinion might make a difference with the queen. She has been maligned by a host of King George's men."

Silently, Kate admitted these were good points. "And if I still refuse?"

Henry shrugged. "I will make do."

Not forbid her to join him or expose her imposture to force her to abandon it. Not shout at her until she conceded. Henry Deeping was everything one could wish for in a man, Kate thought. "The gown I brought is probably a mass of creases," she said. "I will ask the landlady if she can do anything with it."

"You are giving in?" asked Henry, looking surprised.

"No! Having heard your arguments, I am agreeing that they make sense."

The gratification that showed in his face was one of the finest compliments Kate had ever received.

They washed and changed into the finer clothes they had brought. When Kate emerged from her room as a young lady, their two guides looked startled but not entirely surprised.

She had given herself away in the close confines of the boat, she decided. She'd never tried to keep up the illusion for such a long period.

Resuming their travel-worn cloaks, she and Henry put the hoods up and followed Jordaine through Saint-Omer to the queen's lodgings.

"They say her household is managed by an Italian man called Bartolomeo Pergami," the guide murmured as he showed them the way. "He is her majordomo and…so it is said, very good friend."

"So he is someone we will have to take into account," Kate replied. "Well, if I were married to King George, I would be looking for very good friends."

A sputtering laugh emerged from the hood of Henry Deeping's cloak.

Jordaine brought them to a house near the center of town. When he had pointed it out, he said, "It is better if I am not seen."

"A watch will be kept on Rankin and his men?" asked Henry.

"*Bien sûr.*" Jordaine faded back into an alley.

Kate put back her hood. Henry followed suit. They walked to the door, and he knocked. When a maid opened it, he said, "We have come from England to see Queen Caroline." He spoke in English, then repeated the sentence in French, using her title very clearly. He did the same repetition with, "I am employed by the Foreign Office."

The woman looked uncertain, but she let them in and asked them to wait while she inquired. They stood in the small front hall for several minutes. Then the servant returned and told them they could come up. Leaving their cloaks with her, they walked upstairs and into a cramped parlor. It was an odd place to find a monarch.

The plump fair-haired woman who sat in a chair by the blazing hearth and examined them with somewhat prominent blue eyes did not look particularly queenly. Her gown was rich but not perfectly clean. Her nails were a bit grubby as well. Her expression was mocking. They were not asked to sit down. "What does the Foreign Office want now?" she asked them without preamble. Her English had a slight accent. "Besides for me to go away, eh? Always they want me to go away. Up in smoke, if I would. *Poof!* But I am the queen, no matter what George may wish was true. And I mean to go and tell him so. The people will cheer me when I arrive."

That was forthright, Kate thought. They said Queen Caroline spoke her mind—too readily, some felt. Others called her loud and vulgar. It must be dreadful to be always under scrutiny. Every word and move picked apart and judged. Especially when one had no support from one's royal spouse.

They had agreed that Henry must be the one to begin. No one would imagine that Kate had any official capacity. They had also decided it was pointless to beat around the bush. "We have come here to warn you, Your Majesty," he said. "We followed a man from England, where he called himself Rankin. We think he wishes you ill."

"Rankin," she answered. She glanced to one side, where there was a small table piled with papers. "Such a man has written to say he brings me letters from George."

"I don't think that is true," Henry said.

"I didn't believe him," Queen Caroline replied with a flip of her fingers. "George does not write me now. He orders others to do that. To threaten and revile me. Accuse me of adultery." Her loud, raucous laugh filled the room. "I have committed adultery only one time, with the husband of Mrs. Fitzherbert."

Kate was startled at this declaration. It was widely known that Mrs. Fitzherbert had been Prince George's mistress for many years, and it was rumored that they had been secretly married, even though the lady was Catholic and thus not legally eligible to be his wife. But such things were not usually mentioned so openly. Queen Caroline was living up to her reputation for frankness.

"It is rather a joke," she continued. "A cruel jest. My mother hated my father's adulteries. And my father scorned her. They tossed me back and forth like a shuttlecock. If I was affectionate to one, the other railed at me, slapped me even. And then the very same thing came about with my own daughter." Sadness crossed her face. "Poor, dear Charlotte."

The death of one's child must be terrible, Kate thought. And when she was also the only heir to a throne, it was catastrophe.

"And so I went my own way," the queen continued. "Set up my own household where I can do as I please. I was not allowed to join in any court functions as a girl, you know, or even to dance. Not a simple dance! Is it any wonder that I want a bit of fun? George certainly has *his*." She looked at them with narrowed eyes. "Do you blame me?"

Kate did not. She pitied her, rather. But one did not say that to a queen.

"We think Rankin may have come here to do you harm," Henry said.

"Harm," the queen repeated, mouthing the word.

"He is a known villain," Henry added. "And he has brought two others with him."

"We have seen him meeting with Quentin Matthews," Kate said, finding she could not stand silently by.

"Him!" Queen Caroline spat the word. "He is a toad-eater. And a liar. He makes up the most insulting tales about me. How he thinks of such things. A vile man, with a vile mind." She looked Kate up and down. "Why have they sent a woman? Are you his wife?" She gestured at Henry. "What do they expect you to do?"

"Nothing," Kate replied. "No one sent me. I came because I wanted to help see justice done."

"Justice." The queen's laugh was more a jeer this time. "Well, you are young. You may believe in it for a while yet."

"One must if it is to continue to exist."

Queen Caroline gave her a benign look. "The people of England love me."

It was true, Kate thought. What was known as the "queen's business"—her ongoing conflict with George—had captivated the nation and excited popular feeling across the country. George was despised for the way he had treated her, as for so much else.

"All classes will ever find in me a sincere friend to their liberties, and a zealous advocate of their rights," the queen added, as if it was a statement she'd made before. Yet she seemed to mean it. The sentiment was beside the point, however.

"We know that Rankin procured poison," Kate blurted out.

Queen Caroline stared.

"If you were to die here in France, far away from the royal court, the king could deny any connection."

"But he would be very glad." The queen put a hand to her stomach. "My people won't let strangers near me."

A door concealed by the paneling opened, and a tall dark-haired man stepped into the room. "We do our best," he said in an Italian accent. "But you are speaking to strangers right now, as you insisted upon doing."

"I am not afraid."

"There is courage and there is foolishness, *cara*. We must see to this."

"George would not go so far, Bartolomeo," replied the queen.

"You think no? After he has sent spies and spread rumors to accuse you of all manner of sins?"

"All talk," she said, waving this aside. "George is a coward, at bottom."

The man, the "friend" they had been told about, Kate concluded, looked uncertain.

"The king may know nothing about it," she said. "Perhaps he would not have agreed with such a plan. Has not the... audacity. But that doesn't matter. Rankin is not all talk. And the men with him are accustomed to violence."

Henry nodded to reinforce her point.

Queen Caroline looked them up and down again. "And so? You wish?"

"To help," replied Kate.

"So I am to trust you, but not these other Englishmen?" The queen's voice was mocking. "Perhaps you are simply more clever, and subtle. The Foreign Office likes its little plots. They always hope to catch me in some slip."

That was certainly true, Kate noted. She wondered how they could prove their good intentions.

"Having spoken with us, you must make your own judgment," Henry replied.

The queen eyed him, looked at Kate again, and then back at Henry. "I am good at that. Am I not, Bartolomeo?"

"Yes, my lady."

"Even though I had no proper education and cannot spell." She continued her examination of them. It seemed to go on for quite a long time. Finally, she made a slashing gesture. "I say they are sincere," she said to the Italian.

He bowed his head to acknowledge her authority. "But young and rash, it seems," he answered.

"Oh yes. All of that. We do not know if they are competent. Or wise." The queen smiled. "Probably they are not wise."

"A watch is being kept," said Henry. He sounded a little nettled. "Rankin won't move without our knowing."

"Describe him to me," said the Italian. And when Henry had done so, he added, "No such man will enter here. Indeed, no unknown man will be admitted."

Kate and Henry returned to their lodgings satisfied with the visit. But when they entered, Henderson rushed up to tell them that Rankin, though not his hirelings, had slipped past their guard. "How?" Henry demanded.

"I do not know." Their guide's chagrin was evident in his face. "Every entry and window was under observation. The roof as well."

"An underground passage?" Henry asked.

"Jordaine says there is no proper cellar. Only a low hole where wine is kept."

Henry suppressed a curse. They had just promised the queen they would keep tabs on the man.

"It is impossible," said Henderson. "But Jordaine had one of the maids search the entire inn."

"If he could only leave by overlooked ways, then obviously he did not go as himself," said Kate. They turned to look at her. "He must have been in disguise."

It made sense that she would think of that first, Henry noted, having been disguised herself for most of this journey.

"I expect he was wearing women's clothes," she added. "Your watchers would pay a bit less attention to the women going in and out."

Henderson's grimace admitted the truth of this, though he also looked annoyed.

"Perhaps he discovered that he is being followed," Henry said.

"I would swear he has not," said Henderson. "We have been careful."

Henry didn't argue. Henderson and his men had been an

invaluable aid and extremely skillful. He and Kate certainly could not have gotten this far without them. If Rankin had noticed something here at the end, he could not complain. "I suppose he is just being cunning," he said. "We must decide what to do now."

"We must go back to the queen's lodgings," said Kate. "Or *I* must. I will take up a position in her kitchen."

"What?"

"If Rankin tries to poison her, it must go in her food or drink."

"That would kill the whole household," said Henderson.

"And you think he would care about that?" she asked.

"You believe he would not? Is he such a villain?"

She nodded.

"Must it be you—" Henry began. He knew she didn't care to be protected, but he couldn't help it.

"A man would be out of place in the kitchen," Kate answered. "Rankin would sheer off before we could catch him."

"And when he recognizes you there? He saw you in Leicestershire."

"I shall just have to be unrecognizable." She considered the matter. "Hair powder, I think. And I will see if I can borrow clothing from our landlady."

Seventeen

A MERE HOUR LATER, KATE LOOKED ENTIRELY DIFFER-
ent. Gray powder covered her honey-colored hair with a
frilled cap atop it. She wore a drab skirt and kirtle, padded
out so that they fit and to make her appear stocky. Wooden
sabots on her feet altered her gait. She couldn't move very
fast in them at first, but that was all to the good. She held
a walking stick and stood bent like a crone, so that her face
was hardly visible.

It was obvious that Henry was reluctant to let her go.
She gave him credit for not saying so. Men often seemed to
believe that all would be well if only they kept a woman by
their side, which was certainly untrue in this case. She bade
him goodbye and set out with the knowledge that friendly
observers were following her progress. Jordaine had also
put a watch around the queen's lodgings, very much on his
mettle after being fooled. Kate was conscious that they were
only paid strangers, however. Henderson and Jordaine were
the ones they could truly rely on.

Notes had been exchanged with the queen's household
and arrangements made. Kate was met by Bartolomeo
Pergami at the back door and escorted into the kitchen. He
told her that all of the staff with them here were well known

to him. They had been subject to sneaking questions about the queen for as long as they'd served her, from agents sent by her royal husband to dig up dirt. There'd been attempts to bribe them as well, to lie about the queen's doings, and they had stood firm. Thus, Pergami hadn't hesitated to tell them of this new threat. All three women—the cook and two maids—looked grim. The cook held a cleaver as if she was ready to do more than chop meat. With a dramatic flourish, Pergami showed them all the pistols he carried in his pockets before he left to sit with the queen.

Kate was settled at the far end of the long kitchen table with a pile of mending. This task let her keep on the fingerless mitts she wore, hiding the undeniable youth of her hands. She'd also requested two paring knives, which lay close by. But before all else, she took off the sabots and put on the sturdy walking shoes she had brought under her cloak. If she had to move fast, she could now do so.

The work of preparing a meal proceeded. Kate plied her needle and wondered how long she would have to wait. She didn't think Rankin would linger over his task. If he knew he had been followed, he would want to be away as soon as possible. If he did not know, he would still wish to get it over. The longer he was in Saint-Omer, the more likely he was to attract notice. The men with him could never pass as French.

Trays had been taken up to the parlor, and the servants were sitting down to their own dinner when a knock came at the back door. The four women looked at each other. The younger maid rose to answer.

"Mademoiselle," said a melodious voice when she opened

it. "I've brought mushrooms, just picked in the forest today. Very fine. Fit for a queen indeed, and so I have brought them only to you." The visitor's French was very good, Kate noted. Perhaps too refined for a humble peddler.

"You must speak to the cook," replied the maid. As they had agreed among themselves, she stepped back and let the person enter. She then closed the door and stood before it.

Keeping her head down, Kate examined the visitor from under her lashes. It appeared to be an old woman. She wore an ancient cloak with the hood up over a shabby gown—head down, face hidden. The figure's shoulders were a bit broad for a woman. They carried a basket with a cloth covering its contents. That wasn't good. Anything could be hidden there. Kate told herself that Rankin would not have come alone to threaten the servants.

"Let's have a look then," said the cook, who was not at all stupid.

The newcomer set the basket on the table and pulled off the cloth, revealing a pile of fresh mushrooms. If they had been imbued with poison, it was a good choice. People sometimes died after eating the wrong sort of mushrooms.

The cook leaned over them. "Looks tasty. But who are you then? Don't think I've seen you before. I like to know who I'm buying from."

The visitor stood still for a moment. Then, with the air of someone making a risky bet, they slowly raised a hand and put back the cloak's hood.

Kate recognized Rankin at once. He hadn't been able to do much about his hair, merely tying a scarf around his head and putting a mob cap over it. And despite some dabs of rouge, his face was unmistakable. "Aye, that's it," she cackled in French. It was the signal they'd arranged.

The cook reached for her cleaver. The older maid grabbed Rankin's cap and scarf and yanked them off, exposing his cropped hair. With a wordless exclamation he spun and knocked her aside, lunging toward the door.

Kate threw one of her knives. It hit the back of Rankin's head, hilt first unfortunately, startling but not impeding him. And then he knocked the younger maid aside, yanked the door open, and was through it. Kate jumped up and ran after him. "It's Rankin," she called out when she was outside, knowing that Jordaine and his team would be listening. Then she picked up her skirts and ran after the figure fleeing down the narrow lane.

She was accustomed to gowns. Rankin wasn't. And so she gained on him as they ran. People turned in amazement as the sight of two women pelting along the streets.

Rankin glanced back, grimaced to see her closer, and went faster. Kate pounded after him, wondering where Jordaine had gotten to. She was not familiar with Saint-Omer, but then neither was Rankin. She thought he was heading for the inn where his henchmen waited. It would be a disaster if they joined in while she was alone.

Rankin darted around a corner ahead. Kate barreled after him and found him waiting for her just out of sight. He raised a fist to hit her. Kate grabbed the folds of his cloak and collapsed onto the muddy street. Rankin flailed, the clasp of the cloak choking him. He loosed it, gave her ribs a kick, and took off.

Kate was struggling to her feet when Henry rushed up to help her. "Are you all right?" he asked.

Kate didn't bother to answer. She ran.

"Jordaine and Henderson are going to cut him off before he reaches his inn," Henry said, running at her side.

"About time," Kate gasped. "Where have they been?"

"You're fast on your feet. They didn't expect such speed."

She would have sneered at this, but she had to save her breath for the sprint.

They came out into a small square with lanes leading out on all four sides. Rankin was halfway across it. He suddenly paused, and Kate saw that Jordaine and two other men stood in the exits, obviously blocking them. She and Henry held the fourth. "Stop," called Henry. "*Arrêtez-vous.* You cannot get away."

Paying no heed, Rankin turned in a circle, then darted toward a wrought-iron fence on one side of the square. It was more than seven feet tall, Kate judged, with points like spears. Not climbable.

But Rankin swarmed up it. The strength of his arms was prodigious. He seemed about to escape them. And then his feet tangled in his skirts as he tried to plant one on a crossbar. The foot slipped. He fumbled, strained, lunged, and came down hard on the iron points of the fence rather than clearing them.

Kate's cry of dismay was echoed by others from around the square. She ran toward the fence and was horrified to find that the spear points had entered Rankin's chest and abdomen. He dangled there, too high up to be lifted off.

"Someone get a ladder," commanded Jordaine in French. "Two ladders. At once. Hurry."

Several townsmen raced away.

Rankin stared down, his face twisted with pain, his eyes darting around the small crowd that had gathered. He spotted Henry. "You," he said. "And your…grandmother? Ah, no, it is one of the harridans from Leicestershire." Blood bubbled from his lips. "What a way to end."

"We will get you down," said Henry.

"If you cannot see that I am finished, you are a fool." Rankin bared his teeth, horridly reddened by the welling blood. "Beaten by fools and women. Bah!" He shuddered, clawed at his chest, and went limp.

Kate turned away from the blood trickling down the iron. "I never meant for anything like this to happen."

"Of course you didn't," replied Henry. "None of us did." He put an arm around her. With no cloak and the dreadful outcome of the chase, she was shivering despite her exertions. Henry stepped back, took off his cloak, and put it around her. She could not find the energy to refuse.

The townsmen returned with three ladders. As they set two against the fence at Rankin's head and feet, one of them said, "*Mort.*"

There were nods and sidelong glances from around the square.

Henderson materialized at Kate's side. "Madame must be overcome by this terrible sight," he said in his fluent French, loud enough to be overheard. "The fellow tried to steal from her, and so we gave chase. But to try such a climb." He gestured at the grisly fence. "A madman, I suppose. No sight for an older lady to endure. Let us take her away." He urged Kate and Henry toward one of the streets leading out of the square.

"Shouldn't we stay and—" Henry began.

"Become embroiled with the authorities?" Henderson murmured. "To what end? What do you propose to tell them?"

They had no answer to that. Mentioning the queen would cause a great scandal. She would not thank them for that. And they had no official standing here.

"I think it best that we disappear," Henderson added. "At once. The lady can become Rob Jones again, and we will depart for Calais with all possible stealth. Unless there is some other matter we must address?" He looked apprehensive at the idea.

"The mushrooms Rankin brought should be checked for poison," Kate murmured. "I am sure we are right, but…"

"Signor Pergami is well able to attend to that," their guide replied. "You have warned him. He will double his vigilance." He gestured along the street. "Walk quickly, with purpose, but do not run." They went.

"The men who came with Rankin," said Henry.

"They will take to their heels when they hear what has happened to him. That is what their kind does."

"You don't think they would try some other attack?"

"I wonder if Rankin even told them what he planned?" asked Kate. She still felt shaky. "They weren't the sort to trust with any secret. Let alone one that would be worth a great deal if they chose to betray him."

Henderson nodded. "Well reasoned. With their employer gone, and in such a way, they will steal whatever he left behind and flee." He offered a grim smile. "We may see them on the road back to Calais."

They reached their inn soon after this. Kate left the others and went to a small courtyard at the back where she removed most of the powder from her hair by vigorous shaking and brushing. A few traces remained, but a bath was not possible in this simple place. She blinked back tears at the thought of sinking into steaming water and soaking this day away. She was trembling with the cold, and perhaps with something else.

In her room, she paused to take a series of deep breaths. Anyone would have a strong reaction to the events just past. It would be inhumane not to feel it. Certainly not a weakness.

She removed the landlady's clothes and the padding beneath. She folded them carefully, washed her face and arms with tepid water from the washstand, and donned her breeches, shirt, and coat. She was putting the tight braids into her hair when a knock came at the door. "Yes?" Kate said.

"Henry," replied a familiar, welcome voice.

She stepped over and opened the door.

"I came to see how you are," he added. "Because I am shaken, I admit."

Kate walked into his arms.

They closed around her like sanctuary. He moved them both over the threshold, closed the door behind them, and held her.

"I never meant for anything like that to happen," Kate murmured into his shoulder.

"Of course we did not."

"I can't get the sight out of my mind. That horrible fence. The blood." She shivered. His arms tightened around her.

"Nor I," he said. He rested his cheek on the top of her head.

"If we hadn't been chasing him," she began.

"It was an accident, Kate. Which came about because of the man's villainy, trying to poison the queen, and then his reckless attempt to escape."

Kate drew back to look up at him. "What if he wasn't? What if we made a mistake?"

"You think Rankin had some other reason to go to her kitchen in a dress with a basket of mushrooms? And then to run?"

"No." The case was clear. "Still, I feel responsible for his... dreadful death."

Henry nodded. "We did not wish it or arrange it. But we...participated."

"Yes." She looked up into his dark eyes and saw revulsion and regret. He was not putting on some "manly" stoicism. She loved him for that.

"It is hard that something like this happens when one is trying to do good. To see justice done," he added.

Kate nodded. "Rankin set out to kill," she said slowly.

"And we to prevent it."

"He would have let the queen's whole household die from that poison. Without a qualm, apparently."

"While we are a quivering mass of qualms," Henry replied with the ghost of a smile.

She loved him for his quick wits too, and his tender touch and so many other things. "I suppose it is better so."

"I haven't the slightest doubt of that."

She felt a fierce longing for the comfort of his arms tonight.

"Monsieur?" asked Henderson's voice on the other side of the door. "I have news."

Slowly, reluctantly, they drew apart, hands clinging to the last moment.

Henry opened the door.

Henderson and Jordaine stood in the cramped hallway. "Signor Pergami sent word," the first man continued. "The mushrooms showed the marks of a needle. He took them to an apothecary to be cut open, and the fellow said they'd been infused with a strong poison. Only a little would be required to kill."

Without conscious thought, Kate laced her fingers together with Henry's.

"The queen sent her thanks," Henderson went on. "She wishes she might give you a proper reward and hopes to do so in the future when she is on her throne."

Kate wondered if she ever would be. The new king seemed ferociously determined that she should be discarded.

"Pergami assured us that they would keep a sharp watch for any further trouble."

"We introduced him to the men we made use of here," said Jordaine. "They are good fellows. They are spreading many conflicting stories about this Rankin. There is much confusion."

"And his hirelings have run, as I predicted," added Henderson. "So I think we have nothing to do but return home." He sounded relieved. He held out Kate's cloak, which she had abandoned in Queen Caroline's kitchen. She had to let go of Henry to accept the garment.

"It is too late today. We will lie low, not stirring from this inn or speaking to anyone, and leave very early in the morning. As soon as there is light." Their guide was clearly determined on this course of action. Kate wondered what he would do if they raised objections. Not that she had any. She was beset by a sudden longing for her cozy home.

"Yes," said Henry.

Henderson sketched a salute, and the two men turned toward the stairs and left them.

Henry hesitated. Kate didn't know if he meant to depart as well. She couldn't bear the idea. "Please stay with me," she said.

And so he did.

⸻

They left with the first streaks of dawn. Saint-Omer was quiet. A cold mist drifted down the lanes, and the sound of their horses' hooves seemed to echo off the walls. No one accosted them, and they were soon out of the town and on the road back to Calais. The sky brightened to a deep blue. It was frigid but not bitingly damp.

Henry rode behind Kate, keeping an eye out for fatigue. They had no reason to drive themselves now. Jordaine had headed off at a gallop to warn Captain Bailes of their return. But Kate didn't need to strain on this leg of the trip. If she tired of riding, they would stop and rest.

She had cried in his arms in the night, and he wasn't ashamed to acknowledge that he had cried a bit with her. Rankin's had been such an ugly death. He had never imagined an outcome like that when they started on this pursuit. And though he knew it wasn't his fault, and the man had been a blackguard, it was still dreadful to recall.

Much later they had made love with feverish intensity. The desire burning through him, and so evident in her demanding kisses and urgent hands, had been a kind of redemption, Henry thought. Or life triumphing over its opposite. Or love offering itself as a cure. All of those perhaps. The tenderness that lingered afterward had eased them both, he was certain.

The sleep of exhaustion had come over them then. There hadn't been time to talk of their future, just as there had not been in the rush of departure this morning. He meant to do that before they reached England, however. He just had to get her alone with no risk of interruption. Tonight when they stopped would be best. He knew what he wished to say. His only worry was her response.

They rode steadily through the short February day. As the sun began to set, Henderson turned them toward a village inn. "We'll reach Calais tomorrow. Perhaps in time for you to sail. I don't know the tides."

Henry nodded. Kate had been quiet on the ride, and he wondered what she was thinking.

The hostelry was another of the small ones they had frequented on this journey. It had only two rooms to rent. "I can sleep before the fire in the taproom," Henderson offered.

"Nonsense," said Kate. "You will take the second room."

Henry was glad to hear it, but the crisp tone of her voice and the sharp look in her violet eyes bothered him. This was the old Kate back, the one he'd met in Leicestershire and found sharp-tongued. He helped Henderson see to their horses, and then went up to the room they would share. He could wait no longer.

He found Kate brushing out her hair with almost savage strokes. He shut the door and said, "I wanted to speak to you."

"Yes, I was afraid you might."

"Afraid?"

"Let's just get it over with, shall we?"

"Over with?"

"Yes, Henry. We are going home. The great oppressive hand of society is descending upon us. It grows heavier with each step we take."

Given the way she was frowning at him, it didn't seem politic to kneel and do the thing in form. The tender phrases he'd prepared went out of his mind. "I wanted to ask you to be my wife," he said simply.

Kate sighed. She set down the brush. "I do not regret anything we have done together. Indeed, it has been rather... glorious. But I'm not going to marry because of it. To avoid a scandal, which will not arise."

"I didn't…"

"Who would tell? Henderson? Jordaine? Do you think they are acquainted with the London gossips?"

"I'm sure they aren't," Henry replied. Though they might tell Tereford, Henry supposed, if he asked them. They were his men. He wouldn't mention that. "I don't intend to wed for such a reason either," he began.

"And I won't marry to worm my way into the Foreign Office," she said, looking grim. "Whatever your uncle might think, or Jerome, blast him, I am not some scheming, cold-hearted creature who…"

"Of course you're not," Henry interrupted in a loud voice. "You're the complete opposite of that. You're fire and tenderness and quicksilver wit."

Kate blinked and gazed up at him.

"*I* intend to marry for love and nothing else," he continued. "Which is why I asked *you*. Because I love you with all my heart, and I cannot imagine being married to anyone else. In fact, I refuse to be!"

"Don't!" Tears filmed her violet eyes. She held up a forbidding hand.

"Don't?" Henry repeated, his heart sinking toward despair.

"Your family disapproves of me."

"Only because they have never met you."

"Your uncle has. He doesn't like me."

"He will get over it." And if he didn't, that was too bad, Henry thought, but he would not allow it to destroy his happiness.

"They have sensible, practical reasons."

"You are not saying the thing that would silence me." She hadn't claimed she didn't love him. Henry clung to that.

She looked almost desperate. "I am not a good match for a rising diplomat. Have you forgotten what your uncle said? I could ruin your prospects. Do you want…?"

"I want you."

"Henry."

"I am not such a brilliant match either, you will recall." He tried to sound cocky when he was actually desperate. "I have only a small income. And an uncertain future."

"You could have an illustrious career, while with me your life would be…"

"An endless adventure," Henry interrupted. "As would yours with me. I promise."

"How can you be sure?"

"I just am."

"You can't be."

"Can I not? Didn't you notice how splendidly we worked together over these last weeks? You cannot have missed how we *dared*?"

She looked struck by this.

He reached out and took her hands. "Do you not love me, Kate? That is the only consideration that would make any difference."

"I don't…"

"The truth, Kate. We tell each other the truth, don't we?"

"Not when it would hurt," she murmured.

"Even then." He squeezed her fingers. "Perhaps especially then, so that we may mend things."

Her hands tightened in his. "Yes, of course I love you. Do you think I would have...? But it doesn't matter."

Wild elation coursed through Henry. "Nonsense. Nothing else matters." He started to pull her close.

"Stop!"

He did so.

"If I were to..."

"Marry me and make me the happiest man on earth," he finished.

She frowned at him. "I wouldn't be a...an ordinary wife. What if you are sorry in the end?"

"Never. You are exactly the sort of wife I have longed for."

She pushed at his chest. "You are being ridiculous."

"Not at all. I simply didn't know what I really wanted until I found you."

"You disliked me at first!"

"I am a slow learner at times. I admit it."

"Henry! Are you *sure*?"

"Completely. Can you not be as well?"

"Oh, I am. It's just that I don't think I should."

"Should?"

"Take what I want so very much."

A laugh trembled in Henry's chest. "Of course you should. Just as I am. Grasp it with all your might. Never let go. Won't you? Won't you say yes?"

Kate stared up at him, the hint of tears in her violet eyes. "Yes," she said. "Yes, I will."

Fortunately, the bed was right there.

Epilogue

ON A MARCH MORNING WITH SPRING JUST MAKING ITSELF felt in London, a hired carriage pulled up before St. Paul's Church in Covent Garden. This was not the great domed cathedral near the city but a small porticoed building at the edge of the busy market square. Frequented by theatricals and other denizens of the colorful neighborhood, it was often referred to as the actors' church. Tom had recommended it.

Henry Deeping emerged from the vehicle and turned to hand Kate Meacham down. They stood together before the pillared edifice designed by Inigo Jones. "You are sure?" he asked her.

"We cannot conflict with Charlotte's wedding," she replied. "That would be rude."

"But you don't want something grander? At St. George's in Hanover Square perhaps?"

"This is not a high-society wedding, Henry."

"No."

"And we decided to present your family, the world, with a fait accompli. Easier to beg pardon than ask permission."

"Yes, but I don't want you to regret it later. I want you to have happy memories."

"You know I prefer subterfuge and stealth," she said with a smile. "They are my…hallmark."

Remembering the first time he'd seen her in London, slipping out of a hidden doorway to sneak into a diplomatic reception, Henry smiled back. "I just thought all ladies wanted big festive weddings."

"I am not exactly a lady, I think. More of an unmanageable female."

"I manage," he replied with a grin.

"Because I allow you to."

"True. I look forward to a long life under a lovely cat's foot."

She elbowed him.

A splendid carriage with a coat of arms emblazoned on the door swept into the square and pulled up behind theirs. The Duke and Duchess of Tereford emerged and came to stand beside them. Henry, who had thought himself quite nattily dressed in his new coat from Weston, overseen by proud apprentice Ned Gardener, immediately felt overshadowed. Warm fingers twined with his, and he turned to meet Kate's violet gaze. "Stealth," she whispered. "We don't want to be the center of all eyes. Let them do that." A wave of love washed through him. She really was the most wonderful creature in the world.

"All is arranged with the rector," said the duke.

"By you?" Henry asked.

"Cecelia," he replied.

"Oh, all should be well then."

"Mind your impudence, or I will withhold your wedding present," teased the duke. "Where are the others?"

As if in answer, a hack trundled into the piazza. It disgorged Daphne Palliser, Oliver Welden, and Tom Jesperson.

"All present and accounted for," said Tereford. "Shall we go in?"

The group entered the church together and found the rector waiting for them at the altar. Two documents rested on the lectern before him. "This is most unusual," the small plump man said. "Quite interesting."

"They said in Lambeth that I was the first person ever to request two special licenses at the same time," replied the duke.

"It's fortunate you're acquainted with the archbishop," said Tom.

"He is a duke," said Welden. "Everyone toadeats him."

"Not quite everyone," murmured Tereford as the rector gave Oliver Welden a startled glance. "You don't ever change, do you, Welden?"

"Yes, he does," replied Daphne. "He was joking this time."

The duke raised one dark eyebrow.

"I was," said Welden. "I owe you a great deal, Your Grace, and I am…very grateful."

"He said that almost without choking," Tereford observed to his wife.

The duchess merely smiled.

"Shall we begin?" asked the rector.

Henry and Kate took hands before the altar. Daphne and Oliver Welden joined them. The other three sat in a wooden pew, friends and witnesses, as the lines of the double marriage service began. When he made his vows, Henry decided he'd never been happier in his life.

Afterward, they all went to Tereford House. The duchess had begged to be allowed to host the wedding breakfast, and like everything she did, it was elegantly perfect. "This spread deserves a larger crowd," Henry said, as he admired the lavish cake in the middle of the laden table.

"Are you sad that your family isn't here?" asked Kate.

"Only a very little bit," he answered. "And mostly because I am eager for them to know you. We will go and visit. They will hold a large party for us then."

"Will they?" She looked uneasy.

Henry took her hand. "Yes."

"Won't they rather be disappointed? Or angry that you have thrown your chances away?"

"I haven't done that."

"Your uncle's note was…sharp."

Henry had written a detailed report on the events in France and handed it over to his superiors in the Foreign Office. He hadn't mentioned the king or Quentin Matthews, which had rather begged the question of how he'd discovered the plot in the first place. But his uncle would have been able to put those pieces in place if he had read it. And of course he must have. He seemed to have a finger in every diplomatic pie, and he was Henry's patron, connected to anything his nephew did. "We are seeing my uncle tomorrow. We will settle everything then."

"Have you told him I'm coming?"

"Easier to beg pardon than ask permission," Henry repeated.

Kate grimaced, but nodded.

The duke stood and raised a glass of champagne. "To the brides and the grooms. May you be as happy in your marriages as I am in mine."

People smiled, drank. Henry looked around the table. The duchess was laughing at something Tom had said to her. Daphne Palliser, now Mrs. Welden, looked serenely contented. And her new husband appeared as mellow as Henry had ever seen him. He doubted the mood would last. Welden's irascibility was deep-seated. But he did seem glad to be wed. Kate had told him that Daphne meant to help her spouse move up the ranks of the Bow Street Runners, perhaps even to chief constable. She might well be able to do it, Henry thought. She was nearly as clever and subtle as his own wonderful wife.

The word, the idea, delighted him. His wife. Whatever came, they belonged to each other now. They would shape their future together.

———

Kate had suggested that they meet Henry's uncle at the tea shop where he had rejected her. It brought things full circle in a way that satisfied her. His uncle had made no objection, but he checked a little when he entered and saw both of them sitting there. Henry rose to greet him.

"Why am I not surprised?" said Brinsley Gerard when he joined them.

"Because you are a very intelligent man, Uncle. May I present my wife?"

The pride and joy in his face made Kate blink back a tear. She braced herself for his uncle's reaction.

He showed none. Too experienced a diplomat to reveal himself, Kate decided. He simply sat down and looked at them for what seemed like a long while. "Whose idea was it to go haring off to France?" he asked then.

"Mine," said Kate and Henry simultaneously.

Kate started to object. Then she realized that Henry meant to take the blame, if that was what came next. It was a gallant impulse, but perhaps a bit annoying too. "It was a mutual decision," she said.

"But *you* must have gone to Tereford for his boat and the men that came with it," Gerard said to Henry. "He is your friend."

"Yes."

Kate waited for the scold that must be looming.

Instead the older man asked, "Would he do such a thing again?"

"Lend me his yacht?" Henry asked, looking as confused as Kate felt.

"Aid you, if you required it. Asked it of him."

"I–I suppose so." Henry looked at her. Kate stared back, puzzled by the direction the conversation had taken.

"That is a valuable resource," said Henry's uncle. He put the tips of his fingers together and contemplated his stee-pled hands. The small sounds of the tea shop rose around them—the clatter of cups and saucers, the murmur of the few other patrons, none within earshot. "There is conventional diplomacy," the older man continued after a bit. "And then there are other…avenues of foreign policy. Less visible and…rarely acknowledged. It had not occurred to me that you might be suited for the latter, Henry. Or the least interested. You seemed to me a conventional, steady young man." Gerard raised his eyes, glanced at his nephew and at Kate. "Miss Meacham…Mrs. Deeping, I should say, was another matter. But a lone young lady…"

"Is a fairly useless thing," she finished.

"Not useless," he replied. "But limited by the strictures of society. Which were not mandated by me, you know."

Kate sniffed quietly.

"When I thought you were dragging Henry into…"

"I was not dragged!"

"So I learned with this wild venture." Gerard paused, sipped his tea, then continued. "A married couple both with a bent toward…initiative is a different matter."

A number of strands suddenly came together in Kate's mind like a puzzle falling into place. "My parents were involved in the less visible avenues of foreign policy," she declared.

"Quietly, please," replied Gerard.

"But they *were*," she said more softly.

Henry's uncle nodded. "They could be sent, a pleasant young couple, amiably touring about, into places an official could not venture."

"And gather information officials could not get at," said Kate. Her dream of the perilous cliff ran through her mind.

"Often."

"We could do that," Kate said, more to Henry than Gerard.

"It can be dangerous," answered the latter. He seemed to be waiting for Henry to hang back or object. Expecting it even.

"Didn't I promise you adventures?" Henry said to Kate.

"You knew about this?"

He shook his head. "Oh no. I merely trusted and believed that we would find our way." He turned to his uncle. "We are ready to serve."

Brinsley Gerard examined them closely and at length. "We might have a few things for you to do," he replied at last. "There is a situation out East where you could most likely help. If you will agree to follow a few *vital* instructions."

He was looking at Kate. She nodded.

"You would have to give your word of honor to do so," Gerard added.

"I would." The future opened out before her in a thrilling panorama. She would follow in her parents' footsteps, travel the world with her love at her side, and do as much good as she might. It was all she'd ever dreamed of, just as Henry was more than she'd dared hope for.

It was agreed that Gerard would put together the necessary information and meet them again to explain what they would be asked to do. He left them then to gaze at each other with excited amazement.

The proprietress came over with fresh hot water. "More cakes?" she asked.

"No," said Kate as Henry said, "Yes."

"We must go," she added.

"Where?" he asked as the woman walked away.

"Home. I want to show you some things my parents collected on their travels."

"What sorts of things?"

"You'll see," she said with tingling anticipation. "Or wait. We will ask for some of those cakes to take along. For later."

His dark eyes ignited at the look she gave him. They rose together. "I'll follow you anywhere," he said.

"I know," Kate replied.

About the Author

Jane Ashford discovered Georgette Heyer in junior high school and was captivated by the glittering world and witty language of Regency England. That delight was part of what led her to study English literature and travel widely. Her books have been published all over Europe as well as in the United States. Jane was nominated for a Career Achievement Award. Born in Ohio, she is now somewhat nomadic. You can sign up for her monthly newsletter.

Website: janeashford.com
Facebook: JaneAshfordWriter

Also by Jane Ashford

THE DUKE'S ESTATES
The Duke Who Loved Me
Earl on the Run
Blame It on the Earl
A Gentleman Ought to Know

THE DUKE'S SONS
Heir to the Duke
What the Duke Doesn't Know
Lord Sebastian's Secret
Nothing Like a Duke
The Duke Knows Best
A Favor for the Prince
(prequel)

THE WAY TO A LORD'S HEART
Brave New Earl
A Lord Apart
How to Cross a Marquess

A Duke Too Far
Earl's Well That Ends Well
Once Again a Bride
Man of Honour
The Three Graces
The Marriage Wager
The Bride Insists
The Marchington Scandal
The Headstrong Ward
Married to a Perfect Stranger
Charmed and Dangerous
A Radical Arrangement
First Season/Bride to Be
Rivals of Fortune/The Impetuous Heiress
Last Gentleman Standing
Earl to the Rescue
The Reluctant Rake
When You Give a Rogue a Rebel

EARL ON THE RUN

Captivating new Regency romance from
beloved, best-selling author Jane Ashford

Fuming at her tyrannical grandfather's demand that she marry a
man with a title, Harriet Finch plunges into a reckless, rebellious
flirtation with a charming rogue. Imagine her chagrin when she dis-
covers that her provocative new love is actually an earl...

**"Effervescent... slow-burning romance
spiked by witty dialogue."**

—*Publishers Weekly* for
The Duke Who Loved Me

For more info about Sourcebooks's books and authors, visit:
sourcebooks.com

BLAME IT ON THE EARL

A delightfully scandalous Regency romp
from beloved author Jane Ashford

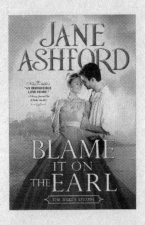

Sarah Moran might be the only unmatched lady relieved to return
to the country after a busy London season. But when she saves
Kenver Pendrennon from nearly falling into the sea while reveling
in the fresh air of Cornwall, the rising tide forces them to seek shel-
ter for the night. By the time they return in the morning, rumors
have already begun to spread, and Sarah and Kenver—who is heir
to an earl—must marry quickly to keep scandal at bay...

**"Sweetly romantic Regency romance
expertly spiked with danger."**

—*Booklist* for *Earl's Well That Ends Well*

IN THE EYES OF THE EARL

Kristin Vayden takes you straight to
the heart of Regency England

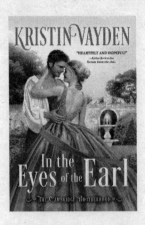

Collin Morgan, Earl of Penderdale, has discovered that someone is committing crimes in his name, leaving him suspended from his work in the war office. Elizabeth Essex, the daughter of a well-respected Cambridge University professor, longs to be recognized for her own scholarship—unheard of for a gently bred lady.

But with Elizabeth's secret threatened and Morgan's confrontation with his adversaries at a fever pitch, working together may be the only way to get to the truth that will set them free.

**"Flawless storytelling! Vayden is a
new Regency powerhouse."**

—Rachel Van Dyken, #1 *New York Times* bestselling author

AN EARL TO ENCHANT

Dazzling opposites-attract Regency romance
from bestselling author Amelia Grey

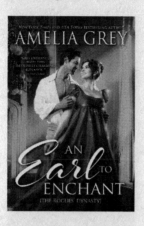

Arianna Sweet knows her father's death was anything but acciden-
tal. Someone is after his groundbreaking medical discovery and
now they're after her. Alone and with no one to turn to, Arianna
has almost given up searching for an ally—until a chance encounter
leaves her and her father's research in Lord Morgandale's strong and
trustworthy hands...

"What romance dreams are made of."

—*Love Romance Passion* for
A Dash of Scandal

For more info about Sourcebooks's books and authors, visit:
sourcebooks.com

THE DUKE IN QUESTION

James Bond meets *Bridgerton* in this steamy enemies-to-lovers historical romance by bestselling author Amalie Howard

Lady Bronwyn Chase leaves London on her brother's passenger liner bound for America with a packet of secret letters that could get her into trouble. Serious trouble. The kind a duke's sister shouldn't be in—the kind that puts spymaster Valentine Medford, the Duke of Thornbury, on her trail. But as the duke gets closer to Bronwyn and the secrets she's keeping, he'll have to decide between the mysterious woman who calls to him, or his allegiance to the Crown.

"[Howard's] prose is delightful, her writing masterful, her characters unforgettable."

—Kerrigan Byrne, *USA Today* bestselling author